THE BURIED FACES

Ivy Bishop Mystery Thriller

Book 3

ALEX SIGMORE

Dark Woods Press

THE BURIED FACES: IVY BISHOP MYSTERY THRILLER BOOK 3

1st Edition

ebook ISBN 978-1-957536-65-1

Print ISBN 978-1-957536-66-8

Description

In the quiet, close-knit community of Oakhurst, the brutal murder of a beloved local priest sends shockwaves through the town. Detective Ivy Bishop, coming off two of the toughest cases of her career, is thrust into an investigation that seems straightforward but quickly unravels into something far more sinister.

As Ivy delves into the priest's life, she uncovers hidden connections to an underground crime network operating right under the town's nose. The deeper she digs, the more she realizes that the priest's death is just the tip of the iceberg. The investigation twists and turns, revealing secrets that Oakhurst's elite would kill to keep buried.

Each clue leads Ivy closer to the heart of something far darker than the shadows of an empty church, exposing a web of corruption, betrayal, and greed that extends to the highest echelons of society. As she navigates this treacherous terrain, Ivy finds herself confronting the darkest aspects of humanity.

With stakes higher than ever, Ivy must untangle the intricate conspiracy before it claims more lives, including her own. "The "Buried Faces" is a gripping mystery thriller from Alex Sigmore, where every revelation peels back another layer of a town's façade, and the quest for justice becomes a perilous journey into the unknown. Prepare for a tale where trust is a luxury, and the truth is more elusive than ever.

Prologue

HER HEART IS POUNDING.

As Lorelai adjusts the necklace her mother gave her for her sixteenth birthday a few weeks ago, she can't believe what she's about to do. The necklace is of a dolphin— her favorite. In some ways it feels like a betrayal to wear it tonight, but she's already said yes and she's not backing down now. How many times is she going to get another opportunity like this? It might never come around again. And she'll have missed her chance.

"You look pretty," her mother says as she rounds the corner and comes into the small living room. Their house isn't what anyone would call "nice," but it's been good enough for Lorelai and her mother for the past seven years. It's more of a home to her than any of the places before because they've been here the longest. But it doesn't offer much in the way of privacy. She can barely get out of her room without her mother hearing her. Which meant she needed a cover if she was going to get out of the house tonight.

"Brit said she wanted to mess around with some new apps," she says, trying to intercept her mother's interjections before they start. She has always been something of a "hover-er," hardly ever leaving Lorelai alone. It probably has something to do with Lorelai's father, whom she's never met and never hopes to. The man left them all alone when she was still in her mom's belly; she has no desire to ever meet someone like that.

"No dating apps, right?"

"No, Mom."

"No boys?" her mom asks.

"No," Lorelai says, already exasperated. "I told you before."

Her mother gets up from the couch and wraps her in a brief hug. "I know. I just worry about you. You're growing up so fast."

"Mom, you're going to mess up what little makeup you let me wear," she complains.

"Sorry, sorry," she replies, stepping back but still holding Lorelai by the shoulders. "God. You could have been my twin sister. We just need to fix your hair a little bit and you'll look like your ol' mom." She reaches out for Lorelai's hair teasingly, causing her to giggle.

"Mom, stop," Lorelai says, though she won't admit she likes knowing she takes after her mom. Sometimes she wonders what she was like when she was Lorelai's age. But then she remembers that her mother was only a few years older than she is now when she got pregnant. She was still in high school when Lorelai was born.

"I know, I know," her mom teases. "Listen, I have the late shift tonight, so I won't be home when you get back. Make sure you lock up and text me when you get to Brit's house and when you get home."

Lorelai turns toward the door. "I know the drill."

"Okay." Her mom finally relents, heading back to the couch. "You two have fun tonight. Tell Brit's mom I said hi."

She heads to the door; thankful she's going to make a clean getaway. "I will. Don't worry."

"Sweetie, I always worry. It's part of being a parent." Her

mom smiles as Lorelai gives her a final wave and heads out the door.

∾

TEN MINUTES LATER, LORELAI WALKS RIGHT PAST BRIT'S house. She lives three blocks over from them in the same neighborhood. She and Brit grew up together, and have stayed best friends all through school. Except last year they redrew the school districts or something weird which meant Lorelai had to start going to a new school this year. Her sophomore year of high school too. Which meant she had to start all over after working so hard to make friends at her old school. And it hasn't been going well. Back at Oakhurst High, it was easy, because she and Brit had been a team. But coming into Pine Ridge North, she didn't know anyone. She begged her mom to do anything to get them back into the right district, but there was nothing she could do. Times were tight enough as it was without even thinking about moving.

That's the shitty thing about being poor. There's never enough for anything.

Lorelai turns the dolphin pendant over and an over again in her hand as she continues down the street, the butterflies finally sneaking into her stomach. She deserves this, doesn't she? After all the crap she's had to endure at the new school, after missing out on all the parties with Brit? And after, despite months of asking and pleading, her mom presented her with a necklace instead of a car for her sweet sixteen? They hadn't even had a party— just invited a few of Lorelai's friends over for some cake. She was embarrassed, especially after attending some of the other kids' sixteenth birthday parties.

But tonight will make up for all of it. She and Brit have been planning this for weeks, and it was finally here. Lorelai can barely believe it. As she rounds the corner, she catches sight of the group gathered under one of the big trees that lines the street. It's already dusk, and what few streetlights that exist in the neighborhood have already begun to come on. But in the shadow of the tree, the people she is there to meet are barely visible.

"Lori, hey," Brit calls out, trotting up to meet her. "Any problems with your mom?"

"None," she says giving Brit a quick hug. "She said to tell your mom hi."

Brit rolls her eyes, grabbing Lorelai by the hand and pulling her to the group. "Moms, right?" Brit is only about three months older than Lorelai, but in some ways, she seems a lot older. A lot more mature. She's developed in ways Lorelai hasn't yet, especially after last year. And she's gotten a lot more popular.

"Guys, this is Lori," Brit says as they reach the group. She recognizes one of the faces, but not the other two.

"Hey Lor, how's that new school?" Oscar asks. Oscar moved to the area about five years ago and went to the same middle school as Lorelai and Brit. When they drew the new districts, he was spared having to move schools.

"Sucks, but what can you do?" Lorelai replies, trying to remain relaxed. They can always tell when you're nervous.

Oscar agrees, then looks to the ground, kicking a rock away.

"This is Donnie," Brit says, turning to the guy beside Oscar. She thinks she remembers him, even though they aren't in the same grade. He's tall, with dark hair that falls into his eyes. A low-slung backpack is on one shoulder.

"Junior, right?" Lorelai asks.

"Yeah," he says sticking out his hand and giving hers a shake.

"And this is Lukas." Brit turns Lorelai to the other guy in the group. While not as tall as Donnie, Lukas seems bigger. Like he has a lot more muscles under there somewhere. He just gives Lorelai a quick nod.

"We doing this or what?" he asks.

"We're ready when you are," Brit says, hooking her arm around Lorelai's.

The three boys turn and start walking while Brit and Lorelai bring up the rear. She's nervous to say the least, but she can't let it show. And if she knows her best friend at all, she can tell Brit is nervous too.

"Have you done this before?" Lorelai whispers as they make their way down the street, passing under the increasing glow of the streetlights.

"Just once at Donnie's house," she says. "It was a few weeks ago. Kind of an… impromptu thing. No big deal."

"Yeah, I'm sure that's all that happened," Lorelai chuckles. "How was it?"

Brit shrugs. "Not as great as you think."

"How far is this place?" Lorelai asks as they leave the last streetlight behind. A chill creeps into the air that hadn't been there before. It's been an unseasonably warm March, but she's still glad she brought her jacket.

"I think it's right up here. You've passed it before," she says.

"I know, I just haven't been paying attention."

Brit scoffs. "That's something you need to do if you ever want a car. You have to know where you're going, don't you?"

"That's what GPS is for," Lorelai says, taking a deep breath and trying to calm her nerves. She's snuck out of the house before—as much as possible in a house like hers, but that's usually just to Brit's house or occasionally to the school. But she's never done anything like this before. When Brit first floated the idea, she wasn't even sure she wanted to. Then she remembered being cut off from her old life by some idiots on the city council and reconsidered. Even if it was trespassing, so what? They owed her for what they took away.

"Okay," Lukas says as they reach the next corner. There are no houses on this end of the neighborhood, only the church which looks like it's been here since the dark ages. It's all dark gray stone, with stained glass windows and two large towers in the front. There's a large spire in the middle atop a pitched roof. The building looks older than dirt.

Behind the church is an old cemetery with a stone fence. At the front are a pair of iron gates that lead into the cemetery from the back of the church, while the fence itself extends all the way out to run along the road.

"Here," Lukas says, pointing to a low bend in the stone from where it has worn down over time.

Lorelai stares at the wall. It's at least as tall as she is. "We're going over that?"

"Yeah, it's easy," Oscar says. "Done it a dozen times before."

"And they don't care?" Lorelai asks, pointing at the church. The lights inside illuminate the stained glass, almost making it glow. She's always heard Catholic churches are the prettiest. Staring at this one in the night, she's inclined to agree.

"The maintenance guy goes home around six," Lukas says. "We don't have anything to worry about."

"Yeah, except that one time he stayed late," Oscar replies, laughing. "You almost pissed your pants."

"Shut up," Lukas says. "Get the girls over first. We'll follow."

"Here, I'll help you," Donnie says, coming up behind Lorelai.

She doesn't want to go over into the cemetery first. All of a sudden this seems like a very bad idea. What if she falls into an open grave? What if there are sticker bushes on the other side? Or what if there's someone still in there, despite Lukas's assurances? She's never even visited a cemetery before, much less snuck into one.

But Brit is right there beside her, her eyes pleading. Lorelai can't let her down. And she isn't about to chicken out in front of the guys.

"Sure," she says, and Donnie's big hands wrap around her waist, lifting her up to where she can pull herself up on top of the wall. Her jeans scrape on the stone.

"All clear?" Oscar asks from below.

She surveys the cemetery. It's dark, the only light coming from the church. But she doesn't see any movement among the gravestones. It's literally dead. "Yeah," she calls back in a hushed whisper.

Donnie lifts Brit up beside her just as Lorelai is trying to figure out how to get down. She can't tell if there's anything below her or not, so she pulls out her phone and turns on the light, shining it down to the ground. It looks fine to jump down to.

She gathers up the courage just as Oscar and Lukas are pulling themselves up on the wall. As her feet hit the dirt on the other side, she can hear the grunting from the guys. She only hopes it's as easy to get back over when all this is done.

A second later Brit lands right beside her, a huge grin on her face visible in the darkness. Before long, they're all in the cemetery, Lukas leading them around beside the wall until they reach some tall gravestones near the front.

"Isn't this a little exposed?" Lorelai asks. She's looking directly at the back of the church which is connected to the graveyard from here. A small path winds from where the cemetery begins to a back entrance.

Lukas sits down on the other side of one of the gravestones. "Nah. No one ever comes out here."

"Especially at night," Oscar says, winking. He sits down beside Lukas while Donnie pulls off his backpack and gently sets it on the ground. He opens it, removing a long glass bottle the color of fire. It has a bulb at one end and a small pipe sticking out which has been blackened with use.

"Man, don't you ever clean this thing?" Lukas asks, taking the bong.

"Can't," Donnie says. "It'll ruin the flavor."

"You're full of shit," he says. He pulls out a bottle of water and pours some into the glass vessel, swirling it around. He then packs some weed in the bowl before pulling out a lighter and lighting the bowl piece. The bong fills slowly with smoke. He removes the front piece and takes a hit, sucking in the smoke before exhaling it. "Ah. Perfect."

He hands the bong to Oscar who follows suit, a smile on his face the whole time.

"Here," Oscar says, passing it to Brit. The girls still haven't taken a seat and Lorelai isn't sure she's going to. She doesn't want to get her jeans dirty in the mud. And something seems wrong about sitting on the ground where dead people have been buried. Like getting closer to them will disturb them or something.

She watches as Brit takes a hit from the bong, meticulously analyzing what she does and how she does it. She doesn't want to look like a newb. Brit holds the smoke in her mouth a moment longer than the boys, then blows it out, passing the bong to Lorelai.

Her heart is nearly beating out of her chest. This is it. This is the moment she's been thinking about for almost three weeks straight. She can't back down, not now. She closes her eyes and takes the hit, sucking in the smoke and holding it in her mouth, no matter how bad it tastes and no matter how much she wants to blow it all out. She counts to three, then lets the breath go.

For a brief second she sees spots, and has to try and cover the fact she's taking shallower breaths.

Donnie laughs as she hands the bong over to her. "First time, huh?"

Damn.

"Next time don't hold it in. Just inhale, exhale," he says

before lighting the lighter and taking in a huge hit. His eyes glass over as he passes the bong back to Lukas.

All of a sudden, the world seems to shift on one end and Lorelai feels dizzy. She grabs hold of Brit who starts giggling uncontrollably. Before she knows it, Lorelai is also giggling and she doesn't even know why. Everything feels lighter. Better. It's like all her worries about her mother, school, money, popularity, it has all slipped off her shoulders. She can't believe how free she feels. How... empowered.

"Wow," she whispers.

"Good, right?" Donnie asks. "My cousin sent it to me from New Mexico. They have some sweet hash down there."

"Is it always like this?" Lorelai asks, staring at her hand as if she's never seen it correctly before. It's almost glowing.

"Well, this is a good batch," he says. "But yeah."

"Lukas, look out!" Oscar yells. Lukas jumps up, nearly clearing the top of the headstone before Oscar breaks out in a fit of cackles. "He's gonna get ya!"

"Dick," Lukas says, kicking at Oscar and missing spectacularly to the point where he almost falls back on his ass.

Oscar nearly doubles over in laughter. "He might still be in there, you know."

"Who?" Brit asks.

"The maintenance guy who caught us that one time," Donnie says. "He takes care of the church."

"Hey, I've got an idea," Lukas says, trying to recover some of his bravado. "How about one of you sneaks up to check? I'd rather not have my night ruined." Lorelai can't help but feel his attention is on her. Brit said they were just coming out here to smoke, but now Lorelai realizes it was probably naïve to believe that.

"I'll do it," she says before she can talk herself out of it.

"I meant one of the guys," Lukas says.

"What? Think I can't handle it?" she asks, feeling more

emboldened now than she ever has in her life. She could probably bend steel right now if she tried.

"Fine," he replies. "Go ahead."

"What do I do?" she asks.

"He sometimes leaves the back door open," Donnie says. "Just go up and check to see if it's locked. If it is, he's probably gone for the night."

"Doesn't seem so hard," she says, looking at the glowing windows of the church.

"Then show us how it's done," Lukas says.

His mocking tone only serves to piss her off. Lorelai doesn't waste any time making her way across the cemetery, determined as ever. She doesn't care if someone can see her right now; she feels amazing. She follows the path to the back of the large church and finds the nearest door inset into the stone. She gives it a small pull, finding it hasn't been locked. It moves under her force.

The movement surprises her for a second and she looks over to the group, four pairs of eyes watching her from about fifty yards away.

What should she do now? She pulls on the door again, and again it moves.

"WHAT IS SHE DOING?" BRIT ASKS.

Lukas furrows his brow. The new girl— Lori— is just standing at the back door. But then she pulls on it and even he can see it give way. "Shit. It's open. He's still in there."

"Why isn't she coming back?" Brit asks.

"Maybe she's too scared," Oscar says.

"Doesn't look scared to me," Donnie says. Before Lukas can add anything, Lori disappears inside.

"What the hell?" Lukas says as the others gasp. Is this girl insane? She's going to get them found out for sure. And if

Lukas's parents find out what he's been doing, he can kiss all of his free time goodbye.

"Go get her, man, before she screws this all up," Oscar says.

"*You* go get her," he replies.

"This was your idea," Oscar shoots back.

"*Someone* go get her," Brit says. "She's going to get us all caught."

"Yeah, good call, bringing her along," Lukas says, resigned to the fact that he'll have to do this. Everyone else is too chickenshit. He heads down the path before Brit can say anything else. He had hoped this new girl would be cool, and if she was anything like what Oscar said Brit was like, maybe they could have some fun. Now they'll be lucky to get out of here in one piece.

Lukas reaches the back door, mentally preparing himself to go in. Is she just inside the door, or did she go further in somewhere? Or did the maintenance guy pull her in? That was something he hadn't considered until now. Shit. Maybe they should all just get out of here.

But before he can make a decision, the door flies open and Lorelai runs out, falling on all fours. She promptly throws up in the grass, making deep retching sounds.

"Hey, you okay?" Lukas asks. He leans over her, but when she looks up at him, her face has gone completely white. It's so startling Lukas takes a step back. Lorelai throws up again as the others come rushing up.

"What happened?" Donnie asks.

"I dunno man, she just, just ran out here like this." Brit is down on the ground, her hand on her friend's back, rubbing it, but Lorelai is still retching, even though it sounds like she's empty.

"Stuff's not *that* strong," Donnie says.

As Lukas is standing there, he chances a glimpse at the open door. There's no one inside as far as he can see. But all the lights inside the church are on. That's strange for this time of night. Usually only a few of them are lit, but it looks like every light inside the church is glowing. Maybe it's his curiosity, maybe it's the weed, or maybe it's because Lori just came barreling out of there, but he's not about to be shown up by the new girl. He takes a few tentative steps towards the church, crossing the threshold and enters into the main part of the building. There's a name for it, but he can't think of it just now.

The marble floor beneath him is gleaming, like it's just been polished and as he looks around, he finds he was right. The place it lit up like its Christmas morning. He's almost so distracted by the dazzling lights and pretty windows that he doesn't see it.

But then in one terrifying instant he realizes why Lorelai is outside puking her guts out. But he's frozen to the spot. He can't move.

All he can do is scream.

Chapter One

"Do you have to drive so fast?" Jonathan asked, grabbing on to anything he could in the small car.

Ivy pulled it around a sharp corner, not letting off the accelerator. "Do you want to get there after everyone has gone home or sometime today?" Okay, maybe she was taking it a little fast. But the car could handle it. In the three weeks since she'd been driving her new "police-appointed" vehicle, which was really just an old Datsun that had been saved from the salvage yard; she'd put all her extra time and effort into cleaning it up and fixing everything that needed fixing.

If anything, this was a good test. She hadn't been able to push the car to its limits ever since she fixed the timing belt and added high flow air-intake system. So far, she seemed to be holding up well, almost as good as the Corvette.

"I'd just rather not throw up in here," Jonathan replied.

"We both know I'd kick you out of a moving vehicle before that happened." After the events of the past few months, the last weeks had been relatively calm. At one point Ivy had been facing a possible suspension from duty or at the very least a reprimand, but Nat had really gone to bat for her with Captain Armstrong. Not only that, but she had been the one to procure her this new ride after her Corvette was lost when Ivy took matters into her own hands.

Nat hadn't needed to do that. And Ivy had expected a beating once the case involving Mrs. Baker was over. Instead, it was as if things had finally turned a corner for her and Nat. They were getting along better than they had in years. Whatever wall had been between them seemed to have melted away after that case was over. Ivy wanted to question it, but she knew better than to look a gift horse in the mouth.

Instead, she had been working regular cases with Jonathan. She'd been keeping her nose clean, staying out of any drama. And she'd been working hard on finding the connection between Mrs. Baker's captor— a man named John Shepard; and Kieran Woodward, the man who she'd saved on the edge of a cliff after he'd nearly killed a local reporter.

A local reporter who just happened to have once dated Ivy's current partner and had been a thorn in her side more than a few times already.

"I'm glad my health is so important to you," Jonathan said sarcastically.

"My upholstery is more important," she shot back. "It's hard to clean up vomit." There had been a time when Ivy never would have been able to sit in the same car with someone, much less touch them. But she flicked her wrist, catching Jonathan's shoulder in a quick, playful smack, causing him to smile.

Where once Ivy had been unable to process the sensation of touch without going into a near panic, recent events had forced her into physical contact, whether she was ready for it or not. Kieran, for one. She'd had to grab him to save him from killing himself, though it had done little good. He was now in a mental institution, in some kind of self-induced coma. But the experience had opened Ivy up to trying to overcome the problem and for a short time, she thought she had a handle on it. That was, until she realized some kinds of contact came when she wasn't prepared.

Since then, she'd been slowly attempting to build it into her routine, through constant exposure. Sitting in this small car with Jonathan, for instance, was a good way to desensitize herself to physical proximity. She barely even noticed it anymore. And she could now apprehend criminals without getting short of breath.

But close, intimate contact was still a challenge for her. Something her Aunt Carol reminded her of every time Ivy visited. Aunt Carol wasn't the kind of person who pushed you past your comfort zone and she would never intentionally make Ivy feel bad. But still, Ivy could tell the woman wanted to be closer to her adopted daughter.

"Here, it's up here, you can slow down," Jonathan said, pointing.

Ivy grinned. She always found it humorous getting a rise out of him. The self-proclaimed "boy scout" of the office getting flustered. It was her idea of entertainment. It was an especially successful day when she could get him to curse, though those days were few and far between.

"Ivy... *Ivy!*"

She slammed on the brakes, bringing the car to a halt. And thanks to her impeccable skill and timing, she managed to stop them right in front of the two patrol cars that were blocking the street. Officer Perry stood on the other side of the car, his eyes wide and his hand on his holstered weapon.

"Happy now? He wants to shoot us."

"Couldn't help myself," she replied, getting out.

Jonathan followed suit as Ivy made her way around the car to Officer Perry, who had relaxed when he recognized them.

"Detective Bishop," he said, nodding. "Detective White. It's over here." There was already an ambulance on scene, and two paramedics were in the process of strapping a young woman to a gurney. Another man stood off to the side, looking shell-shocked as one of the officers spoke with him. In the middle of the road were the two vehicles, one of which had been flipped over and was upside down. One of the doors had already been cut away by the fire department, which were nearby with their truck, helping to divert traffic to nearby roads.

"No small wreck," Ivy said as they approached. Given the angle of the vehicle which was still right-side up, she wasn't sure how a wreck like this could have happened. The front right side of the car was crushed in, but that couldn't have been enough to flip the other car, could it? Plus, this was a residential road. Maybe with higher speeds, like on an inter-state, this could have happened, but in a place where the speed limit was thirty miles per hour?

"What do we know so far?" Jonathan asked the patrolman.

"We got the call about thirty minutes ago. Bystander called it in. Said this car came flying over the intersection, clipped the other one, causing it to flip over before rolling to a stop over there." He pointed to the car that was upright. "Apparently they came through the intersection at a high speed."

"Who was the driver?" Ivy asked.

"Raymond Burkhard," the officer said. "He's over there." He pointed to where a man sat on the ground on the far side of the scene, close to the fire truck. Ivy watched as the para-medics finished strapping the young woman to the gurney and lifted her up into the ambulance.

"Jennifer!" The man who had looked shell-shocked, speaking with the other officer ran across the scene to the back of the ambulance just as it was closing. "You have to let me go with you. I can't leave her alone."

"Don't worry sir, she's going to County General. You can

meet back up with her there. We need to get her there as soon as possible."

"No, you don't understand," he said. "I'm her father. I *need* to be with her." The officer he was speaking with came up behind him, trying to coax him away from the ambulance.

"Sir, let them go to the hospital. I'll drive you over there myself right now."

"*No!*" he yelled, spinning on the officer. "This is all *his* fault!" He pointed at Burkhard sitting on the curb about fifteen feet away.

Ivy could already see the decision in the man's eyes before he moved. "Hey," she said, getting Jonathan's attention. As Jonathan turned, the man took off in a sprint towards Burkhard, who suddenly looked alarmed, trying to scramble back.

She had one chance, and no time to think about it. Steeling herself, she stepped in front of the man, who duly slammed into her. She had planted her feet and was able to stop him, but it meant full body contact. It was so sudden and powerful she winced, and her vision turned white for a brief moment. But she couldn't let it best her. Ivy pushed the man back, gently, remembering to breathe. "You don't want to do that. Let Officer Perry take you to the hospital so you can be with your daughter."

The distress on the man's face was palpable. Ivy understood. She had experienced that pain. The man was somewhere between fury and anguish. More than likely it would all hit him at once, and it was better if he wasn't at the scene when it did.

"C'mon, Mr. Nash," Perry said, coming up behind the man. "We'll go right now. We can follow the ambulance all the way there."

Nash allowed himself to be walked over to one of the patrol cars. Perry helped him inside before getting in himself and driving off, following the path of the ambulance.

Ivy exchanged a glance with Jonathan. "You okay?" he asked.

"Yeah...I will be," she said. It surprised her she had been willing to do that, but that had been one of the main reasons she'd been working so hard on herself the past few weeks. She couldn't very well do the job if she couldn't trust people. How she ever thought she could was beyond her.

"You're sure? That was a pretty hard hit."

"Let's just talk to Mr. Burkhard about what happened," she said, changing the topic. Ivy didn't want to discuss her issues, especially not with Jonathan. While he was one of the only people who knew the true depth of her phobias, she felt like every time he asked about them it was like Ivy couldn't take care of herself. Like she needed someone to watch out for her. Of course, most of that had been her own fault. There had been a time when physical contact like that would have sent her into a full-blown panic attack. The fact that she was still upright and walking was a testament to just how far she'd come in a short period of time. She wasn't going back, and if she had it her way, no one would ever mention it again.

"Mr. Burkhard?" she asked, approaching the man sitting on the curb. He was flexing his fingers all the way out, then balling them into fists again, over and over, like it was some kind of compulsion.

He looked up, and despite the fact Ivy had been in his eyeline the entire time she approached him, he seemed startled that she was standing right in front of him. She pulled out her badge to show it to him. Beside her, Jonathan did the same. "I'm Detective Bishop. This is Detective White. Can you tell us what happened?"

He began flexing his hands faster. If Ivy didn't know better, she would say he was on something. "I just...I...uh."

"Just take a deep breath, Mr. Burkhard," she said. "Start from the beginning." Looking him over, he couldn't be older than thirty, though his eyes were sunken in, like he hadn't been getting much sleep. Sitting on the ground, she couldn't tell how tall he was, but his hair was thinning on top and his skin was sallow.

"I was just drivin' to deposit my check," he finally said.

"Your paycheck?" she asked. He nodded.

"Where do you work?" Jonathan asked.

"Davis Automotive," he said. "Over on Gran Vista."

"You're a mechanic?" Ivy asked. He nodded. "How long have you worked there?"

"'Bout six months," he said. Gran Vista wasn't in the best part of town. Ivy was aware Vice had been having a lot of issues down there lately. But the fact Burkhard was all the way over here didn't make much sense if he was going to cash his paycheck.

"Where do you normally cash your checks?" she asked.

"Um… at the Walmart," he said, looking down.

"That's clear on the other side of town," Ivy said. "So what were you doing over here? It's nowhere close to Gran Vista *or* Walmart."

"I…uh, needed to visit a friend."

"What's this friend's name?" Jonathan asked.

"Davis."

"Okay," Ivy said. "So you were coming to see Davis. Then what happened?"

Burkhard looked over at his car, then back at the road, then to the stop sign at the intersection. "I dunno."

"Did you run the stop sign?" Ivy asked.

"No, no. I slowed down," he said.

"A bystander said you were going around fifty," Jonathan said. "And you slammed into Mr. Nash's car there coming through the intersection."

Burkhard didn't say anything, just stared at the ground.

"Have you taken any illegal substances today, Raymond?" Ivy asked. "Or had any alcohol?"

He didn't respond, just continued staring at the concrete,

like he didn't hear her. As best she could tell, this was open and shut. Burkhard, probably high, blew through the intersection, took out Nash's car, flipping it, and may have killed a young woman. "Mr. Burkhard, I'm placing you under arrest for reckless driving and endangering the public," Ivy said. "Please stand up." When he didn't move, Jonathan got behind him and picked him up as Ivy handcuffed him. "We're going to do a blood test and see if there is anything in your system. If there is, we'll add driving under the influence to that list."

While Jonathan read Burkhard his rights, Ivy called over one of the other patrol officers. They escorted Burkhard to the nearest vehicle, where he was helped into the back. The man was in no condition to put up a fight, though he might be more resistant when he sobered up.

"Meth?" Jonathan asked once they had him in the back of the patrol car.

"Maybe. Could be H. Hard to tell. But I'm betting this Davis person is his dealer." She headed back over to the cars just as a tow truck arrived. Ivy stared at the door the fire department had to cut off with the jaws of life. The frame around it had been smashed in. It must have been where the young woman was sitting when Burkhard hit them. Odds were Burkhard was in for a long stay. And if the woman didn't make it, they'd add manslaughter to the list of charges as well.

All for what? A high?

"What are you thinking?" Jonathan asked.

"Just about how pointless it all seems sometimes," she replied.

"Try not to focus on it too much. It's a good way to drive yourself crazy. C'mon. Let's finish up. I don't want to be here all night."

"Yeah," Ivy replied. He was right. Despite the fact he never harped on it, Jonathan had about five more years' experience in this job than she did. But it always felt like they were equals, which was how she knew she had a good partner.

Ivy took one last look at the cars, then followed Jonathan over to the small crowd that had gathered. They'd need statements from anyone else who saw the wreck.

With any luck, they'd only be here a few hours. And lately, luck had been on her side.

Chapter Two

IVY PULLED out her phone to check the time. It was closing in on eight PM and they still had to write their reports for the incident. They'd managed to interview everyone who saw the wreck, which more or less confirmed what Ivy had assumed happened. The witness statements along with Burkhard's own testimony would be enough to wrap this one up. She doubted it would even go to court. The D.A. would more than likely offer a deal, and if Burkhard had any sense in that messed-up brain of his, he would take it.

The tow trucks had managed to remove the vehicles and the fire department had stayed to help clean up the scene, which Ivy appreciated. It made the work go faster. And before long, the lanes were open to traffic once again like nothing ever happened.

"Dinner?" Jonathan asked as they made their way back to Ivy's car. "Your choice. But I don't want to take it back to the office. I need a break."

"Shit," Ivy said under her breath. "I completely forgot. I was supposed to have dinner with Aunt Carol tonight." She checked her phone again, but there was no missed texts or calls. Carol knew Ivy's schedule was chaotic, and she never pushed Ivy to break her commitments with the department for her sake.

"How late does she normally eat?"

"Around seven," Ivy said, speed dialing her number. She could at least give Carol her apologies.

"Hey there," the woman's soft voice said over the phone. "Working a late case?"

"I'm so sorry," Ivy said. "There was a bad wreck out here on Winslow. I didn't realize we'd be here so long."

"You don't need to apologize to me. You know that," Carol said. "Did you get something to eat yet?"

Ivy glanced over at Jonathan. "We were just discussing that."

"Well, if you can take a break, come on over. I still have everything ready here. I can throw it in the oven."

"I don't want—"

"Now don't you try and tell me I can't feed my own daughter," Carol said. Despite Carol adopting Ivy when she was twelve, she had never referred to her as anything other than her daughter, even though Ivy didn't reciprocate. Carol never had any biological children, and by the time Ivy came along, she was already in her late forties. Ivy was the only "child" she would ever have.

Ivy's stomach rumbled. "If you're sure it's no trouble."

"Do I need to drive over there to convince you in person?" she asked.

Ivy grinned, despite herself. "No." She glanced over at Jonathan who looked like he was doing his best not to eaves-drop on the conversation. "Do you have room for two?"

"COME IN, COME IN," CAROL SAID, OPENING THE DOOR FOR them. The night had turned chilly and it looked like a storm might roll through. Ivy shivered as she crossed the threshold into the warm foyer of Aunt Carol's house. She hadn't lived in the house since she was eighteen, but a couple of weeks back she had taken up residence for a few days while she sorted some things out with the Baker case. It felt better to stay with someone than be alone back at her apartment. Not to mention this house was really the only home she could come back to. The one that belonged to her parents—the one she grew up in—had been sold long ago after her family disappeared.

"Jonathan, good to see you, thanks for coming," Carol said, welcoming him in and wrapping him in her arms. She would have done the same to Ivy if Ivy would let her, but that was a bridge they had yet to cross. Despite Ivy's foray into desensitization, she still had a barrier when it came to people she knew personally. It was much easier to slap some cuffs on a stranger than it was to embrace a friend.

"Thanks for having me. I hope I'm not intruding," he said, taking off his overcoat. Ivy did the same, taking his coat from him and storing them both in the closet. She leaned in just a little further to make sure the shotgun Aunt Carol had purchased was still there on the inside of the door. While it had a blanket over it, it hadn't moved since the last time she checked. On the one hand, she was glad she had it, but on the other, Ivy wasn't sure she wanted Carol wielding a shotgun.

"There is no such thing in this house and if you mention it again, I'll take it as a personal offense." Aunt Carol smiled and led them into the living room. She was spry for her age, and in good shape, which she attributed to her constant physical activity, yoga and a limited amount of weightlifting. While usually soft-spoken, Carol was the kind of person who was energized by having people around her. And the more people she had, the more energetic she became. She practically flitted her way into the kitchen.

"Now you two stay there for a minute while I finish this. Then we'll eat at the table like civilized people."

Ivy rolled her eyes, leaning close to Jonathan. "She refuses to eat in front of the TV. Something about her parents always doing it when she was little."

"That's right," Aunt Carol said from the other room. "My parents would microwave us meals, pull out the tray tables and sit us down in front of the idiot box for dinner every night. I have seen enough reruns of every sitcom imaginable that if I never watched television again, I wouldn't miss it."

Jonathan approached the doorway to the kitchen, leaning against the frame. "You grew up in Oakhurst?"

"In Portland," she said. "Moved to Oakhurst when I was in my thirties. I'd had enough of city life."

"What part of Portland?" Jonathan asked.

"We had a house in Cedar Hills. Do you know it?"

He nodded. "My family is from Portland too."

Ivy made her way past Jonathan—managing not to touch him, though it was close—and started working around Aunt Carol. The woman would rally and rail against any help, but Ivy had learned long ago to stop asking for permission and to just get started. She began by checking the lasagna in the oven —it still had another ten minutes or so.

"Really?" Aunt Carol asked, the joy in her voice unmistakable. Ivy grinned again; this was Aunt Carol at her happiest. Maybe missing their pre-planned dinner had been a stroke of luck. Because if she had made it, Jonathan wouldn't have been here. But she was glad he was. She liked him more than she was willing to admit to herself, though she wasn't about to let those feelings run away with her. It wasn't like anything could ever happen between them. How would that work? No physical contact? It wouldn't be fair to him.

"What part of Portland does your family live in? Maybe I know them," Carol chirped.

Jonathan sighed. "I'm sure you do. Constance Garson?"

Carol stopped fussing over the green beans for a moment. "*The* Constance Garson?"

Jonathan nodded. "After my father died, she went back to using her maiden name."

Carol cleared her throat. "She has a daughter too, doesn't she? Your sister?"

"Marie," Jonathan said.

"I had no idea you were Constance Garson's son," Carol said, turning to Ivy. "Why didn't you tell me?"

"Because I don't know who Constance Garson is," Ivy said, pulling a tray of rolls already arranged in perfect lines out of the refrigerator. She set it on the counter beside the oven.

"She's only one of the wealthiest and most philanthropic members of the Portland community," Carol said, turning back to Jonathan. "Didn't she donate enough to Randall Children's Hospital to have an entire wing named after her?"

He nodded. "That was for my sister's sake. She has a rare type of blood disease. They're…still trying to figure out what it is."

"Oh," Carol said, taken aback. "I'm so sorry. I had no idea."

"It's not something my mother wants known," he said. "The idea that any of us are susceptible to disease is something she doesn't handle very well."

Carol returned her attention to the beans again. "Sounds like you have a strained relationship."

"It's…complicated," Jonathan said. "Still, I went up to see her and Marie a month or so ago. My sister is doing very well, despite what my mother believes."

"I'm glad to hear that." Carol handed the green beans to Ivy. "Here, put these in under the lasagna."

Ivy did as she was told, not bothering to question it. Carol was a whiz in the kitchen, something that was sorely lacking from Ivy's life. She went about gathering the utensils and cloth napkins before setting them around the table for the three of them while Carol and Jonathan continued to converse in the kitchen. Why hadn't she done this before? For the longest time she'd treated dinner with Aunt Carol like a chore instead of something to be enjoyed, and when she did open herself up to it, she'd been adamant about not bringing Jonathan over, *despite* Carol's repeated requests.

Why? What was so wrong about any of this? That her partner and her adoptive mother would get along? That they might actually have something in common?

"—and so then, I get a call from the principal telling me she's flashed the entire school!"

Ivy's heart jumped as Carol came into the dining room, carrying a bottle of wine and glasses. Jonathan followed her in, laughing hysterically.

"What are you doing?" Ivy asked, frozen to the spot.

Carol set the glasses down before uncorking the wine. "Just relating a few of your more…interesting…times at school."

Behind her, Jonathan was grinning. "Now I understand why you always wear pants."

Her cheeks flashed hot, there was no doubt they were beet red. Now she remembered why she hadn't wanted to do this. Carol was going to trot out every embarrassing story about her. "Look, it was one time and it was a mistake."

"Flashing the entire school?" he asked.

"It wasn't the entire school, it was one hallway," Ivy said, heading back into the kitchen, fuming. "She's exaggerating. And it was only for a second. My foot got caught on my skirt."

"She was suspended for three days," Carol said.

"A rebel from the start," Jonathan said.

Ivy grabbed a pair of oven mitts and pulled the lasagna out of the oven, setting it on Carol's old terracotta trivet. She then shoved the rolls into the oven and slammed the door.

"Honestly, that was probably the tamest thing she ever did," Carol said.

"Okay, that's enough," Ivy said. "Story time is over. How

about we talk about something else? Jonathan? How much does your mom annoy you? Let's talk about that."

Carol chuckled. "You can't blame me. This is the first time you've brought someone over in...well, probably ever."

"You never brought anyone over when you were younger?" Jonathan asked.

"I thought we'd agreed not to talk about me anymore." Ivy hated to admit it, but it was true. After everything that had happened with her parents, she found it hard to relate to people. Other girls her age didn't understand why she didn't like to be touched, which was a surprisingly big deal. Ivy had gotten along with some of the other kids at Mrs. Baker's house because they'd all been in the same boat. But after Aunt Carol adopted her and she started going to a "normal" school again, she just couldn't get on the same level with other people. Eventually, she stopped trying and just focused on her schoolwork.

"I get it," Jonathan said. "I didn't really either. No one wants to be friends with the rich kid. They all think you're too stuck up, that you think you're better than they are. All people ever wanted from me was either money or to beat me up. Sometimes both."

"Oh," Ivy said. "I'm...uh, sorry." Out of the corner of her eye she caught Carol watching them, a serene smile on her face. Ivy immediately turned away from Jonathan and headed back into the kitchen, determined not to think about him or anything else other than getting the rolls out in time.

"I like him a lot," Carol said softly from behind her. Ivy turned to see it was just the two of them. Jonathan must have stayed in the dining room.

"He's a good partner," she said.

"He seems like it."

Ivy waited a full breath. "I know what you're thinking. But it won't happen."

"I never said anything."

Ivy turned to her adoptive mother. Aunt Carol was the most patient, most caring person she had ever met. And Ivy had put the woman through her paces, especially in her teenage years. How Aunt Carol hadn't written her off yet was beyond her. She never judged, never expected anything. Only ever offered support. And as much as Ivy didn't want to disappoint her, some things just couldn't be helped. In the end, Ivy always disappointed everyone. It was in her blood.

Ivy opened her mouth to say something, but thought better of it just as the timer went off. She pulled the rolls out and set them beside the lasagna, both smelling wonderful. Carol grabbed a second pair of mitts and took the lasagna, headed for the dining room. "Let's eat," she said. "You must be famished."

Chapter Three

DESPITE THE EARLIER TENSION, Ivy managed to relax sometime after the third embarrassing story. It was clear Aunt Carol was enjoying herself, and Ivy wasn't about to rain on her parade. Not to mention the food was wonderful. It almost made her forget they still had to head back to the office to write their reports from earlier.

Not only did Jonathan get to hear about all of Ivy's exploits as a teen, but she managed to learn a lot more about him though Carol's ability to keep the conversation flowing no matter what. She learned that he and his mother didn't become estranged until his father passed away when he was still young, and that she had become more and more over-bearing as he got older. And while his sister was content to stay in Portland to "carry on the family name," Jonathan had needed a way out. At first, he'd thought police work would be enough of a barrier between his old life and a new one, but apparently working in a town where everyone knew who your parents were wasn't an effective strategy. Eventually—and against his mother's strict wishes—he moved to Oakhurst just to put a little distance between them.

"Let me guess, she threatened with cutting you out of the will," Ivy said, pointing at him with her fork covered in sauce and cheese. A small bit dripped on the table. She grabbed a napkin to wipe it up.

"Threatened, followed through, and sent me a copy," Jonathan said before taking a sip of his wine. "I guess she thought an ultimatum was the best way to get me back."

"That's terrible," Carol said. "I'm so sorry you've had to endure that."

He shrugged. "I made my peace with it. I never wanted their money anyway. It didn't make my parents happy. Why would it be any different for me? Honestly the only reason I go back anymore is for Marie. She's not as cynical as I am."

"And the doctors don't know anything about her disease?" Carol asked.

He shook his head. "She's the first known person to contract it. They think its genetic, but aren't a hundred percent sure. But they don't think she'll live much past forty. Though to hear my mother tell it, Marie is already on her deathbed."

Ivy averted her eyes. She'd known a little about Jonathan's upbringing, but nothing in this detail. And she hadn't realized just how complex the situation was. "You said she flew her all over the world looking for a treatment."

He took a deep breath. "Just goes to show money can't fix everything."

Carol reached out and placed a supportive hand on Jonathan's. "Thank you for sharing that with us. I know it couldn't have been easy."

He smiled. "I figured I at least owed you that much, for the skirt story if nothing else." He turned and winked at Ivy.

Carol chuckled, looking around the table. "Can I get anyone dessert?"

"Not unless you can put it into a pill about that big," Ivy

said, holding her finger and thumb about an inch apart. "That's all the room I have left."

"This was plenty, thank you. I don't think I've eaten this well in years," Jonathan said, getting up to start clearing dishes.

"No, you sit right there and let things settle," Carol said. "I will take care of the dishes."

Jonathan stood up anyway. "I can't very well let you do that, not after fixing this meal for us. Trust me, I'm a master of the dishwasher."

Carol sat back down, motioning for him to go ahead. Jonathan took the initiative and managed most of the plates in one trip. The whole time Carol couldn't stop grinning at Ivy, despite her repeated attempts to get Carol to stop with pointed looks. When Jonathan had cleared everything and was running the water in the kitchen, Carol made a motion for Ivy to go join him.

Ivy shook her head.

"Why not?" Carol whispered.

"Because…it can't lead to anything good."

"You don't know that. At the very least don't be rude. Go help our guest."

Ivy huffed, feeling like she was seventeen again as she got up from the table and joined Jonathan in the kitchen.

"Did she send you in here?" he asked.

Ivy just glared at him. "Hand me a plate. You rinse, I'll load."

Jonathan handed the plate over as Ivy opened the dishwasher, slipping it in the back. "She likes you. A lot."

"I can tell," he said, handing her another plate. "But she *loves* you."

"I know," Ivy said. "I love her too…it's just…hard."

"I can't imagine," he said.

"Why did you tell us all that stuff about your mom and

your sister? Really? You didn't have to say any of that." Ivy grabbed a couple of the glasses he had already rinsed.

"I don't know," he said. "It's not something I talk about... ever. But being here, with you, it's easy to open up. I don't know why."

"Aunt Carol has that effect on people," Ivy said, adding the smaller plates inside. "She has a way of disarming you without you even realizing it."

"I don't think it's her," he said. "I think it's you."

Ivy stopped loading, looking up at him. "Me?"

"I just feel very...comfortable with you," he said. "I can't really explain it."

Her heart began ratcheting up a couple of beats, despite her best efforts to stop it. She didn't know what to say. The energy in the room had taken a quick turn. It was as if she was standing in the middle of a thundercloud, with bolts of electricity snapping through the air around her.

Ivy had an almost uncontrollable urge to drop the plate she was holding and grab onto him for dear life, never to let go again. She could imagine herself doing it, taking hold of his arm, purposefully feeling that skin-to-skin contact for the first time... it was so strong, it overwhelmed her to the point she was practically shaking.

Only for Ivy to realize she wasn't shaking at all; her pants were vibrating. More specifically, the phone in her pocket. She broke eye contact with Jonathan, turning herself away as she fumbled for the nearby towel to dry her hands. She only managed it halfway before fishing the phone out of her pocket.

"Bishop."

"It's Nat." The voice of her boss came through clear, severing whatever invisible connection she had felt in the moment with Jonathan. He was at high alert, his focus on Ivy's phone. She put it on speaker.

"I'm here with White. We haven't had a chance to get in to file our reports yet, but we're headed to the office now," Ivy said.

"Don't bother," Nat replied. "Something has come up. I need the two of you, right away."

Chapter Four

THE ENTIRE DRIVE to the scene, Ivy couldn't stop thinking about what she had felt in Aunt Carol's kitchen. She didn't think she had ever felt like that before, a *pull* like that, so strong it was almost like being dragged in by a magnet.

At the same time, she did everything she could to bury that feeling under every ounce of willpower she could muster. She couldn't let herself slip up, not with Jonathan. Not with anyone. It would not turn out well. She would just have to suppress the feeling and hope she could keep it from ever popping up again. The last thing she needed to do was lead him on into thinking there could be something between them when there clearly couldn't. It just wasn't in the cards for her, at least not anytime soon. And she wasn't going ask someone to sit around and wait for her to get her head straight.

"Ten o'clock on a Friday night. It's always the crazies that come out on the weekends," Jonathan said as Ivy turned off the main road into an older part of town.

"I guess everyone needs a hobby," she said, hoping he wasn't thinking as hard about what almost happened in the kitchen as she was. Hopefully he just dismissed it as nothing more than a brief interlude, nothing to ruminate on and certainly nothing to ever mention again. If she was lucky, they could just pretend like it never happened.

"There we are," Jonathan said as soon as they saw the flashing lights in the distance. The road was mostly flat, following a series of streetlights that looked like they had come from the 1950s. This was one of the oldest neighborhoods in Oakhurst, but not in a good way. Most of the houses were dilapidated, having been ignored for the flashy, new sections of town. If Ivy wasn't mistaken, this was probably where most people came to live in the town after World War II. The houses had that post-war era look about them. Most were one story and none had garages. In fact, some didn't even have driveways. Instead, they just had gravel pathways which had been overgrown with grass.

About a block out, the streetlights stopped as they approached the large church which sat on the corner plot away from most of the other houses. Ivy had passed it a few times, though she'd never paid much attention to it. It was large, stone, and ornate, as most Catholic Churches from that time were. Stained glass windows shone in the darkness from the front and the sides of the building, highlighting the lights from inside.

Three patrol cars were already on the scene when they pulled up, one of which had been at the wreck earlier. Ivy pulled the car to the side of the road and looked around for Nat before she and Jonathan got out.

"Has Lieutenant Buckley arrived yet?" Ivy asked the patrol officer directing any traffic down this road around the church. He'd been one of the officers at the wreck earlier.

"I think she's inside somewhere," he said. "Hell of a night, huh?"

"Poor guy probably hasn't even eaten yet," Jonathan said as they made their way to the scene. "At least we don't have to do this on an empty stomach."

Ivy supposed it was too much to ask that he not ever

mention the dinner again. But at the same time, it had been really nice. Just those last few moments had been... well, *charged*.

The patrol cars sat alongside the left side of the church, which was one of the two streets it bordered on the corner. However, the large wooden doors at the front were open, with officers coming and going. A small crowd had gathered on the other road, the one that abutted the church's front. And because there was no sidewalk, an officer was doing his best to keep the crowd in a small group off the main part of the road.

"Two scenes in one night," Ivy said as they ducked the police tape already in place. "Why do I feel like we're not going to get back to the office any time soon?"

"Probably because we won't," he replied. "These late-night cases are never the easy ones."

"Anyone seen Lieutenant Buckley yet?" Ivy asked as she approached the doors to the church.

"Here," Nat said, emerging from behind the doors. Her dark red hair was tied back, though some of the wavy curls had escaped. She looked like she hadn't slept in a week. "I need both of you to prepare yourselves."

Ivy stopped short with Jonathan not far behind. In fact, he was as close as they had been beside the sink, if not closer. She could almost feel the heat emanating off him. "Why? I thought you said this was a murder case."

"It is," Nat said. "But it's not like any murder case I've ever seen. I just hope you two have empty stomachs."

Ivy exchanged an anxious glance with Jonathan. "Nat, what is *in* there?"

"Do you know Father Rouge?" she asked. "He's head of this church. Or... he was."

"Someone *murdered* a priest?" Ivy asked.

Nat took a deep breath. "They didn't just murder him." She stepped to the side to allow Ivy and Jonathan entry. Ivy took a tentative step in, looking around as she did. The outer vestibule seemed quiet. But when she stepped into the nave, she could feel something was very wrong.

"There," Ivy said, pointing at the altar which sat at the end of the long central aisle that split the seating area of the church in two. At the end of the aisle stood one officer, though he wasn't looking at the altar.

Ivy couldn't take her eyes off it. A body lay across the ornate stone structure, perpendicular to it so the body's legs were facing her. Ivy nodded at the officer as they approached, who nodded back, then silently excused himself. She could feel Jonathan right behind her as they grew closer, almost like he was a shield in a way. But as they got within ten feet of the altar, an unimaginable stench reached her nose. It was the smell of shit combined with bile. She stopped to gag, nearly throwing up all over the marble floor.

"You okay?" Jonathan asked.

Her stomach roiled, but Ivy had always had a strong constitution. She held her nose, took three deep breaths, then straightened back up. "Yeah," she said, letting go of her nose again. It was still pungent, but not as bad. As she turned back to the body, the white robe was unmistakable. However, it was covered in blood. And as she and Jonathan took the steps to the altar, she could see why.

The figure in front of them, who she assumed was Father Rouge, had been disemboweled. His chest and stomach cavity were open, his intestine having been pulled out of his body and laid across the altar. Some of his other organs had been removed as well, placed carefully beside him, leaving a gaping cavity in their wake.

"Punctured his lower intestine," Jonathan said, covering his nose. "That's where the additional smell is coming from."

It took Ivy a minute to resolve what she was seeing. The man's eyes were open, a look of surprise on his face. And there were small slice marks across his cheeks, like someone had swiped at him with a claw or a sharp blade. He was sliced open from about the middle of his rib cage all the way down to his pelvis and his clothes were soaked in blood. So much, that it had dripped down from the altar to the floor and was pooling to the side.

"Damn," Ivy whispered.

"It's one hell of a scene." She turned to see Nat standing in the middle of the aisle about halfway back. "Like I said. Not your typical murder."

"Who found him?" Ivy asked, stepping back down from the altar, careful to avoid the blood. Jonathan stayed behind, taking a closer look at the body.

"Nobody. We got an anonymous tip on the phone line. They refused to identify themselves. Sounded like they were trying to disguise their voice. Might have used one of those app things." Nat put her hands on her hips, dropping her head. "Patrolman Ellis and his partner came to check it out. They found the doors to the church unlocked, and when they came inside... this."

"Are you tracing the call?" Ivy asked.

"Working on it now. But if they disguised their voice, they could have used a burner phone."

Ivy nodded. This was on an entirely different level than what she was used to dealing with. Headless bodies were one thing. But someone who had been disemboweled...displayed like this...it was something else entirely. Someone had wanted to send a message. And they had called to make sure Father Rouge was found while he was still fresh.

"Forensics?" Ivy asked.

"On the way."

She looked above her as Jonathan rejoined them. "What about cameras? Any inside?"

Nat shook her head. "Only a few security cameras on the outside of the building. One by the back door and another by this door. We're trying to locate whoever would have access to them. You're seeing this one fresh. We only got the call forty-five minutes ago."

"Ok," Ivy said. "We'll get to work. Is Burns on her way?"

Nat nodded. "Should be here within the next ten minutes."

"Good," Jonathan said. Rochelle Burns was the best coroner this side of the state. Hopefully she would be able to tell them something about the body that wasn't evident. As much as Ivy hated to do it, she returned to the body and began snapping pictures with her phone for future reference. She could have waited for the forensics team to do it, but she wanted to get them while he was still fresh, in case something about the scene changed. Time was of the essence here. There was an obviously deranged and dangerous person out there. Someone with a dark agenda. She needed to find them before they hurt anyone else.

"Let's start by checking the perimeter," Ivy said. "See if our killer accidentally left anything behind."

"Agreed," Jonathan said. He'd switched fully into business mode, all trace of his earlier softness gone. Ivy was amazed how he could turn it on and off like that; it was very much something she wished she could do too.

Thankfully, Ivy had some supplies stashed in her car. They headed back out and returned with booties for their shoes and gloves to make sure they wouldn't disturb anything. On the way back, Ivy noticed the crowd outside had only grown larger. When this story hit the news, it would be a full-blown panic.

When they got back inside the church, they donned their protective equipment and began a detailed search of the area around the altar, just as Dr. Burns and her team showed up.

"Jesus, Mary and Joseph," Dr. Burns said, crossing herself as she approached the altar. Ivy took a second from their investigation to go speak with the woman.

"I didn't realize you were Catholic," Ivy said.

Dr. Burns, a woman in her late fifties with short, silver-blonde hair stared for a moment at Father Rouge. "I'm not. It's habit. Grew up in a Catholic school. Never quite shook it." The two techs behind her looked like they might be going a little green. "Made any progress?"

"We just got started," Ivy said. "I took pictures as soon as we got here."

"Send those to me," Burns said. "We'll get our own as well. But I'm expecting him to decompose quick, exposed to the open air like this. We'll need to be efficient." She turned to her team and with one practiced motion, all three of them started to get to work.

"We'll work the perimeter and make our way in," Ivy said.

"And we'll work our way out. Meet you in the middle," Burns said.

Ivy thanked her, then returned to Jonathan, who had stopped by one of the side doors that led to the outside. "Funny. I didn't think coroners were bothered by this kind of stuff."

Jonathan turned to look at Dr. Burns and her team near the altar. "Did she say something?"

"Just crossed herself," Ivy said.

"I guess there's a first time for everything," he said. "She's still human. Honestly, I'd be more concerned if she *didn't* show a reaction."

"I guess that's true."

Jonathan pushed on the door; it swung open with ease. "Not locked."

"Like the front door." Ivy pushed through, finding herself on the back of the church, staring at a cemetery in the darkness. "Could he have escaped through here?"

"Maybe," Jonathan said. "It would make more sense than going out the front door." He looked up. There were no cameras on this side of the building. "It's dark out here, easy to get away. He could jump that stone fence if he was in good enough shape."

Ivy took a few steps into the courtyard, staring out at the cemetery. "What are the odds he's still out there, watching?" The cemetery itself was as large as a city block, apparently having been here long before space in the town became an issue.

"He'd have to be pretty stupid," Jonathan said.

Still, Ivy couldn't shake the feeling something was out among those tombstones, watching them. She was about to take a few steps forward when another pungent smell caught her nose. She pulled out her phone, shining it along the ground until she found the source.

"Look," she said. "Someone seems to have lost their lunch...or dinner." A pile of vomit sat at her feet. Ivy bent down, shining the light in it.

"I'll go get Burns," Jonathan said. "We'll need a sample of this."

"Think it could belong to the killer?" Ivy asked. "Maybe he couldn't handle what he'd just done."

"Maybe," Jonathan said. "One thing is for sure. Someone else was definitely here."

Chapter Five

"HEY, DOC," Jonathan called across the nave. "Got something out here you're going to want to check out."

Burns looked up from her work. "Jiminez, follow Detective White. Take care of whatever he needs." One of the techs stopped her work and got up, trotting over to Jonathan.

"What is it?"

"We found some—"

"Jonathan!" He turned to see Alice Blair, being held back by a very adamant officer Ellis. Alice was doing her best to sidestep him, but Ellis was a big guy, almost bouncer-sized. There was a reason they used him for crowd control.

"Go find Detective Bishop," Jonathan told Jiminez. "She's on the other side of that door. She'll show you."

"Got it," Jiminez said, trotting off. Jonathan turned and headed back down the aisle until he reached the vestibule.

"I'll take care of this," he told Ellis, edging his way around the big man. Alice was practically bouncing up and down on her feet, something she always did when she was in pursuit of a big story. Beyond her was her cameraman, Jimmy. Somehow both of them had managed to avoid the blockade on the street where an even larger crowd was now gathered.

"Detective, can you tell us what happened? There are reports a priest has been killed," Alice said, shoving the microphone in Jonathan's face. The light on Jimmy's camera was on, though Jonathan knew it wasn't a live broadcast. Alice would make sure she had something solid before insisting on breaking into the channel's prime time viewing slot.

Jonathan gently covered the microphone with his hand, moving it out of the way. "Turn that off, please."

"Are you declining to make a statement, detective?"

"Alice. Now."

She screwed her face up, the frustration he'd seen on it so many times before leaking through. He'd seen that same look the day they'd broken up, after he'd decided he just couldn't handle a relationship with her. Alice was a nice enough person; they just hadn't been compatible. And for a while, he thought she was handling it well. That was, until she began letting herself into the police station and trying to get inside information on every case he'd been working. It got so bad that when she uncovered classified information about a recent killer, it ended up putting her right in his crosshairs. Jonathan and Ivy had barely saved her from being Kieran Woodward's final victim. He had hoped that close call with death might have curtailed some of her behavior. Unfortunately, it only seemed to have increased her determination.

"Really? You're gonna deny me this story. I'm the only one here. As soon as Channel Six gets over here, I lose the exclusive."

"A man has died, Alice."

"People die every day, *Jonathan*. It's my job to inform the public."

"At the potential cost of tipping off any suspects," he said. "You'll be the first to receive a statement when we can make one. We're still gathering information."

Alice turned to her cameraman, making a slicing movement across her throat. Ironic, considering that's where her scar remained after her run-in with Woodward. She addressed Jonathan again. "You give me your word?"

"I'm not going to cut you out of an exclusive, Alice," he said.

She peered around him, trying to see into the rest of the church. "Where's Detective Bishop? Isn't she with you?"

Jonathan furrowed his brow. "She's out back, why?"

Alice's gaze lingered past him for a few minutes before pulling back. "No reason. Just wondering. I happened to pass Lieutenant Buckley on the way in. She didn't look too happy."

"It's a...complex case," he said.

She leaned close to him. Close enough he could smell a hint of her perfume. "Off the record, what happened in there?"

"Alice..."

"C'mon," she said. "For old time's sake. None of it will reach the airwaves, I promise."

Despite her hunger for the job, Alice had always demonstrated professional integrity. If she said she would keep something out of a story, she always delivered. However, her determination sometimes compromised that morality, as in the case when she broke into Ivy's computer without authorization. And as much as Jonathan wanted to trust her, he wasn't about to open that door again. It had been hard enough during the breakup and they had just begun to get to a point where Jonathan felt like they could be colleagues without things being...complicated.

He didn't want to screw that up.

"Sorry, I'll have a statement for you later. Just give us some time."

Alice huffed, stepping back. Her eyes darted around the place, then landed back on Jonathan's as a sly grin grew between her lips. "How about this? An information trade. I have some...interesting information about your boss that might be of use to you."

He narrowed his gaze, then pulled her to the side out of earshot of officer Ellis. "What are you talking about?"

"Nothing," she said, though the way she said it indicated the opposite. "Like I said, you tell me; I tell you. Simple exchange."

Jonathan chanced a quick look at Ellis. He was doing his best not to pay attention to them, but he'd already overheard some of that. Whatever information Alice was dealing, it would only lead to trouble.

"I don't have time for this," he said. "If you'll excuse me, I have a job to finish."

"You sure?" Alice said. "I really think you'll want to hear this. Maybe Detective Bishop will be more receptive. In fact, I can almost guarantee she will."

"That's enough," Jonathan said, his voice stern. "This isn't a game. Either wait for an official statement or don't. It's your call. But don't try to weasel your way in here again." He made a motion to Ellis who came back over.

"Come on folks, let's move it back," the big man said.

"You don't know what you're missing," Alice called to him, the vitriol in her voice unmistakable. "Make sure to tell Detective Bishop hi for me!"

Jonathan had no clue what had gotten her so riled up and he didn't care. Alice was more or less out of his life and he preferred to keep it that way. He turned back and headed into the church. They had a job to do.

THE POUNDING ON THE DOOR MATCHED THE POUNDING OF HIS headache.

Jonathan turned over, bleary-eyed, fumbling for his phone. When he found it, he realized it wasn't even six-thirty yet. Who could be knocking so hard that they threatened to break down his door?

His first thought it was someone from the precinct, but why wouldn't they just call? He threw off the covers, pulled on a T-shirt and made his way down to the door. The knocking had an almost rhythmic quality to it, coming in short, quick bursts.

When Jonathan looked through the peephole he immediately recoiled. *You have got to be kidding me.*

"Jonathan? I saw you in there. Your shadow blocked out the light for a second. Let me in."

"Go away, Alice. I'm trying to get some sleep," he said.

She knocked harder. "Not until you let me in."

He gritted his teeth. First he'd been up all night working on a gruesome murder case—not getting home until almost four—and now *she* was at his door again. Hadn't he gotten rid of her last night?

But if Alice Blair was one thing, it was persistent. He unchained the door, threw the deadbolt and opened it to find her standing in front of him, as put-together as always. Her blonde hair was pulled back in a tight ponytail and she had on her signature pencil skirt and blouse she always wore when she was on TV.

"How are you not exhausted?" he asked.

She stepped around him. "Easy. Drugs." She made her way into the kitchen as Jonathan sighed, closing the door. What would happen if he just went back to bed? Would she leave him alone then? Or would she keep berating him until the end of time?

Alice started opening cabinets, getting Jonathan's coffee maker started.

"What are you doing here?"

"I tried talking to you last night and you wouldn't have it," she said. "So we're going to talk now. Where did you move the coffee cups?"

He groaned, sitting on one of the stools that rested against his island and pointed to the top left cabinet. Alice grabbed two cups from the cabinet as the coffee maker warmed up. "You still like the doughnut flavor?"

"What I'd really like is some sleep."

"Sleep when you're dead. It's either doughnut or cinnamon roll. Why don't you have any normal flavors?" She rifled through the bowl of individual flavor cups. "When we were together you at least had more than two."

"That's because you liked more than two," he said. "I don't."

"Aww, that was for me?" she said, her voice chipper. Whatever was going on, she was in a *good* mood, though he had no idea why.

"Can we get to it please? I have to be in the office in three hours and I'd prefer to spend at least one more of those hours in bed."

The light on the coffee maker turned green, indicating it was ready for the flavor. "I guess doughnut it is," Alice said, popping it in before hitting the start button. The black liquid streamed into the cup, filling the air with its saccharine aroma.

Jonathan didn't even need to drink coffee for it to have an effect on him. The smell was enough to begin snapping him out of the exhaustion he felt.

Alice opened the refrigerator, snooping around inside. "Don't you have anything to eat?"

Jonathan resigned himself to the fact he wasn't going to get an answer from her until she was ready, he gave up trying to fight it. "Bottom drawer. There are some eggs."

"Ah," Alice said. "You used to keep them on the shelf."

"Not everything stays the same," he said.

"Let me guess, keeping them in the drawer is more efficient, space-wise," she said, winking as she pulled out a couple of eggs before removing a skillet from under the cabinet and setting it on the stove. When he didn't answer she grinned. "Yeah, thought so."

As the skillet heated up, Alice placed the cup of coffee in

front of Jonathan. Doughnut or not, the smell was heavenly. He took a tentative sip, relishing the taste as it coated his throat. "Alice, why are you in my house, fixing me breakfast?"

She cracked a couple of eggs on the skillet as her own coffee cup filled to the brim. "Two reasons. First, I thought I owed you an apology. That was a dirty move last night, and I shouldn't have done it."

"Okay," he said.

"And two, even though you gave me such a bland state-ment that I could have written myself, I decided I couldn't hold off on the information about Lieutenant Buckley any longer."

He took another sip, watching her carefully. "Then that wasn't just a ruse?"

Alice flipped the eggs expertly, the whites sizzling on the pan. "To tell you the truth, I've been struggling with telling Detective Bishop for weeks."

"Wait, this involves Ivy?" he asked. "What's going on?"

"A couple of weeks ago, during that case with the missing girls, I had a run-in with Detective Bishop. At the Baker house."

"I know," Jonathan said. "She told me."

"It seemed strange to me that she knew the house so well, having never been there. But that was before I learned she had been a previous resident, that her family had disappeared and the Baker woman had taken care of her for a short time before she'd been adopted."

"Okay." None of this was news to Jonathan, but he was surprised Alice knew. Ivy had only mentioned they'd had a casual run-in, not that Alice had become privy to Ivy's personal life.

"Well, you know me. Once you hit me with a good mystery I can't stop until I figure out what's going on. I took a quick look and realized that your boss, Natasha Buckley, had been the officer who found Ivy the night her family disappeared. Not only that, she was assigned to the case to find them." Alice looked up as she plated the eggs, pushing them slowly across the island to Jonathan. "I can see none of this is blowing your socks off."

Jonathan ignored the eggs. "What's the point, Alice?"

She set the skillet to the side and took her cup of coffee between her hands. "I just found it curious that the case had never been solved. And when I looked into it further, I found it even more curious that very little, if any, progress had ever been made. Two adults and a ten-year-old child go missing, leaving behind a twelve-year-old girl with no memory of what happened? I even pulled the articles from the time. It was a *big* story back then."

"A lot of cases go unsolved," Jonathan said, taking a sip of his coffee. Though he didn't like where this was heading. Alice looking into Ivy's case? That couldn't lead to anything good.

"Yeah, I suppose. Still, something didn't seem right. No trace of these people. Their house and possessions all sold off; their lives erased like they never even existed? Smelled fishy to me. Like someone didn't *want* them to be found. I asked Lieutenant Buckley about it a few weeks ago. She flat-out denied it, of course. But I got the feeling she knew more than she was saying. Like she was trying too hard, you know? So I pushed the issue."

"Wait, you asked *my boss* if she was participating in a coverup?"

Alice winced. "Well…yes. I admit, I shouldn't have been so direct. But I have a good instinct for these things. And I can tell when someone is lying. Tell me this all adds up. Tell me it makes sense to you."

Jonathan stood, his coffee forgotten. "It doesn't matter if it makes sense or not. You can't just go around accusing people without evidence. You should have come to me."

"And let you talk me out of it? No way. The look on Buckley's face told me all I needed to know. She's guilty of something. I just need to find out what."

"So now you're a detective," he said, his sarcasm plain. *No wonder the Lieutenant sent out a memo about reporters in the office.* At the time he thought it had been nothing more than a simple reminder, but now the reasoning was clear.

"All I'm saying is I think Detective Bishop should know," she replied. "I mean, I assume she's looked into it."

"I wouldn't know," Jonathan said. Ivy wasn't the kind of person who talked about her past very much. Last night at dinner had been the most she had ever opened up, something he hoped would continue. "But if you think I'm floating this idea to her, you really must be on drugs."

"You don't think it's possible?" she asked. "Who else would be in the perfect position to cover it up? Think about it. No leads. No witnesses. No evidence? Three people gone without a trace?"

Jonathan had only been working with Ivy a couple of months, so they hadn't had a lot of time to develop that rapport that naturally comes with time for partners. He wasn't about to insert himself into something that had nothing to do with him. Not only was that an invasion of her privacy, but it would undermine the trust they had built so far.

"Why can't you just let things alone?" he asked. "It was the same when we were together. You never knew when to let go."

"Hey," she said, her voice stern. He even detected a hint of hurt. "I can't help the way I am. If you couldn't deal with that, then that's your problem. But I think something is going on here, and Ivy has a right to know."

"Then why not go to her yourself? Why come to me?"

"Because, dummy. She'll be a lot more receptive to hearing it from you. I barely know the woman. Out of the few interactions we've had, most of those have been combative."

"And you're just doing this out of the goodness of your own heart? Is that it?"

Alice worked her jaw, staring daggers at him. She might pretend to have the greater good in mind, but Jonathan knew better. Alice wanted the story behind what happened to Ivy. And if she could be the one to break it, it would make her career.

"You know what?" Alice said. "Fuck you. Maybe I am a little selfish. So what? At least I'm honest about who I am around people. At least I don't pretend to be some goody-two-shoes when really, I'm just as selfish as everyone else." She headed for the door, grabbing her purse off a nearby chair as she went.

"Alice—" Jonathan called after her, but all he got in return was the slamming of a door.

He glanced down at the eggs growing cold in front of him, sighing. There was only one word for how he had acted.

Shitty.

Plain and simple.

Chapter Six

Ivy PULLED up to the now-familiar house, grinning as she did. What had once seemed so intimidating and uninviting was starting to feel like a second home to her. As she got out of the car, she could hear tiny barks coming from inside. She made her way to the large gate in the middle of the fence, pushing her way through to the overgrown yard, which still hadn't been cut. But that wasn't surprising. Oliver wasn't the type of person to be out every Saturday with his lawnmower, making sure his house looked like every other on the block.

She stepped up to the door, looked into the camera staring down at her and waved. A second later the bolt on the door unlatched and she walked in.

Immediately, Hero was at her feet, yipping and running circles around her. She bent down to try and pet the French bulldog mix, only for him to think it was a game and tried to go after her hand, jumping up then getting down on all fours with his butt in the air, his tail wiggling like crazy. Finally, she managed to wrangle him and give his head a good rubbing.

Satisfied he'd both been petted and played with, Hero took off down the hallway, his little feet tapping against the hardwood floors. Ivy stood and followed him into the back bedroom where Oliver sat, surrounded by three screens and more computer equipment than she could count. The servers were running hot today, as Oliver had fans on each of the large machines, trying to keep them cool. But the temperature in the room was a good five degrees warmer than the rest of the house.

"How do you not suffocate in here?" she asked, stepping inside.

"You get used to it," he replied without turning around. "That and a lot of water."

Hero was panting at his feet, looking up at them.

"And him?"

"He falls asleep right at the door," Oliver said, turning in his chair to point. "See?"

Ivy looked to see a small bed just a hair larger than Hero in the doorway. She hadn't even seen it when she'd come in.

"What's the case?" Oliver asked.

She took a step back. "What?"

"I assume you're here because you need help with a case. So what is it?"

"Can't I just come around and say hi?" she asked.

He held out his hand. "C'mon. Give it to me."

Ivy rolled her eyes. That was the problem when someone knew you as well as Oliver knew her. Even though they hadn't talked for years, when they reconnected, it was like plugging two ends of a disconnected cord back together. They immediately fell back into their old habits with each other, as if no time had passed at all.

"We got it last night," she said, opening her phone and scrolling to the pictures she'd taken of Father Rouge. "But brace yourself. This isn't a nice one."

Oliver gave her a *really?* look before taking the phone. But as he looked at the pictures she caught him wince a few times before finally setting the phone to the side.

"Told you."

"Who was that?" he asked, turning back to his computer.

"Father Matthew Rouge," she replied. "A priest with twenty-two years in the Catholic Church. He's lived in Oakhurst his entire life from what I can find. Never married, obviously. No children. Other relatives are deceased."

"Okay, so what do you need from me?" he asked.

"I was wondering if you'd ever seen anything like this before. You know, in your...exploits on the dark web."

Oliver barked out a forced laugh. "What kind of stuff do you think I get up to in my spare time? I don't go for torture porn."

"So you've never seen this before."

He shrugged, handing the phone back to her. "I mean, there are all kinds of sick things people do to each other. And it's just not in the modern era either. There were some truly messed up torture devices used back in the olden days. Things that would cut a person in half while they were still alive, or devices meant to strip the skin from people. Humanity has never had any trouble coming up with new ways to kill each other."

Ivy scoffed, looking around for a place to sit, though there was none. Oliver lived a solitary life. The only place he had extra seating was around his kitchen table. "I'm looking for this specific signature," she said. "Someone who unwinds the intestine like this. Who places the organs beside the body in this orientation. Does anything about this strike you as familiar?"

"If you mean 'have I ever seen anyone use this exact setup before?' No. But I'll have to do some looking. Like I said, it's not my area of expertise. I don't even like going down that road because it's too easy to find the truly depraved stuff."

"If you can't do it—"

He turned around again quickly. "I never said that. Just give me a few days. Searching for these things...it's not easy."

"Neither is seeing them in person." She leaned up against

the nearest server, but it was hot to the touch and Ivy pulled away quickly. Hero, who was panting harder, left the room, headed for the kitchen. "Can we talk somewhere else for a minute? It's sweltering."

"Yeah," Oliver said, getting up. "You want something to drink?"

"Just water," Ivy said, following him into the kitchen. Despite his insistence that it wasn't hot in that room, beads of sweat had broken out across his brow. When they arrived in the kitchen, Hero was already lapping up water from his bowl.

"Why is everything in there so warm, anyway?" Ivy asked. "It's never been like that before."

"I'm working on a job for a new client," Oliver said reaching into the refrigerator to retrieve a couple of bottles of water. "It's taking a lot of processing power."

"What kind of job?" Ivy asked. Oliver shot her a look that said she shouldn't have even asked. "You know, there are legitimate jobs out there that need doing. Plenty of people need help setting up websites. Or building apps. That's big now, right?"

"It also pays next to nothing," Oliver replied. "If you want the big bucks, you have to swing for the fences."

"And what are you going to do with all these *big bucks*?" Ivy teased, taking a seat at the kitchen table.

"I dunno, maybe buy myself a jet. Fly off to Hawaii whenever I want." He cracked open the water and drank more than half of it without taking a breath.

"Right," Ivy said, opening her own bottle. "It's not warm in there at all."

"Ok, fine," he said. "But what do you want me to do? I need the processing power."

Ivy glanced over at Hero, who had finished drinking, though water was dripping from his jowls all over the floor. "Just make sure he stays cool. It's technically still winter, you know."

"Only for another week or so," he replied, draining the rest of his water. "Well, I need to get back to it." He stood, suddenly.

"No rest for the weary, huh?"

"This is a particularly...demanding client. Plus, now I have to do your homework on top of it." He said it jokingly, but Ivy could tell there was something else there, a kernel of truth somewhere. Whatever this job was, Oliver was worried about it for some reason.

"Hey, you know you can talk to me about anything," she said. "Even if it's not exactly... legal. It isn't like I'm going to arrest you."

"I know," he said, stopping in his tracks. "Don't worry, it's nothing big. Just...demanding. Like I said."

He sure seemed in a hurry to get back there. Ivy stood, her water barely touched. "Let me know if you find anything. And if you don't have time for it—"

"Nah, don't worry," he said. "I was just messing with you. If there's documentation out there of someone else doing this, I'll find it."

"Thanks, Oliver. That means a lot."

"Sure," he said, heading back into his office. "Good luck with the investigation."

Ivy bent down to pet Hero, giving his head a good rub. "Keep him straight, okay?" The dog just looked back at her with his big brown eyes. For a second she thought she should stay, press the issue. But if Oliver wanted to tell her what he was into, he would. It wasn't her business to get in the middle of his.

She let herself out, checking the time again. Another thirty minutes before she had to meet Jonathan back over at the church so they could start interviews this morning. It was already shaping up to be a long day.

Chapter Seven

BY THE TIME she arrived back at the church, a crowd twice the size of the one last night had already gathered. Two different news crews were on site, including the channel Alice Blair worked for, though she didn't see the woman anywhere. Jonathan had told her Alice showed up last night, asking about the case, but Ivy had been too busy to ever look for her. She hadn't had an encounter with Alice since Mrs. Baker's house and Ivy was happy to keep it that way. Alice was unpredictable, and Ivy still wasn't sure what side of the fence she fell on.

Ivy drove up to the police barrier and waited for the officers to remove the stanchions so she could park closer to the church. She pulled in behind Jonathan's car and stepped out, a small bag in her hand. They'd already arranged to do another sweep of the church this morning in the daylight. Burns had gathered as much evidence as she could last night, including a sample of the vomit beside the back door. Ivy and Jonathan had stayed until they removed Father Rouge from the scene, then had stationed officers around the building so no one could get in overnight.

Not that they'd been away for very long. They hadn't left

until sometime around three or three-thirty. And if Ivy hadn't already had three cups of coffee this morning, she doubted she'd be standing upright.

"Hey," Ivy said, making her way back into the church's vestibule. Next to the door was a small office area where the church administration happened. Jonathan was already there, looking as bleary-eyed as Ivy felt. "I brought egg sandwiches."

"Oh," Jonathan said, reluctantly taking the one Ivy offered him. "Thanks."

"Something wrong?"

"No, just…nothing. I appreciate it." He held on to it like it might bite him. "The secretary is already here and the maintenance supervisor is on the way. Want to get started?"

Ivy put the egg sandwich and his odd behavior out of her mind. "One second. I want another look at the altar." She walked up the aisle, taking in the scene, this time in the daylight. Beams of light filtered through the stained-glass windows, bathing the altar in an ethereal glow. But that glow was marred by the sight of dried blood that had yet to be cleaned from the surface. And given that it was white marble, Ivy doubted if it would ever truly come off. They'd have to end up replacing it.

She took a second to see the scene with fresh eyes, hoping it would spark something in her head about what happened here. But it was as nebulous as it had been the night before. A man, murdered in the middle of his church, displayed for all to see. And an anonymous phone call alerting them to it.

Other than a small pile of vomit outside, that was all they had. No witnesses, no other evidence.

She turned back around and headed for the office. "Let's see if we can't at least establish a timeline."

"Right," Jonathan said. Ivy noticed the egg sandwich was conspicuously absent.

She made her way through the vestibule and into the office, which was more modern than the rest of the church. It had glass doors and a suspended ceiling with florescent lights. The first desk in the office was labeled "Church Clerk", though there was no name.

"She's in the back," Jonathan said.

Ivy made her way around the few cubicles until she reached a small break room, complete with vending machines. It had its own door that could be closed off from the rest of the office area. Inside sat an older heavyset woman, probably in her mid-fifties. Her curly brown hair had been permed and she wore pink glasses, though they were off and beside her on the table as she sipped from a paper cup.

"Eloise Banner?"

The woman looked up. "Yes?"

"I'm Detective Bishop. You've already met my partner, Detective White?"

She nodded. "A few minutes ago. He was nice enough to bring me some water." She indicated the cup clutched tightly in her hand. "I just can't believe this is happening."

Ivy took a seat across from her while Jonathan sat at the head of the break room table. "Do you think you could answer some questions for us?"

"I'll do whatever I can," she said. "Matthew was such a sweet man. How could someone do this to him?"

They hadn't released the condition of the body to the public for fear of a possible copycat killer. That was information Nat wanted kept secret for as long as possible. But this was already turning into a media storm. Ivy surmised they only had a few days before the truth got out one way or another. Regardless, all Mrs. Banner knew was Father Rouge had been murdered, nothing more. "You were here yesterday?"

She nodded. "All day."

"What time did you leave?" Ivy asked.

"Around six. It's when I normally leave."

"Did anything about yesterday seem different to you?"

Jonathan asked. "Anything about Father Rouge's behavior perhaps?"

She shook her head. "Nothing."

"Did he have any appointments with anyone yesterday?" Ivy asked.

"Several. Matt—Father Rouge was a pillar of this community. He met with Gregory Wisle with the city council before lunch, then he had another meeting with M.A.A."

"M.A.A.?" Ivy asked.

Banner lowered her voice. "Mothers Against Addiction. They meet regularly at the church on Tuesday nights."

Ivy noted Jonathan was writing all of this down. "What did Father Rouge's typical day look like?"

"That's really about it. He'd get in around nine or ten, have a few meetings, sometime a lunch meeting. Occasionally he'd go out and volunteer with the community or participate in a fundraiser. Then he'd come back and is here the rest of the day. He usually did his writing and other work in the afternoons and evenings."

"For services?" Ivy asked.

She nodded again. "He said the only time he could concentrate was in the quiet of the evenings."

Jonathan stopped jotting notes for a moment. "Did he often stay late to work?"

"Almost every night. It was rare he ever went home before I did," she replied.

"And you're sure he didn't have any appointments after you left yesterday?" Ivy asked.

"I'm sure. I can show you his calendar if you'd like."

Ivy sat back in her seat, exasperated. "Yes, we'll need a copy and a list of everyone he's met with in the past two weeks."

"Have you spoken with Deacon Lutz yet?" she asked.

Ivy and Jonathan exchanged glances. "Who?"

"He supports Father Rouge during services, sort of like a second in command," she replied. "Has anyone notified him?"

"Not that we're aware," Ivy said. "How can we get in contact with him?"

"I'll get his number for you," she said. "He's been on sabbatical since Tuesday."

"Sabbatical where?" Ivy asked.

"Deer Ridge Correctional Facility," she said. "It's a medium-security prison a few hours east."

Ivy nodded. They would check with the facility to confirm Deacon Lutz was actually there. "I'm sure someone will let him know."

She gave them a small smile in return. "Let me get those other names for you. If you'll give me a few minutes."

Ellis stuck his head in the room. "The groundskeeper is here."

"Didn'ja hear me? I'm not the groundskeeper. Ah'm the church *custodian*," a ragged and rough voice from behind him said.

As Ellis moved to the side, Mrs. Banner got up and embraced the man behind him, a man who was probably in his sixties, though his arms looked like they were carved from solid oak.

"Oh, Arch, did you hear? Isn't it just awful?" Mrs. Banner said, burying her head in the older man's chest.

"I know, I know," he said, patting her back. "He didn' deserve it."

"I just can't believe it," she said again, her words muffled.

"Mrs. Banner," Ivy interrupted. "If you wouldn't mind."

"Of course," she said, pulling away from the custodian. "I'll get those items for you."

"Please give them to Officer Ellis," Ivy said, nodding for Ellis to follow the woman.

The custodian, however, remained in the doorway. "You wanted to see me?"

Ivy and Jonathan stood. "If you wouldn't mind…Mr. Suntree?"

"Jus' call me Archie. Everyone else does," he said, coming in and taking Mrs. Banner's seat. He was tall with short gray hair that was balding. Deep lines snaked across his face, one that had seen a lot in its lifetime.

Ivy walked around to close the door behind him before taking her seat again. Banner and Suntree were the only two permanent employees the church had on staff. Everyone else was either part of the clergy or were volunteers, other than Father Rouge, of course. "What can you tell us about yesterday, Mr. Suntree?" Ivy asked.

"Not much to tell. Was a normal day, s'far as I could see. I came in around six, like always. Did my rounds, took lunch at eleven, then was back at twelve and stayed until 'bout five."

"And when you left there was no one else in the church other than Mrs. Banner and Father Rouge?" Jonathan asked.

"Nope. Jus' them two. It was a slow day."

"Can you tell us what you do on a daily basis?" Ivy asked. Suntree looked to her like a pretty strong guy, despite his age. Not to mention he had keys to the property and would be able to come and go as he pleased. She didn't want to tip him off that he could be a suspect, but at the same time they needed information.

"I take care of the property, fix whatever needs fixin'. The grounds too. Keep the cemetery mowed. Stuff like that." He sat back in his chair, almost relaxed.

"Did you interact with Father Rouge often?" Ivy asked.

"Not really. We talked every now an' again. He's a baseball fan, so gave us somethin' to chat 'bout. But I know he was a busy man, so I stayed out of 'is way."

"Can you tell us where you were between six and ten p.m. last night?" Ivy asked.

His mouth drew into a line. "Lessee. At six I was with my grandkids at the park until 'bout seven. Then I had dinner with my son's family. After that I went bowlin' with a couple of the guys. Was there 'till about eleven or so."

"Can you give us the names and phone numbers of the people you were with?" Jonathan said.

"Shore. Ain't got nothin' to hide."

Ivy sighed. They would check out his alibi anyway, but she suspected it would hold. Suntree didn't strike her as the kind of person who could kill a man in cold blood and display his organs beside him. "Do you know anyone who had a grudge against Father Rouge? Anyone who might have wanted to do him harm?"

"Not really," he said.

"What about Deacon Lutz? Do they get along?"

The man threw out a laugh. "Those two? Never saw a bad word pass between 'em. Look, you want someone to blame, you check out those kids who are always trespassin' in the cemetery."

Ivy glanced up. "What kids?"

"Bunch of dopeheads, think it's funny to smoke their *dope* in my cemetery," the man said, working himself up. "It's disrespectful is what it is. I'm all the time findin' cigarettes and discarded beer cans out there. But I know what they're really doin'."

"Dope?" Ivy suggested. Jonathan shot her a smile.

"Damn right. Caught 'em a few weeks back. Made 'em give me their names and even took their pictures. Told 'em I'd be callin' you folks if I caught 'em out there again."

"You believe they were here last night?" Jonathan asked.

"I'd bet my hat on it." Ivy noted the man wore no hat. "Always get bolder on the weekends. Out for a good time." He leaned forward. "If there's one thing I can't stand, detectives, it's disrespect. And these kids these days…"

"How many kids are there?" Jonathan asked.

"Three. Want me to get you their names? I got 'em pinned up over my desk."

"That would be helpful," Ivy said. Suntree was up and out of the room in an instant. "What do you think?"

"I doubt kids could have done that to Father Rouge, but it's an avenue worth exploring. If they were here, they might have seen something."

Ivy flexed her hand open and closed. "I dunno. Sounds like he has an axe to grind. I'm not entirely sure he's trustworthy."

"We'll keep our eye on him," Jonathan said. "With so many local ties I doubt he's about to go anywhere."

Within moments, Suntree was back in the room and tossed three polaroids on the table before sitting back down. Ivy studied the photos. She hadn't seen a Polaroid camera in years. Each photo showed the face of a teenage boy, eyes wide. The pictures were close to their faces and almost blown out, so the finer details were lost. The backgrounds were almost completely dark. At the bottom of each one was a name.

"Oscar Hernandez, Donnie Klinger and Lukas Winchell," Ivy read aloud.

"That's them."

"Do you have any other information on them? Ages? Phone numbers?"

"Naw, I figured I put enough of a scare into 'em they wouldn't bother me again. But you never know. I think they all live in the neighborhood. Never seen any bikes or cars or nothin' when they been around."

Ivy gathered up the photographs. "Thank you, Mr. Suntree. We'll take a look."

"If there's foul play about, you can bet those three were involved," he said.

"You think they're capable of murder?" Jonathan asked.

"Buddy, I think kids are capable of anythin'. You seen what's happenin' on the internet these days?"

Ivy put the pictures in an evidence folder. "Have they ever

broken into the church itself? Anything other than the cemetery?"

He pulled back a little. "Well, no. Not to my knowledge."

"Anyone else you know who might not like Father Rouge?" Jonathan asked.

"Naw. Most everyone loved 'em. Nice guy, friendly. Worked in the community…the man never met a stranger."

"Any suspicious people around the church lately? Other than the kids."

He sat back in his seat, taking a deep breath. "Not that I'm aware."

Ivy had to admit, it wasn't much to go on. She pulled one of her cards out of her wallet, sliding it across the table to him. "Okay, Mr. Suntree. Thanks for your help. If you think of anything else, please give us a call."

"That's it?" he asked. "What about the church?"

"It will have to remain closed for the time being," Ivy said. "Until we can complete our investigation.

"But tomorrow's Sunday. And there's a Mass tonight."

"I'm afraid those will have to be cancelled," Jonathan said. "This is an active crime scene."

Suntree got up. "Yeah. I understand. But a lot of people ain't gonna be happy 'bout it. Have you spoken to the bishop?"

Ivy exchanged a look with Jonathan. "Not yet."

"Well, best be on it. He's gonna want to name a replacement for Father Rouge." Suntree nodded again then headed back out, leaving Jonathan and Ivy sitting there.

"Seemed really torn up about the man," Ivy said.

"I'm assuming that's sarcasm."

She turned to him. "He's already asking us to help usher in his replacement."

Jonathan pulled out his phone, snapping pictures of the polaroids Suntree left. "If there's anything I know about Catholics is they don't let anything get in the way of their faith. They'll want someone down here to help honor Rouge and perform services in his stead."

"Great," Ivy said. "So now we have to consider maybe someone wanted his job?" She had hoped this would have been someone local. But if someone from outside of town was looking at Rouge's job, they could have orchestrated a hit. It certainly wasn't out of the realm of possibility.

"C'mon," Jonathan said. "Let's check out the kid angle first. We'll worry about the diocese later."

Chapter Eight

THEY HEADED BACK to the station to run the names of the kids Suntree had provided. Unsurprisingly, nothing came up in the system, meaning they probably weren't the hardened criminals Suntree had made them out to be. However, after a few calls to the local school board, Ivy managed to find all three boys attended Oakhurst High. From there she was able to obtain a copy of their phone numbers and addresses. Suntree had been right; two of the boys lived in the same neighborhood as the church: Lukas Winchell and Donnie Klinger.

After grabbing a quick and too-greasy lunch, Ivy drove them back out to the neighborhood, passing the church as she did. A crowd was still gathered and one of the news reporters stood out front, delivering a report on what had happened. So far, they hadn't released many details to the news outlets in an attempt to contain the story. But Ivy knew it was only a matter of time. Which made her wonder: where was Alice Blair? Ivy figured she'd be the first back on the scene this morning but so far there was no sign of her. Had Jonathan said something to her last night to put her off the story?

"Ikenberry, here," Jonathan said, noting the street sign. Ivy had almost missed it as it was mostly covered by overgrown trees. She turned down the side street, noting there were no sidewalks and the road looked like it hadn't been paved in a while. On both sides of the street were older, run-down houses in serious need of maintenance.

"This was probably a really nice place back in the forties and fifties," Jonathan said as if he were reading her mind. She couldn't help but smile. Thankfully his attention was out the window. She wasn't sure why, but she didn't want him to see her reaction.

"Now everyone lives in the suburbs and leaves places like this to rot," she said. The house they were looking for was up on the right. Number 882. She pulled up in front of the one-story building, noting there was no car in the driveway. The shades on the large picture window which faced the street were drawn. It didn't look like anyone was home.

As they got out of the car, Ivy surveyed the street. It was quiet. No one was out mowing their lawns, or doing chores. Strange for a Saturday morning. She got the feeling this wasn't the friendliest neighborhood in town.

They made their way across the lawn since the house didn't have a walkway, and took the steps to the covered porch. Ivy made sure her badge was on display before Jonathan knocked. As he did, she kept a close eye on the shades of the picture window. At first there was no response, but finally when Jonathan knocked a third time she saw the shades move ever so slightly. "Someone's home."

"This is the police," Jonathan said. "We're looking for Lukas Winchell."

Finally the bolt on the other side of the door slid and the door cracked open, still on the chain. On the other side was a grizzled face with a haggard beard. "Whatchoo want Lukas for?"

"We just have a few questions to ask him," Ivy said. "Are you his legal guardian?"

"Yeah," he replied. "Lukas ain't here."

"Do you know where he might be?" Jonathan asked.

"No."

"What about when he'll be back?"

"He comes back when he comes back," the man replied. Ivy caught the distinct reek of whiskey on the man's breath, even from where she was standing.

"Is Lukas your son?" Ivy asked.

"Grandson," he replied. "His daddy's with you people. In lockup."

That hadn't come up in her search. Then again, she'd only been looking for the teen. Not any relatives. She'd have to look into the matter further when they were done here. "Do you know of how we can get in touch with Lukas?"

"His phone, I suppose," the man replied. "Never leaves the damn thing behind."

Ivy knew the chances of a teenager answering a call from the police were slim to none. Even if the call came up unidentified, he'd more than likely just let it go to voicemail. And she didn't want to spook him. Especially if he had been at the church last night.

"Do you know where Lukas was last night, Mr…"

"He don't tell me," the man replied. "Now if you don't mind, I'm tryin' to enjoy my only day off." He closed the door on them before Ivy could get out another word.

Jonathan pursed his lips and knocked again. But Ivy knew it was pointless. Mr. Winchell wouldn't be answering any more of their questions.

Finally, they headed back to the car. "You want to try the phone number?" he asked.

"He won't answer," she replied. "Hell, half the time I don't answer if I don't know who's calling me. Let's just try the next kid."

They got back in the car and drove three blocks over to Decker Street. The house of Donnie Klinger looked much the same as the Winchell property. But no one answered the door when Ivy and Jonathan approached. And this time, she couldn't even tell if there was someone inside or not.

Frustrated they weren't getting anywhere, Ivy stepped off the porch, looking around the neighborhood. Two houses down, a man in a wife-beater sat on an old rocker on his porch, watching them. "Hang on," she said. "Lemme check something."

Jonathan, who had been heading back to the car, looked over. "What are you going to do?"

But she was already on her way across the street. She kept her pace slow and calm as not to alarm the man, who didn't take his eyes off her. As she reached his house, she could see he had a six-pack of beer at the base of his rocker, with a half-empty bottle still in his hand.

"Good afternoon," she called. The man nodded back. "Do you happen to know the Klingers? At six-sixteen?" She pointed to where Jonathan stood in front of the house.

"Yeah," he replied. "Known 'em for years."

"Do you know if they're home?"

"What do you want with 'em?" The man's tone was more combative than she'd like. Odds were she wasn't going to get much from him. She was about to forget the whole thing when she saw a small cross nestled above the man's door.

"We're looking to speak with the boy, Donnie," she said, softening her tone. "He may be a witness to what happened at the church last night."

The man put his bottle down. "You mean that thing on the news with the priest?"

She nodded.

The man's entire demeanor changed. "Oh, God, really? Donnie saw what happened?"

"He may have," she said. "We need to find him to ask."

The man's eyes went glassy for a minute. "Yeah, well I saw him leave this morning around ten or eleven."

"In a car?" Ivy asked.

The man chuckled. "That boy don't have any business driving a car. You crazy?" Ivy didn't get it. She looked at the man quizzically. "That boy smokes more pot than a chimney. He does good to stay upright."

Maybe there was something to what Suntree told them after all. "Which way did he go when he left?"

"He's probably down at the park," the man replied. "Ah seen him down there all the time with his friends. Shame. They take over the place so the little-uns don't have a place to play."

"Which park?" Ivy asked.

"Renwood. Just a couple blocks that way," he said, pointing to his left."

"Great," Ivy said. "Thanks for your help."

"Ah hope you find who did it," he said. "Ah really liked that priest. He was a good man. Man o' the people." Ivy regarded him a second before shaking it off and rejoining Jonathan.

"What was that about?" he asked.

"C'mon, we need to get to Renwood Park."

MUCH LIKE THE CHURCH, IVY HAD PASSED RENWOOD PARK probably five dozen times in her life but had never paid much attention to it. As they pulled up, she spotted a couple of teenagers sitting on the ground near the jungle gym, right where the man said Klinger would be. She couldn't tell if they were the kids in the photos from this distance, but it was worth a shot.

"Try not to spook them," Jonathan said as they got out.

"Have you ever *met* teenagers?" Ivy asked. "They're not five. Trust me, they'll stand their ground." It wasn't so long ago that she was an angry teenager herself and she could very much remember what it felt like being in that headspace all the time. Feeling like she was smarter than all the adults, like she had it all figured out, despite the fact no one listened to her. And then there was the constant onslaught of emotions. Thankfully those days were behind her. Youth might be nice for some, but it was something she never wanted to experience again.

As soon as they pulled up, Ivy could already feel eyes on them. And as they approached the small group, three gazes were locked on theirs, watching the entire way. One of them was Donnie Klinger, while another was Oscar Hernandez, looking just like their polaroids. Lukas Winchell was nowhere to be found, but the two boys were sitting with a teen girl with bright blonde hair.

"Donnie Klinger?" Ivy asked as they approached.

"Yeah?" the boy replied. His eyes were bloodshot and lidded; more than likely he was already high. In fact, all three of them were from the looks of things. A small stream of smoke emanated from a nearby backpack.

Ivy nodded at the pack. "You might want to take that out of there before you burn something."

Klinger looked at the pack, then back at her. "What?"

"Your pipe or whatever is in there." The three teens shared worried glances. "Look, we're not here to bust you on whatever miniscule amount of pot you have on you. We need to ask you about last night."

"W-what about it?" Oscar asked.

Despite the high, Ivy could tell all three of them were worked up over something. The girl in particular looked like a rubber band about to snap. She was softly rocking forward and back, shooting glances at the other two, who couldn't take their eyes off Ivy and Jonathan.

"Where were you, for one?" Jonathan asked.

"At a friend's house," Oscar replied.

Ivy nodded, playing along. "What friend?"

"Lukas's," he said. "My friend Lukas."

"That's funny," Ivy said. "Because we just came from Lukas's house and his grandpa said he wasn't home all night."

The three of them shared another glance before the girl ribbed Oscar. "Just tell them."

"Tell us what?" Ivy asked.

"We went to the church last night," she said before Oscar could say anything else. "But we didn't do anything."

"*Brit,*" Oscar hissed.

"*Why* did you go to the church?" Jonathan asked.

"Because they said it was a good place to relax," the girl said, ribbing Oscar again. "Said it was quiet and no one would bother us out there."

"Unlike here," Donnie added.

"And you are?" Ivy asked the girl.

"Brit...Britnee Masterson. I live off Birchwood."

Ivy crouched down so she was on the same eye level with Brit. "Were you the only ones out there last night?"

"No, I brought my friend Lorelai with me. And Lukas was there."

"Okay, so what happened?"

Donnie put his hands in his long hair, pulling at it. "We didn't do anything. I swear. We just jumped the wall to have a little smoke. That's it."

Ivy turned her attention back to Brit. "What happened?"

She nodded. "It's like he said. We just jumped the fence and lit up in the cemetery. That's it."

"You didn't see anything? Or hear anything?"

The three of them exchanged glances again.

"Look guys, either tell us the truth here, or we take you down to the station and get your statements there," Jonathan said, clearly losing patience.

"Lorelai, she...she went into the church," Brit said. Ivy turned back to Jonathan. Surely a teenage girl couldn't have done that to Father Rouge. Jonathan pinched his features.

Ivy returned her attention to Brit. "Then what happened?"

"I'm not really sure. It all happened so quick. She came back out...and then Lukas...he went inside after her because she came out vomiting. But then he came running back out and told us all to run. And that's it."

"That's it," Ivy said. "Really?"

"Yeah," Brit said, looking to her two friends for confirmation.

"Where are Lukas and Lorelai right now?" Ivy asked.

"Haven't seen Lukas since last night," Donnie said. "He wasn't at home this morning and hasn't been answering texts."

"I think Lorelai is at home, sick," Brit said. "Her mom said she wasn't feeling well."

"Yeah, that was some strong stuff last night, wasn't it?" Donnie said, nervous laughter building in his throat. Now Ivy understood what the man on the porch had been talking about.

"Did either of them say anything about what they saw inside the church?" Jonathan asked. "You said the other girl came out vomiting?"

"Yeah," Brit said. "But they wouldn't talk about it. We all just went home afterward. Lori was sick the whole way."

"You guys know what happened last night, right? At the church?" Ivy asked.

The three of them exchanged confused looks. "What?" Oscar asked.

"Don't you watch the news?"

"No," he scoffed. "Why would we?"

Ivy stood back up, not sure if she believed them or not. But if Lorelai and Lukas saw Father Rouge, they might have seen something else, too. They had potential witnesses out there, and needed to track them down. "What's Lorelai's address?" Brit rattled it off to her without even blinking. Ivy fished out a card and handed it to her. "If anyone hears from Lukas, call me immediately. We need to speak with him."

"You're not going to arrest him, are you?" Brit asked. "He didn't do anything."

"We could arrest all five of you for trespassing," Jonathan said. "But all we want to do is speak with him. If he's willing to cooperate, no one will get in trouble."

Brit nodded, though she still seemed apprehensive. "Yeah, okay. We'll keep trying."

Ivy and Jonathan made their way back to the car. "Think they'll do it?" she asked.

"Doubtful, but it was worth a shot. We may need to put an APB out on Winchell. He may have never gone home last night."

"You're not thinking he's involved?"

"If what they're saying is accurate, no. But if he saw something and someone saw *him*, he might be in trouble."

"And this other girl, Lorelai...Sylvester? Wouldn't she be in danger too?"

"Maybe," he said, getting back in the passenger side of the car. "Let's find out what she knows. Then we can decide what to do about Winchell."

"Do you believe them?" she asked. "About not knowing what happened?"

"Do you?"

She turned the engine over and stepped on the gas. "Not in the slightest."

Chapter Nine

"Yep, got it," Jonathan said as Ivy pulled up to the Sylvester home. It was in slightly better shape than the last two, but obviously still in need of some work. An old Subaru sat in the driveway and the name *Sylvester* was written on the mailbox in reflective lettering. He hung up. "Burns said she can match the vomit found at the scene to Sylvester if we provide her with a spit or blood sample."

"Really?" Ivy asked. "I didn't know that was possible."

"Neither did I, but she is one of the best," he said, putting the phone back into his jacket pocket. "That has to be a grisly process, though."

Ivy couldn't agree more. She didn't see how Burns did her job without losing it. She couldn't dig around in people's body cavities all day without throwing up herself. Maybe it was something Burns had just gotten used to over the years. Or maybe it took the kind of person with a different constitution. Regardless, she was just glad it wasn't her.

"Third time's a charm?" Ivy asked as they approached the house.

"I'll let you take the lead on this one," he said, allowing her to climb the short, concrete stairs first.

"Why, because this is a girl?" she asked.

"No, because I think you're better at it," he replied. "You had a way with those kids back there. I'm not sure I could have gotten them to admit as much as they did."

She scoffed. "I'm sure you could have. Though it may have taken you longer. And a trip down to *lockup*."

"Hey, teens can be real jerks. You have to be firm with them," he said, though she saw a smile creep on his face.

"*Some* teens. Just like some adults."

"I guess," he replied. Some of that hard edge that he put on when he was on the job melted away. Ivy smiled in return.

As she knocked on the door, she tried to think about how they were going to approach this. Would Lorelai even speak to them? And what had she seen last night?

Unlike the other two houses, the door to the house opened right away, revealing a middle-aged woman in a baggy sweatshirt and pants. Her dark reddish hair was pulled up, revealing bits of sandy white at the edges and a pair of thick glasses sat on her nose. "Yes?" she asked, looking down at the badges Ivy and Jonathan wore on their belts.

"Are you Mrs. Sylvester?" Ivy asked.

"Are you with the police?" she replied.

"I'm Detective Bishop. This is Detective White," Ivy said.

"Thank goodness," she replied, which elicited surprise from Ivy. "I wasn't sure if I should call you people or maybe the hospital." She seemed on edge, almost frantic.

"What's wrong?" Ivy asked.

"There is something wrong with my daughter. She's never acted like this before and I just don't know what to do."

"May we come in?" Ivy asked, suddenly on edge.

"Oh, yes, please," the woman said, stepping aside. "I'm sorry, I've just been out of my mind with worry."

Ivy and Jonathan entered the small house. It was nicer than Ivy had anticipated. The carpeted floors were a little worn, but clean and everything carried a scent of furniture polish, like it had all just been cleaned. Ivy spotted a bunch of cleaners on the kitchen table.

"Oh, sorry," Mrs. Sylvester said, hurrying over to the table and grabbing the towels and bottles. "I clean when I can't sleep. I've been up all night checking on Lorelai."

"Where is your daughter?" Ivy asked.

"In her bedroom. She won't come out. She won't even speak to me," she said. "She's *never* done that before. I know I can sometimes be... overbearing, but she's never acted like this before. I think...I think something happened last night and she just..." The woman collapsed into a nearby recliner, her head in her hands.

"Here, take it easy, Mrs. Sylvester," Ivy said, bending down in front of her just like she had with Brit. "Tell me what happened last night."

The woman took a few deep breaths. "I had to work the late shift, so I didn't get home until around two-thirty. By then she was home. I went to check on her and found she was wide awake, but she wouldn't say a word. She just stares at the wall. I tried to get her to talk, to eat something or at least drink some water, but..." She shook her head. "I kept checking on her all night...no change."

"What about before that?" Jonathan asked. "What happened before you went to work? Did you see Lorelai go out?"

She nodded. "She just had her sixteenth birthday last week. She said she was going over to Brit's house to hang out. But when I called Britnee's mother this morning, she told me that Brit told her she and Lorelai were hanging out at *my* house last night."

Classic parent dupe. "Did Britnee tell you where they really were?" Ivy asked.

"I didn't think to ask. I've been so worried," she said.

"We think they were at Oakhurst Catholic last night," Jonathan said.

Mrs. Sylvester looked up at him, her face going a shock of white. "What? The one on the news?"

Ivy nodded. "We think Lorelai may have seen something. Something that may have been...well, traumatizing."

"Oh, my God." She buried her face in her hands. "Oh my God, oh my God."

Ivy winced, then steeled herself and placed a hand on Mrs. Sylvester's knee. It was like putting her hand on a hot stove, but she kept it there, forcing the sensation away. "I know this is hard. May I speak with Lorelai? I've had experience with trauma in the past. I may be able to get her to talk about what happened."

Mrs. Sylvester withdrew her hands. Her face was streaked with tears. She sniffed, nodding. "Of course. If you think you can help."

"I'll do my best," Ivy said, removing her hand. Immediately the world snapped back into focus. "Which way to her room?"

The woman pointed down the hall. "It's the second door down there. The one with the flowers and stars on it." She stood back up.

"I'll hang back here," Jonathan said in a soft tone. Ivy was grateful he didn't feel the need to accompany them. She didn't think both of them charging into Lorelai's room would be very productive.

Still, she had to prepare herself. Lorelai could be the key to Father Rouge's murder. She had one shot at this; she couldn't screw it up.

Mrs. Sylvester approached the door, first listening to see if she could hear anything on the other side. Then she knocked lightly. "Lorelai? Honey? Can we come in? The police are here and want to ask you some questions."

There was no answer. Mrs. Sylvester turned the handle, and the door gave way. Inside light streamed in through the two windows, one along the side and another at the back of the room. A large bed took up most of the room, with a dresser, a nightstand and an old rocking chair the only other furniture. A laptop sat on top of the dresser, charging. The room was colored in muted pastels, but was neat and tidy. Under the covers lay the person Ivy assumed was Lorelai, covered almost to her head. Like her mother, she had dark red hair, though that was all Ivy could see of the girl. She remained at the door while Mrs. Sylvester walked around and took a seat on the bed, rubbing the girl's hair. "Sweetie?" she said. "Can you please speak with the detective? She says she knows about last night."

It might have been Ivy's imagination, but she thought she saw the form under the blankets stiffen. Mrs. Sylvester tried a few more times, but to no avail. Finally, she got up. "You're welcome to try, though I don't know if she'll say anything. Should I call a doctor? My job doesn't have health insurance, but I'm just—"

"How about you go speak with my partner," Ivy said. "He can help you with that."

She nodded, shooting glances back at Lorelai before finally heading back down the hallway.

"Lorelai," Ivy said in a soft voice. "My name is Ivy. I'm a detective with the Oakhurst Police." She entered into the room a few steps, but maintained her distance. "I'd like to talk about what happened last night."

Ivy watched as the form under the covers finally started to turn to face her. The covers came down to just below her chin, revealing a young girl with a fair complexion and a strong resemblance to her mother. She stared at Ivy with wide dark brown eyes.

"We spoke to Brit earlier," Ivy said. "She told us you guys were at the church last night. That you and Lukas went inside."

The girl sank back into her pillow further, like she was trying to get away from Ivy.

"You saw something, didn't you?" Ivy asked. "I know what that's like. I saw something bad happen when I was young too."

"What?" the girl squeaked.

"Something so bad that I haven't talked about it for fifteen years," Ivy said. "Something that my brain just blocks out. I can remember snippets...but not all of it." The girl's eyes grew even wider. "But I don't want that to happen to you. Memories are funny sometimes. And they can get... stuck. Especially if we bury them and don't let them out. And then you end up carrying them around, like this big weight on your back." Ivy smiled. "And you don't deserve that. Whatever happened, I can help you. At the very least, I can listen."

The girl sat up a little more, the covers falling away, revealing she was wearing regular clothes, not pajamas. Ivy noticed a tiny golden dolphin pendant suspended from her neck. "That's a nice necklace."

"Thanks," she said. "My mom gave it to me."

"She's very worried about you," Ivy said.

"I know, I just...she wouldn't understand." Her eyes took on a glassy look, like she was looking beyond the house. Beyond the world, even.

"Brit said you guys were in the cemetery," Ivy said. "What happened after that?"

"I...I um..." She began blinking quickly and Ivy could see she was about to relive it again. She didn't want to retraumatize the girl, but at the same time, she'd probably been living that moment since she got home last night.

"It's okay," Ivy said. "Just go slow. Take deep breaths. Like this." She demonstrated her breathing technique. "Don't focus on the emotions. Just tell me step by step what happened. Pretend like you're reading a report for school."

"For school?" she asked.

"Right, like a history report. That's all it is. It's history now, right? It's all over. And whatever happened can't hurt you right now."

Lorelai took a few more deep breaths. "Like a history report," she repeated under her breath. "Lukas...Lukas was being a jerk."

"Good," Ivy said. "Keep going."

"He acted like...like I couldn't handle myself. He dared me to go to the door."

"Which door?" Ivy asked.

"The...um, the side door...the one that was open."

"Did you know it was open before you got there?"

She shook her head. "No. I didn't think it would be. I thought it would be locked. But when I pulled on it, it opened."

"Then what happened?"

She furrowed her brow. "I couldn't chicken out," she said. "Brit had already vouched for me. I couldn't let her down. I... went inside."

"Did you hear or see something that made you want to go inside?" Ivy asked.

"Not at first. It was just...I was supposed to be seeing if the maintenance guy was still there or not. We didn't want him ruining the night. Lukas said the church was supposed to be closed, but all the lights inside were still on."

"What happened after you went inside?" Ivy kept her voice soft and without any urgency. Lorelai needed to get to this in her own time, and Ivy didn't want to rush her.

"I...uh..." She pulled the covers back up to her neck, squeezing her features together. "There was a sound...like... like...I don't know."

"That's okay," Ivy said. "What else."

"I heard a voice. At first I thought it was the maintenance guy, so I hid behind one of the pews."

"What did this voice sound like?"

"Rough. Angry. *Really* angry."

"Was it a male voice?" Lorelai nodded emphatically. "Did you recognize it?"

"No…it was almost like a growl."

"Did you hear what it was saying?"

"*Liar. Cheater. Betrayer.*"

A chill ran down Ivy's spine as Lorelai whispered the words. Someone obviously with an agenda. This was no random killing. Someone *wanted* Father Rouge dead. "Did you hear anything else?"

"No," Lorelai said, her voice going higher in pitch. "Just those words, over and over."

"Ok, what happened next?"

"I waited until it stopped. I didn't want to get caught," she said. "When it was quiet I peeked over the pew, thinking whoever was there had left. But then I saw…him and I just…I just…" She began sucking in air, like she couldn't get enough. Ivy moved to the bed, sitting beside her.

"It's okay," Ivy said. "Deep breaths, remember? Deep breaths."

Lorelai nodded, taking in deeper and deeper breaths until she calmed down.

"You saw Father Rouge, didn't you?" Ivy asked. Lorelai nodded, keeping the covers tucked up close.

"Did you see anyone else? The person whose voice you heard?"

She shook her head. "I just ran back out the same door. Almost knocked Lukas over."

"Lukas was standing at the door?" Ivy asked.

She nodded. "Then I threw up."

"I probably would have thrown up too," Ivy replied, which elicited a small smile from the girl. "What happened after that?"

"I…don't really know. There was some yelling. I just remember walking back with Brit. She kept talking about how Lukas had run off somewhere. But I wasn't really listening."

Ivy made sure she looked in the girl's eyes. "Lorelai, thank you very much. That is very helpful."

"Lori?" They both turned to see Mrs. Sylvester at the door, tears in her eyes again. "She's talking?" Jonathan stood behind her, a sheepish look on his face.

"Hi, Mom," Lorelai said. Ivy moved off the bed just in time for Mrs. Sylvester to wrap her daughter in a hug.

"Oh, my baby girl," she whispered. "I'm so, so, sorry. Whatever happened, I'm so sorry."

"I'm okay, Mom," Lorelai finally said.

Mrs. Sylvester released her, turning to Ivy. "Did she help you?"

Ivy nodded. "She did. She helped a lot."

"What happens now?" Lorelai asked.

"First, you get some rest," Ivy said. "We may have some more questions for you later. But you need sleep, and a good meal. See if your mom won't make your favorite for you."

"Yes, anything you want, sweetie," Mrs. Sylvester said.

"We can show ourselves out," Ivy said. "But I'm going to leave you my information in case Lorelai remembers anything else. And we'll be in touch in a day or two."

Mrs. Sylvester got up and wrapped Ivy in a hug before she could stop it. "Thank you, both of you. Thank you for coming."

"You're welcome," Ivy said, doing everything she could to keep the pain out of her voice. Though she did notice Jonathan looked like he was about to say something, or interrupt in some way. Thankfully, the hug was short-lived. Jonathan led the way back out to the car after they had said one last round of goodbyes.

"I'd call that a resounding success?" he said.

"Half of one," she replied. "I'll explain on the way back to the station."

Chapter Ten

IVY YAWNED. It had been a long night, followed by an early morning. After gathering all the information from Lorelai, they had spoken with Nat, who agreed putting an APB out on Lukas Winchell was warranted. No one had seen him since that night and even though he wasn't considered a suspect—seeing as there was no way he could have perpetrated the crime according to Lorelai Sylvester—he *was* missing. And Ivy couldn't help but wonder if the killer hadn't in some way targeted him. Though that didn't make sense, given no one seemed to be after Lorelai, the actual *witness* to the crime.

Still, she wanted to find and speak with Lukas, if for no other reason than to see if his story matched up with the others'. But until then, she and Jonathan still had to work the case.

Even though there wasn't a service Saturday night, there had been a candlelight vigil in Father Rouge's honor, held right outside the church beyond the barriers. The local news had even reported it, and yet still no sign of Alice Blair, something Ivy found more curious by the day. She figured she must be off on some big assignment, maybe out of town.

But Ivy and Jonathan had been at the service to watch for

anyone who might seem suspicious. Killers sometimes returned to the scene of the crime to witness the aftermath of their actions. And until they found something more concrete than what little Lorelai witnessed, they had to explore every possible avenue.

This morning was no exception. There was another service being held outside the church, despite the drop in temperature, with at least fifty people in attendance. The bishop had arrived from Portland, and would be the officiant conducting the service this morning. Ivy leaned up against the hood of her car, watching the man from a distance as Jonathan walked over, handing her a cup of coffee.

"Thanks," she said, taking it in her gloved hand. "Where's this from?"

"Shop about a block that way," he said, pointing east. "Never had this brand before, so try it at your own risk."

Ivy took a sip. It was okay, not the worst she'd ever had.

"Anything?" he asked, settling in beside her.

"Just a bunch of parishioners as far as I can tell," she replied. "Just like last night."

"Probably won't amount to anything," he replied, taking a sip as well before screwing up his features and setting the cup down beside them on the hood of the car.

"Hey," she said.

He grabbed the cup again. "Sorry, force of habit." He dumped the cup out beside the car into the grass. As they continued to watch the crowd, Ivy could practically feel him chomping at the bit. Maybe that was because he was physically close to her again—they hadn't been this close since Aunt Carol's house. She wasn't sure she wanted to open up whatever can of worms was brewing between them, but it was driving her crazy and she just had to know what was on his mind.

"Out with it."

"What?"

"You're practically vibrating with energy," she replied. "Just say it already."

"I'm not *vibrating*," he replied. "I'm just cold."

"If you expect me to believe that, then you must think I'm the worst detective in the world." She shot him a pointed look that said she wasn't about to put up with any bullshit this morning.

He exhaled, the vapor disappearing into the air. "I was just…I was concerned about what happened yesterday. At the Sylvester house. Mrs. Sylvester…and then Lorelai…"

Ah. So that's what this was about. Apparently, Ivy had misjudged him after all. He wasn't thinking about the night at Aunt Carol's. He was worried she might fall apart on him.

"It's fine," she replied. "I can handle it."

"No," he said, "I didn't mean it like that. I just…I worry about you. I know that kind of thing is difficult. I wasn't sure if I should have stepped in or not."

"I can take care of myself, Jonathan," she said, feeling the need to scoot away from him.

"Crap, I'm just making this worse," he replied. "I'm sorry. I shouldn't have said anything."

Ivy stared at the ground. Now *she* felt like an ass. Why did this have to be an issue? Why couldn't she just touch people without it being a big deal? What she wouldn't give not to have to deal with this.

Jonathan had been the person who had helped her the most through her issues, even though he really didn't understand them. And unlike Oliver, he'd never pressured her in any way, similar to Aunt Carol. But it wasn't like she knew what was going on herself. Sometimes she could grab someone and yank them to the ground without an issue. Other times, she couldn't even gather the courage to touch someone's hand. And what had happened yesterday had only reinforced the fact she wasn't ready for close physical contact. Supporting Lorelai had been hard enough, but when Mrs.

Sylvester wrapped Ivy in a hug, it was like being electrocuted. She'd been lucky she hadn't passed out.

Ivy glanced up, prepared to try and lay it all out for him, only to see someone in the crowd of parishioners staring at her. "Heads up," she said. "I've got one, eleven o'clock."

"Got her," he replied. The woman looked away, turning her attention back to the bishop, who continued speaking. But then she turned to look at Ivy again. "Think we've got a runner?"

"Let's see," Ivy said and began walking toward the crowd. But the woman didn't move. If she wanted Ivy's attention, she'd gotten it. But if she was connected to the crime, Ivy figured she would have taken off by now.

"I'll circle around," Jonathan said. "Come up from behind." He peeled off to her left, but the woman's eyes never left Ivy's. She momentarily glanced at the bishop again, then began making her way towards Ivy, near the edge of the crowd. Finally, she reached the back where it was harder to hear the bishop's message.

"Good morning," Ivy said as the woman approached. "Is there something I can help you with?"

"You are with the police investigating?" she asked. She was on the shorter side, probably in her mid-forties with dark hair and a medium complexion.

"I'm Detective Bishop, and yes, I'm looking into what happened here."

"I might have something that can help you," she said.

"And you are?" Ivy asked, noticing Jonathan had set himself up fifteen feet behind the woman in the event she tried to get away.

"Lana Orellio. I used to work for Father Rouge."

"Nice to meet you, Lana," Ivy said. "What can you tell me?"

The woman looked over her shoulder at the crowd of people gathered. "Not here. Can we meet somewhere?"

"I think there's a coffee shop around the corner over there," Ivy said. "Would that do?"

The woman nodded. "Yes, please. I don't feel right speaking about it here."

"Speaking about what?" Ivy asked.

"First, coffee."

Ten minutes later Ivy and Jonathan sat at a small table across from Lana Orellio. All three of them had fresh coffees in front of them, the smell of beans wafting into the air. Though Jonathan leaned back away from his cup. Ivy couldn't help but smile to herself that he'd been forced to order another out of politeness.

"I wasn't sure if I should say anything or not," Lana said after taking a sip of her coffee. "I didn't want to get anyone in trouble."

"Just tell us what you know," Ivy said. "At this point, anything would be helpful. What was your relationship with Father Rouge?"

"I used to clean for him—the church," she replied. "But I was let go a few weeks ago."

"Why was that?"

Lana ran her finger around the rim of her cup. "He said it was because of budget cuts, that the church wasn't bringing in enough tithes. But I knew the real reason."

Ivy exchanged a quick glance with Jonathan. "Why don't you tell us what you mean."

Lana dropped her voice. "The powder."

"Powder?" Ivy asked.

Lana glanced around the shop again before leaning forward. "Father Rouge always kept his desk locked. And I'm not the kind of person who snoops. But when I was cleaning one afternoon a few weeks back I noticed he'd left it unlocked.

He *never* left it unlocked."

Ivy wasn't about to ask how she knew that if she wasn't trying to get into it. "Keep going."

"Well, I couldn't help myself, could I? I'd never even seen inside the desk. But I didn't understand what I was looking at. They were these little baggies with what looked like sugar in them. At first I thought that's what they were, but when I looked online later, I found out the truth."

"What truth was that?" Jonathan asked.

"That it was…" she dropped her voice to a very low whisper. "…cocaine."

"Did Father Rouge catch you looking through his desk?" Ivy asked. She wasn't sure what to make of this cocaine angle.

"No, no. He wasn't there. And I put everything back where it belonged. But he brought me in a week later and fired me. I think he knew."

"How would he know?" Jonathan asked.

"Maybe he had a secret camera set up somewhere," she said. "That must have been it. And when he figured out I knew his secret, he had to get rid of me."

Lana struck Ivy as someone either too paranoid, or prone to fantastic ideas. She hadn't had a lot of personal experience with it, but Jonathan had told her sometimes there were people who would lie and make up details about a case just so they could feel like they were part of it. That's how Lana seemed to Ivy. Too desperate to have some connection to something important that she was willing to seek them out. As far as Ivy knew, forensics hadn't found any small white packets in Father Rouge's desk during their initial search.

One look with Jonathan told her he was thinking along similar lines. "Why would Father Rouge have drugs in his desk?" Ivy asked.

"I don't have the slightest idea," the woman said. "But when I heard he'd been killed, I figured that had to be the reason. People get killed all the time when drugs are involved, right? Maybe he thought I told somebody about his stash."

"How would that get him killed?" Jonathan asked.

"Well, if he moved it," Lana replied. "And someone caught him. I mean, how much cocaine can one person use?"

"How much did you see in the desk?" Ivy asked, wondering if they were missing something else important while they wasted time with this woman.

"Oh, there had to have been twenty or thirty of the little packets," she replied. "It was a lot."

"I don't suppose anyone else knew about this," Ivy said. "The deacon? Or Mr. Suntree, or Mrs. Banner?"

She screwed up her features. "I wouldn't know. I never said a word to anyone. I didn't want to get Father Rouge in trouble." She leaned forward again. "Is it possible he was using it for medicinal purposes?"

"Cocaine?" Jonathan asked.

"Yeah, like for addicts who might be trying to cut back, but couldn't go cold turkey. That's possible, right?"

Ivy stood, having heard enough. "Thank you so much for your time, Mrs. Orellio, but we really need to get back."

"So you'll investigate?" she asked as Jonathan took his cup and placed it in the dish tray behind them.

"We'll look into it," Ivy said. "If you think of anything else, please let us know."

"Oh, I definitely will," she replied. "Trust me, I want to find whoever did this as much as anyone. Whatever Father Rouge was into, he was a good man. That much I know."

Ivy and Jonathan bid her a farewell and headed back out into the cold, rounding the corner as they made their way to the church again.

"Well?" Jonathan asked, a smirk on his face when they were out of view of the café.

"Well, what?"

"How much of that do you believe?" he asked.

Ivy wanted to discount the whole thing, but then again Orellio had tried to help. To Ivy she seemed too desperate to give up what little information she had, which was always in itself suspicious. Sometimes people just wanted to help, but more often than not they were out for something. "Waste of time."

"Yeah?" he asked.

"You don't think so?"

He shrugged, putting his hands in his coat pockets. "We could take another look. Just to be sure."

"Why? Forensics has already been all over that office. We would know if they'd found cocaine on the scene. Don't tell me you actually believed her. Rouge, a drug lord?"

"That's the thing," Jonathan said. "It's so far out of left field it's making me curious. Maybe she didn't see cocaine, but I think she found *something* while cleaning."

"Okay," Ivy said. "I just hope it's not a waste of time."

"Got any better ideas?" he asked.

In the distance the crowd from the service was dispersing. "Unfortunately not."

Chapter Eleven

THEY WAITED until everyone had finished dispersing before entering the church again. Thankfully, the vigil last night and the service this morning seemed to have placated people and the gathering crowds were no longer lingering. That would make their jobs easier. The news vans had dispersed, moving on to the next story until there were new developments. And as long as they kept the condition of Father Rouge's body a secret, odds were it would fade into the background as just another murder, albeit a prominent one.

Ivy and Jonathan removed the police tape on the side door, unlocking it and letting themselves in. But before they could get all the way across the threshold, the clearing of a throat from behind them caused Ivy to turn.

"Morning," the man clad in a black cassock said, his white hair cut close. He wore a wide purple "belt," though it was more like a sash that had been wrapped around his midsection and had a pleasant smile on his face.

"Good morning," Jonathan said. "Can we help you?"

"You are the detectives working the case?" he asked, holding out a hand. "Frazier Bain."

Jonathan took the steps and shook the man's hand. "Detective White. And this is my partner, Detective Bishop."

Ivy held up her hands. "I've had a cold, sorry."

Bain smiled, dropping his hand and placing it back in his pocket. "Bishop, huh? Aptly named for such a case." His smile grew wider.

"What can we do for you, Bishop?" Jonathan said.

"I was hoping to find out when I could access the church. There will be a lot of work that needs to be taken care of, and I'll need all of Father Rouge's records. As you can imagine, this is a major disruption and we don't want to leave the church without a leader for very long."

"Of course," Jonathan said.

"It's still an active crime scene," Ivy added. "We'll let you know when we're done."

The bishop took a few steps closer. "Will that be in the next day or so?"

"I doubt it," Ivy said. "You're probably looking at a week. At least."

"A *week*," he said. "But I need to assess the state of the church, reassign the personnel to cover the duties, the charitable matters, the fundraisers. This community relies on this church. I'm not sure I can—"

"Sir," Jonathan interjected. "I'm sorry, but Father Rouge was killed in here. And until we have completed our investigation, it will have to remain closed."

The man grimaced for the first time, though it looked to Ivy like there was something else under there. Malice, perhaps? The bishop really didn't like being told no. All hints of his former pleasant demeanor had disappeared. "I'll at least need copies of his records. Immediately."

"We'll work on getting those to you," Jonathan said. "Now if you'll excuse us, we are in the middle of our investigation."

Ivy thought she heard him mutter something under his breath as he left, heading for a black Mercedes parked on the other side of the street. "Looks like the church pays pretty well."

"Some parts of it anyway," Jonathan replied. "C'mon. Let's see if Lana's theory holds any water."

As they entered into the large nave, Ivy was struck by the grandeur of it all. She could almost forget that a man had been brutally murdered and displayed in here. And despite the body having been removed and the area cleaned, sure enough there were still pink stains on the marble altar. And a lingering odor Ivy wasn't sure would ever fully go away. "What happens when Bishop Bain sees that?"

"Hopefully we'll have some more answers by then," he replied.

"Do you really think we're going to find anything here?" Ivy asked, moving past the altar to the front of the church where the offices were located.

"Burns has a solid team," Jonathan said. "But it never hurts to take a second look."

Ivy huffed. This isn't what she wanted to be doing. They should be out looking for Lukas Winchell, or trying to find whoever Lorelai heard that night, despite the fact forensics wasn't able to come up with much. The entire church was full of fingerprints, footprints, hairs, fibers, and all manner of contaminants. Trying to weed out the one person who killed Father Rouge would take a miracle from the heavens.

"We need to get Lorelai to listen to an audio lineup," Ivy said, making her way towards the offices.

"Of who?" Jonathan asked. "If we had a suspect that would be great. But right now—"

"Suntree, and maybe Deacon Lutz," Ivy said.

"Both of whom have an alibi."

"You know how easy it is to get friends and family to lie for you," Ivy said, opening the door to the office, though the Deacon's time at the prison would have been a little harder to fake. They'd confirmed he'd been there for five straight days, staying on the property. "Suntree has access to the property, he's certainly big enough, and he had a personal relationship with the victim. I'd say he looks as good as anyone right now."

"You want to look into his alibi further? See if we can find some cracks?"

"Wouldn't be the worst idea," she replied. "If nothing else we just end up eliminating a suspect." She made her way into Father Rouge's office, pulling out a pair of gloves and slipping them on.

Jonathan followed her inside. "Hey, got another pair of those? I forgot mine."

Ivy handed him a pair, making sure not to come into physical contact with him. Even through gloves she could still feel it, and she didn't need any more distractions right now. Her goal was to get through this search as quickly as possible so they could go out and take a second look at Suntree. The more she thought out it, the more it made sense that he would have something to do with this. He hadn't seemed particularly upset about Father Rouge's death, and he'd even said they didn't really get along that well.

Though not getting along with someone was a long way from disemboweling them.

"Shall we start with the desk?" Ivy asked. She tugged on the small metal handle, but the door didn't budge. "Locked."

Jonathan furrowed his brow. "The keys have to be some-where around here."

"Why would Burns' people lock it again?" Ivy asked. "They *did* look in here, didn't they?"

"I'm sure they did," he replied, searching the room. Near the door was a set of keys hanging on a keyring. "Here." He tossed the keys to Ivy.

She didn't find the correct one until the fourth key. "Moment of truth," she said, giving him a placating grin. "Let's see if your instincts were right."

"Wait," he said, holding up a hand. "Want to make this interesting?"

Her shoulders slumped. "Interesting how?"

"A little wager?"

She had to hold back a laugh. "A bet? From *you?*"

He shrugged. "It's not against the law."

It was just funny, coming from Detective Jonathan White, the appointed Boy Scout of the precinct. But then again, that hadn't been a name he'd given himself. He'd built up a reputation for always doing the right thing, and he'd been berated for it. And Ivy wasn't going to join in on that. "Sure, what's your bet?"

"I win, and *I* get to drive us around for the next week."

Ivy winced. He knew how to get to her. But at the same time there was no way there was anything in this drawer. "And if I win?"

"Choose your prize."

Ivy's eyes grew wide with anticipation, a huge grin coming over her face as she weighed the possibilities.

"Actually, wait. I changed my mind."

"Oh no," Ivy said, letting go of the drawer. "You opened this pandora's box. I agree to your *wager.*"

"Nope, I changed my mind. It's too late," he said. "I forgot how devious you can be."

"Who, me?" she asked as innocently as she could. God, it was so *easy* to slip into herself with him. And for a moment, she didn't want to think about the implications of that. Instead, she'd much rather win this bet. "You just know you're going to lose. That woman was full of it and you're getting cold feet."

He narrowed his gaze at her, working his jaw. "Ok. Fine. Hit me with your best shot."

So much glee and anticipation filled Ivy's chest she thought she might burst. "The next time we arrest a perp, you have to cuss him out." Jonathan went to object. "And I don't mean just a one-word insult. I mean an unending stream of the foulest language your virgin ears have ever heard."

He huffed, clearly in conflict. But she could also detect the hint of a smile on his lips. "Fine. Deal."

Ivy chuckled. "Oh, I cannot *wait*. I'm gonna record it." She grabbed the drawer door again. "You ready? This is for your personal honor."

He rounded the desk to stand closer to her, making sure he had a good view. But he was a little *too* close. As close as he'd been the other night. And yet, Ivy didn't mind it. She actually liked it. "I just can't wait to drive around at normal speeds for a week."

"Big talk from a man who is about to have a potty mouth," she replied. She yanked the drawer open.

Inside were all manner of pens, notepads, a box of staples, some documents and various odds and ends. But there was no trace of any small white packets.

Immediately Ivy felt elation at what looked like an easy win. She turned to grin at Jonathan.

"Wait, pull it all the way out," he said. "Let's make sure."

"Whatever you say, *loser*." She pulled the drawer until it wouldn't go any further, but there still weren't any small packets. However, at the very back of the desk was a magazine of a somewhat *questionable* nature.

"Tsk, tsk, tsk, Father Rouge," Ivy said, pulling it out. A busty topless woman was featured on the front. "Who buys magazines anymore? I thought people got all their porn from the internet these days."

"I guess some people are just stuck in the past," Jonathan said, looking deeper into the drawer. He even pulled out his phone, shining the flashlight into it as far as it would go.

Ivy quickly flipped through the magazine to make sure there was nothing hidden between the pages. But it was empty of anything other than lewd photographs. "I have to say, this makes me have more respect for him."

"Everyone has needs," Jonathan replied. "We are just animals, after all."

"Speaking of which," Ivy said. "I can't *wait* until the next arrest. In fact, I might just have to go out and issue a speeding ticket right now."

Jonathan grumbled, checking the other drawers of the desk. None of the rest had locks on them and most were filled with folders or papers relating to the church. "I would have sworn she was telling the truth."

"Why?" Ivy asked, closing the main drawer again. "She didn't seem that credible to me."

"I don't know," he said. "Just something in the way she said it. Like she didn't want to get Father Rouge in trouble, but at the same time, she wanted someone to know what he was into."

Ivy wondered if she'd also found the magazine. "She was probably just upset at being fired and invented the cocaine story as a way to get back at him."

"But that doesn't make any sense," Jonathan said, closing the last drawer. "If she wanted to get back at him, wouldn't she start that rumor when he was still alive? Or at the very least, start spreading it as soon as he was dead? To tarnish his reputation?"

"Maybe that's what she was doing with us, planting the seed," Ivy suggested.

"If that's the case, she's a horrible judge of character," he replied. "We're not about to go out and start besmirching a man who just died."

Ivy took another look at the magazine and decided to take it with her. It wouldn't help for Bishop Bain to find it later. "Yeah, that's a good point."

Jonathan went to the far wall and began looking at the bookcases there. "Maybe she mis-remembered. There might be something else here."

"Wow, you do not take losing well, do you?" Ivy asked, but

he didn't reply. Instead, he was opening every book that lined Father Rouge's shelves. She wasn't sure what he hoped to find, as she doubted Rouge would hollow out a book to hold his "drugs." They were looking at another dead end. If Father Rouge was guilty of anything, it was not knowing how to use "incognito mode" on his computer.

In an effort to placate him, Ivy opened the drawer again, and rooted around. But it was just as they had seen. Nothing but supplies. It seemed the only reason Rouge had kept it locked was to keep anyone from finding the magazine. But the more Ivy looked at it, the more something didn't sit right with her. The pages of the magazine were crisp, as if they'd barely ever been opened. And when she checked the date, the magazine was over a year old.

Why would Father Rouge keep a year-old magazine in his desk? He clearly hadn't looked at it very much, if at all.

Ivy bent down and took a closer look at the desk drawer, opening it all the way again. The desk itself was oak, and very well constructed. Ornate details ran along all the edges, and each of the drawers were dovetailed. Clearly someone had put a lot of work and time into this desk. It might have even been a one-off custom, for the church itself.

As Ivy ran her hand along the inside of the drawer, she thought she felt something at the very back, almost like a small indentation. She ran her finger back and forth over it, before pressing down on it.

To her surprise the bottom of the drawer popped up, as if on a spring, revealing a hidden compartment underneath.

"Hey," she said. "I might have celebrated a bit too early."

Jonathan came back over. "Is that a secret compartment?"

"Sure looks like one." There were no baggies of white powder inside, but there was a small black book. "I don't remember seeing this on the manifest from Burns."

"Me either," Jonathan said, pulling out his phone.

Ivy flipped through the book. It was a list of names, along

with numbers on the side in three different columns. It looked like the kind of ledger a bookie would use. And it was all handwritten. It wouldn't take long to determine if this was Father Rouge's handwriting or not.

"Yeah, got it. Right away," Jonathan said, hanging up. "She said they never found a compartment in the desk."

Ivy handed him the ledger and while he flipped through it, she took a closer look in the secret compartment. Something else inside caught her eye and she shone her light into the corner.

"What do you have?" Jonathan asked.

At the very corner of the compartment looked like a very small amount of white powder that had accumulated.

"I think…" she said. "This means you win."

Chapter Twelve

WITHIN THE HOUR, one of the forensic techs was back out to the church to gather a sample of the white powder for evidence. Ivy would have taken it herself, but there was so little of it, she didn't want to risk contaminating what was there. She figured it was better if someone with the proper tools took it into evidence. If it turned out to be what Lana Orellio had suspected it was and not just sugar from a packet that had spilled once upon a time, then they might actually be on their way to establishing a motive for killing Father Rouge.

"Can you imagine how much digging that woman must have done to find that compartment?" Jonathan asked, his arms crossed as they watched the tech bag up the evidence. "Even *our* people didn't find that."

"I guess some people are just naturally nosy," Ivy replied. "And in this case, it turned out to be a good thing." She held out her keys for Jonathan.

"Hang on to those until we get confirmation. I don't want to celebrate too prematurely." He wiggled his eyebrows at her.

"Very funny," she said.

"Ok," the tech said. "All done. It's in the chain of evidence. We'll get this tested and back to you asap. Burns also wanted me to let you know to come see her. She has some information about the body."

"Sure," Ivy said. "We can head there now. And while you're at it, take this in too." She handed over the ledger. She'd already taken pictures of all the pages, but wanted to make sure it was included in the evidence gathered.

"You got it. Have a good evening." The tech headed back out, followed by Jonathan and Ivy, who locked up and replaced the police tape. As they headed down the stairs back to the car, Ivy noticed the black Mercedes was still sitting across the street. But the windows were tinted so she couldn't see if Bishop Bain was inside or not.

"Think we need to get patrol out here to watch the church?" she asked.

"Do you really think a bishop would break into a crime scene?" Jonathan asked. "What could be in there that he wants so desperately?"

She stopped, considering the question. "Do you think he knows what Rouge was involved with?"

"That's a good point," he said. "I didn't consider that. Let me call the lieutenant."

"I can do it," Ivy said as they headed back to her car. She called Nat up and explained the situation and what they had found, along with their encounter with Bishop Bain.

On the other end of the phone the woman sounded tired. "We don't have the manpower to keep someone there overnight, but I'll have unit 212 run by every hour or so. At least let him know someone is watching."

"Thanks Nat," Ivy said.

"No problem," she replied. "And good work finding the powder. Here's hoping it comes back as something significant."

"We'll let you know what we hear," Ivy replied and hung up. She still couldn't get over how much their relationship had improved in the past few weeks. It was like working with a completely different person.

"She's sending Pawlowski and Harman by later on their patrol. Hopefully Bain isn't stupid enough to try anything." As they reached Ivy's car, she was grateful Jonathan wasn't rubbing her face in the fact she lost. At least, not yet.

"Let's hope not," Jonathan said. "Between this and that missing kid, this case is starting to get a lot more complicated."

Ivy turned on the engine, the heat going at full blast. "Not to mention this," she said, holding up her phone. On it were the images of the ledger.

"Let me see that real quick," Jonathan said. He took the phone and flipped through the pictures, going back and forth a few times. "Wait. I know these names. Two of them, at least. These people are from Portland."

"Which ones?" Ivy asked.

"Whitney Pierson. Friend of the family. My mother used to play tennis with her mother when they were younger. She's big in the art scene up there. And Douglas Lefler. He's a big-time lawyer who used to work in the area. I think he moved out to the coast." Jonathan furrowed his brow. "I wonder if the rest of these names are somehow connected to money."

Ivy took the phone back and flipped through the pictures. She didn't recognize any of the names, but then again, she wasn't as plugged in to the social pipeline as Jonathan was. Or at least, as much as he had been, once upon a time.

"You think they might know something?" Ivy asked.

"I'd say it's at least worth investigating," he replied. "You fancy a drive up to Portland?"

"Sure," Ivy said. "But let's see what Burns has for us first."

HAVING FOLLOWED BURNS'S TECH BACK FROM THE SITE, THEY headed into the M.E.'s office right behind him. He peeled off to the right to check the evidence in while Ivy and Jonathan headed left down to Burns' office. The medical examiner herself was sitting behind her computer when Ivy knocked, and took her glasses off as she looked up.

"Ah, good. I won't take much of your time, but I thought you should see this." She stood and led them down to the examination room where the body freezers kept the dead. While stark and clinical, Ivy could never get used to a place like this. It was too creepy, being here with all these bodies all the time. She'd never be able to keep her imagination in check.

"This certainly was a first for me, so thank you for that," Burns said, pushing into the examination suite. She walked over to one of the freezers and opened the third drawer at the bottom, squatting down over the body of Father Rouge.

She moved with such ease and purpose, Ivy had no doubt the woman was in the right profession. None of this bothered her at all, that much was plain. And she was good at her job, thankfully. Otherwise, they would have been forced to send Father Rouge to Eugene, or even Portland for a proper analysis.

"Cause of death was obviously from massive trauma to the chest. He bled out within twenty to thirty seconds, but for those precious seconds, he was alive and awake."

"Ouch," Jonathan said.

"Indeed. Though the shock probably helped him mask a lot of the pain. The injuries were caused with a small, sharp blade, and each cut was made with extreme care and purpose. This wasn't someone who just started hacking at the body. See here?" She pointed to where the skin had been sheared off across the rib cage. "No knicks on the bones themselves. You're looking for someone who knows how to skin an animal."

"Skin an animal?" Ivy asked. "But he wasn't skinned."

"No, but whoever did this has experience in the area.

They know their way around opening a body up. It's the only thing I can find that would be close. Unless your killer has a lot more human bodies out there that they practiced on first."

"We'll check it out," Jonathan said. "Anything else?"

"I had expected to find some material under his fingernails or any other indications that he may have fought back, but there is no indication he managed to scratch or even hit his attacker."

"So you're saying he just sat there and took it?" Ivy asked.

Burns eyed Ivy. "No one would be able to withstand this kind of pain and not have a visceral reaction. My guess is he was restrained in some way."

"But we didn't find any restraints at the scene," Jonathan said, standing back up. Ivy and Burns stood up as well.

"Just telling you what the evidence shows, Detective. We don't have anything matching this kind of M.O. in our records, so whoever this person is, they haven't killed anyone around here before. What that means, I'll leave up to you."

"So either Father Rouge is their first victim or they're new to the area," Ivy said. "Great." She wondered if Suntree was a hunter. He said he enjoyed bowling. Maybe he enjoyed deer hunting and field dressing as well.

"Thanks, Doc," Jonathan said. "This is a big help."

"I wish I had more," she said, snapping off one of her gloves. "But until another body shows up, this is it."

"Let's just hope that doesn't happen," he replied.

Chapter Thirteen

WAS IT JUST HIM, or was Ivy taking it easy on the roads? Usually, when they were in the car together, she would drive like a madwoman, pedal to the floor. That had been bad enough in her old Corvette, but that car hadn't been very reliable. Now she had this Datsun, which could take a lot more of a pounding than the old sports car ever could. And ever since the lieutenant had "gifted" it to Ivy, she had been putting it through its paces.

But as they drove towards Portland, Jonathan noticed she wasn't driving as offensively as normal. Was it because he had won the bet? Or was there something else on her mind?

While he'd tried to preoccupy himself with the case, Alice's words from the other day had been like a warped record on repeat in his head. He'd thought about broaching the subject with Ivy numerous times already, but it just hadn't seemed like the right timing.

And now, here they were on a long drive together which would be the perfect time to bring it up. Except, he wasn't sure it was his business to get involved. Ivy and the lieutenant had a contentious relationship. One that, up until a few weeks ago, looked like it would only get worse. But then things had turned around on a dime and now Ivy was happier in this job than he'd ever seen her. Was it his responsibility to potentially shatter that happiness? Especially when Alice even admitted she didn't have hard evidence?

He wasn't sure he could bring himself to do it.

"You're thinking pretty hard over there," Ivy said, glancing over as she drove.

"Just wondering why your foot isn't all the way to the floor."

She shrugged. "Don't want to get a speeding ticket."

He watched the farmland pass by as they drove. "You sure you're not being a...what did you call it? Sore loser?"

"Well, technically I haven't lost yet. Let's see what forensics comes back with." He could tell she was trying to keep things light, but it only served to darken his mood. If he didn't get this off his chest, it might end up caving in on him. But at the same time, was his comfort or relief worth tearing apart what little stability Ivy had achieved? He didn't think so.

"Hey," she said. "What is going on with you? Usually I can at least get a snappy retort."

"A lot on my mind," he replied.

"Family?" she asked.

"Not really," he replied. Thankfully his mother had stopped bothering him so much lately. Maybe he was finally getting through to her. "It's nothing to worry about."

"Weren't you the one just lecturing me on being 'operationally ready?' If there's something going on with you, let's get it out now. The last thing I want is to be in a tense situation wondering if your head is on straight."

He let out a long breath. "Would you have any reason to suspect the lieutenant's attitude lately has been... insincere?"

"Nat?" Ivy asked. "Why? What's going on?"

He had to be careful here. Maybe he could tiptoe around the subject without actually falling all the way in. Then again, maybe he was just kidding himself. "I received some intel that may call into question some of her...decisions."

"Jonathan," Ivy said, glancing over. "What are you talking about?"

And down he went. "Has Alice spoken to you in the past few days?"

"Alice?" she asked. "*Your* Alice?"

He winced, not liking how that sounded coming from her. "She came to my place the other day, after that first night at the church. Remember I told you I gave her a statement?"

"Yeah, I figured she'd be glued to that scene, but I haven't seen her at all. I've been meaning to ask you about it. Where is she?"

"No clue. The last I saw her was Saturday morning. But I thought she might have approached you." He sighed again. "That's not true. Because if she had, you would have told me."

"Okay, now you're starting to worry me," Ivy said and the car slowed even further. "What's going on?"

"I didn't want to mention it because I know your relationship with the lieutenant is... unique. And things have seemed so much better these past few weeks. But at the same time when Alice came over, she started making these...accusations."

"What kind of accusations?" Her posture had become noticeably stiffer, like she was preparing for someone to kick her. Gone was the playful nature from before.

"She said she spoke to the lieutenant about your case. She believes there is a coverup going on."

"Wait," Ivy said. "She's been looking into *my* case?"

"Apparently. I didn't know anything about it until she came to see me. She said she's been deciding whether to approach you or not. But I guess she figured you wouldn't flat-out reject the idea if it came from me."

"What kind of coverup?" Ivy asked.

"She didn't specify. She only said that she believed since the Lieutenant was still the case officer, she was hiding something. She apparently did a deep dive into what happened to your family and from her end, the facts don't make sense."

Ivy stared directly ahead, long enough that the silence in the car became uncomfortable. "Personally, I think she's just looking for a story and yours is too unique to pass up. She's the kind of person who, once she gets her hooks into something, doesn't like to let go."

Ivy still didn't respond. Jonathan couldn't imagine what was going through her head at the moment, but the fact that she'd shut down wasn't a good sign.

"I'm sure it's nothing. She didn't even have any hard evidence. Just a *feeling*."

The car began to accelerate, the landscape on either side of them blurring as it went past. "How much does she know?" Ivy finally asked.

"I'm not sure, I didn't ask for details," he replied. "But I told her you had already looked into the case and if there was anything to find there, you would have found it." He paused. "I assume, anyway."

The silence stretched between them again. Ivy was a quiet person by nature, but this was a different kind of quiet. One that he could almost touch. Was she upset that Alice had looked into her personal case? Or was it anger? He'd been reading people for years and yet he couldn't read his own partner. It was like she was behind some kind of glass shield he couldn't penetrate.

"Of course, it doesn't make any sense," Jonathan finally said, desperate for someone to say something. "Otherwise, why would the lieutenant have defended you so much when they found your name carved into Mrs. Baker? And a coverup? For fifteen years? I just don't believe she's capable of it."

"Maybe she's just trying to get a rise out of you," Ivy said, her voice ice cold.

He turned to her. "What do you mean?"

"Anyone with a pair of eyes can see she still has feelings for you. Maybe this is her way of trying to get back into your life," she said.

"Alice may be many things, but she's not dumb. She knows it's over between the two of us. And she knows I'm not the kind of person who can be 'influenced' in that way." He paused, because even though she wasn't a part of his life anymore, he felt a duty to defend her integrity. "Maybe you should talk to her. Clear all of this up."

"Maybe," Ivy said, her voice a little softer.

"I didn't mean to upset you," he added. "I wasn't even sure if I should tell you. It's...complicated."

"I understand," she added.

More silence. What he wouldn't give to go back and start this conversation over again. He never should have said anything. He should have just buried it along with the rest of his skeletons and never mentioned it. Alice even said she wasn't going to talk to Ivy without more evidence, so why had he felt the need to?

And now he may have done irreparable damage to their relationship.

Chapter Fourteen

AFTER MAKING a few calls on the way up to the city, Jonathan was able to confirm Whitney Pierson was attending a fundraiser for the Boys and Girls club in Portland and would be there most of the day. They managed to locate the fundraiser taking place at a local Presbyterian church, a fact both of them found ironic.

Thankfully, he hadn't brought up the subject of Alice any more during the drive. At first, Ivy had wanted to dismiss the woman's accusations out of hand. The possibility that someone—especially Nat—could be covering up the details from Ivy's case was ludicrous. But some small part of Ivy's mind wouldn't let her dismiss the idea. In fact, it wanted to *explore* the possibility. Ivy hoped that was because she wanted to prove it wrong. But the more she thought about it on the drive, the less confident she felt.

And what did it say that all it took was a single unfounded accusation for Ivy to start questioning Nat's motives? Had she just been blind these past few weeks? Or willfully ignorant? Or maybe it was just because she had wanted her relationship with Nat to improve so badly that she was willing to overlook what was staring her right in the face. The fact was the only difference between her and Nat today versus a month ago is Nat was being nicer to her. Had that been enough to lull Ivy into a false sense of security because it had reminded her of the relationship they used to have all those years ago?

Unfortunately, once that illusion had been cracked, it was hard not to allow it to shatter. The entire rest of the drive Ivy found herself going back over every interaction with Nat, looking for anything that might come across as deceptive. Before the Baker case they had been at each other's throats.

But after?

Ultimately, she decided it wasn't something she was going to figure out on a quick drive up to Portland. Part of her resented Jonathan for introducing the idea into her head in the first place, but another, *older* part of her was grateful. The part that knew the world wasn't all sunshine and rainbows. If Alice—someone who couldn't have done more than a few hours' worth of work on Ivy's case—was suspicious, then why wasn't Ivy? It wasn't as if she had any hard evidence one way or another. Ivy knew the details of the case better than anyone, and she had just willfully ignored those details in exchange for a non-contentious relationship with Nat.

No, that wasn't fair. Ivy *had* begun looking into her case. But between the Kieran Woodward case, the Baker emergency and now this case with Father Rouge, her time had been limited. And what little she had done had led nowhere. The case file was as dry as a creek bed in the badlands. Alice had probably seen the same thing. So she had turned her suspicion—rightly so—towards Nat.

So why hadn't Ivy done the same?

"Looks about right," Jonathan said as she pulled into the church's parking lot. The lot was filled with fancy-looking cars including BMWs, Mercedes and Range Rovers.

"Nice crowd," Ivy said, getting out of the car.

"Can't fundraise if people don't have money," he said, joining her in front of her car looking up at the Presbyterian monolith. Energy radiated off him. It had taken a lot for him to tell her what was going on and she wasn't surprised that he hadn't wanted to say anything. But she was glad he did. Even if it made things more difficult.

"Thank you, by the way," she said, causing him to turn to her. "For telling me about Alice."

"I feel like I only made things worse," he said, worry coloring his cheeks.

"I'd rather know an uncomfortable truth than an easy lie," she replied. "And I want you to feel like you can be honest with me. Even when it comes to…personal matters. We're partners. We have to be able to trust each other."

"I agree a hundred percent," he replied. "It's just…this was something of a unique situation."

Was it her, or was he actually inching closer to her? His hand couldn't be more than a few inches from hers. She could practically *sense* his presence from his proximity alone. If there was one thing that not touching people did, it was make her hypersensitive anytime they were close. And it had been going on so long it was almost like a sixth sense.

"Still," she said, taking a step forward. "Thanks anyway. Now let's see what Mrs. Pierson has to say. You said you know her?"

"I do," he replied. "For a while we ran in the same circles up here. Of course, when she went off to Stanford I lost track of her."

"Think she'll remember you?"

"Only one way to find out," he replied and took the lead. They climbed the stairs and headed inside the church. Signs on artist boards indicated where they should go to find the fundraiser. Unlike the Catholic church which was basically just one large room with a couple of annexes, the presbyterian church was much more maze-like. After leaving the main area, they followed the signs down a variety of hallways until they reached what looked like a multi-purpose room. Basketball hoops that once hung down from the ceiling had been drawn up for storage and a large stage stood at the far end of the room. Collapsable bleachers on either side of the court had been pushed all the way in so they were flat against the wall, and a variety of high-top tables had been placed around the room, each covered with a black tablecloth that was cinched around the bottom.

On the stage stood a man behind a podium, auction style as different women brought up items for the crowd to bid on. And while it all seemed casual enough, Ivy could tell just from one glance that none of these people were hurting for money. They might not be dressed up in tuxedos and evening gowns, but most of the men wore well-knit sweaters over collared shirts while the women wore A-line dresses. It looked to Ivy like church had probably ended an hour or so ago and the fundraiser took place directly afterward.

"Next up we have—what do we have?" the auctioneer said from the podium. A woman in a dark green dress with bright blonde hair walked up on the stage holding what to Ivy looked like a telescope. "Ah, yes. Courtesy of Mr. Scott Thompson, a genuine nineteenth century spyglass." The auctioneer took a small card from the woman in the green dress. "This spyglass was used on board the USS Centaur on the twenty-first of May, 1918, by captain Nathanial Woodruff as he spotted a German U-boat off the coast of western France. The Centaur would go on to sink that U-boat before returning to port. This spyglass has been examined and authenticated by the Museum Conservation Institute of Maryland."

He held up the spyglass for everyone to see. The crowd murmured with excitement.

"Looks like we got here for the main event," Ivy said.

"We'll start the bidding at a thousand dollars," the auctioneer said.

Whoa. Was that normal for these things? To Ivy's left a man raised his hand.

"I have a thousand," he said. "Do I hear two?" Another man across the room raised his hand.

"Let's hear twenty-five hundred," the auctioneer said.

"Five," a man called out.

"I have five-thousand, thank you." The auctioneer pointed at the man who had called out the number. "Do I hear fifty-five?"

"Six," a woman close to Ivy said, raising her hand.

"Thank you, Mrs. Fischer, always a generous contributor. How about seven?" No one else raised their hands. "How about sixty-five?"

"Sixty-five," another woman on Jonathan's side called out. She was tall, with dark hair that had been classically styled.

"That's her," Jonathan said.

"Whitney Pierson?"

"Yep."

"Seven thousand," Mrs. Fisher called out beside Ivy, shooting daggers at Pierson. But Pierson didn't even glance over.

"Ten," she said.

"*Ten-thousand*," the auctioneer called out. "I think we can safely say that is the top bid for today. If there are no objections—" He held his gavel towards Mrs. Fisher, who just gave a subtle shake of her head before turning around and leaving the room. "—Very well! Ten-thousand dollars to Mrs. Whitney Pierson. Thank you, Mrs. Pierson."

"Anytime, Horace," she called out, eliciting a few chuckles from the crowd.

The auctioneer continued. "Our next item—"

"C'mon," Jonathan said, the hint of disgust in his voice. "I'm not sure how much of this I can take."

Ivy just couldn't believe she'd watched someone drop five figures on what was essentially an old piece a maritime junk. Then again, she never had been the sentimental type…except when it came to cars. But a telescope?

She followed Jonathan over to Mrs. Pierson, who was enduring a round of congratulations from her fellow bidders.

"Whitney," Jonathan said, approaching her.

The woman's brow formed a "v" before recognition dawned on her and a smile broke out across her face. "Jonathan White. I didn't see your name on the register. Are you here to bid?"

"Unfortunately not," he said, pulling his coat back to reveal his badge. The smile on her face dropped. "This is my partner, Detective Bishop."

"Hello," she said to Ivy before turning back to Jonathan. "How are you?"

"Now this item is a real gem," the auctioneer called out loudly.

"Can we speak in the hallway?" Jonathan asked. "It's important."

The woman, whose posture had been relaxed and carefree when she'd been spending a ton of money on a relic, was now tight and guarded. Ivy kept a close eye on her as they exited the auditorium into the hallway, blocking out all the noise from the auction.

"How long has it been?" Mrs. Pierson asked. "Fifteen years?"

"At least," Jonathan replied.

"You're looking well," she said. "And a Detective. So you did it after all. I bet your mother was pissed." She grinned.

Jonathan's businesslike wall cracked a little, something Ivy found very interesting. It was clear these two had a past. She wondered how deep it went. "Let's just say she didn't come to my graduation. I see you're doing well for yourself."

Pierson blushed. "Oh, that was just a bit of fun. The church does this charity auction every year. It's all goes to a good cause."

"So then you're a member of this church?" Ivy asked.

Pierson turned to her. "Yes. I've been a member here ever

since I got married." She looked between the two of them, confusion on her brow. "Why?"

"We're investigating a murder," Jonathan said.

"Oh," she replied. "Here? In Portland?"

"Oakhurst," Ivy said. "It's a few hours south of here."

"Oh, yes," she said. "I've been there a few times. Beautiful town."

"Your name came up in our investigation," Jonathan said.

"My name?"

Ivy stepped forward. "Do you know a Father Matthew Rouge? Of Oakhurst Catholic Church."

The air around them seemed to shift and change in front of Ivy's eyes. "Um…I don't think so."

"You're sure? Your name was written in a ledger of his."

"A l-ledger?" she asked. Ivy pulled up the picture on her phone and showed it to Pierson. "That's very strange. Maybe it was another Whitney Pierson."

"We checked," Jonathan said. "There aren't any others in Oakhurst. Not to mention another prominent Portland name on the list. Someone who runs in the same circles."

"I'm sorry, Jonathan. I don't know what to tell you," she said. "I haven't been to Oakhurst in years."

"And you're sure you've never met Father Rouge before?" Ivy asked. "If we check, we're not going to find any transactions between the two of you?"

"No, of course not. What kind of transactions?" she asked.

Jonathan sighed. "Thanks for your time, Whitney. Congratulations on your win." He motioned to Ivy that they should head out. Ivy could see they weren't going to get much out of Whitney Pierson. They could try to press the issue, but that would probably only end up making her clam up and call her lawyers.

"Okay," Mrs. Pierson said. "I still don't understand."

Ivy had the distinct feeling they were getting the run-around, but there was little they could do about it. If the woman wasn't willing to talk, they'd need to find another angle.

Back outside, Ivy headed for the driver's side of the car. "Well, that was a bust."

"I guess we shouldn't have expected her to admit it outright," Jonathan said. "What's she going to say? 'Yes, I was buying drugs from Father Rouge'."

"You think that's what was happening?" Ivy asked. "Assuming the powder comes back positive."

"It's the only thing that makes sense at the moment," Jonathan replied. "Why else would she be in that ledger?"

"Why would she go all the way down to Oakhurst when she can get as many drugs as she wants here?"

He shrugged. "I don't know."

Ivy opened her car door and got inside. "I still don't know if I buy this Priest selling drugs bit. If that's what was really happening, then he must have had a supplier. It wasn't like he was manufacturing the stuff himself."

"Like I said, it was just a theory that seemed to fit. Otherwise, I don't have another explanation as to what these names are doing in that ledger."

"Do you believe her?" Ivy asked. "She seemed surprised to see her name there."

"She may not have been aware he was keeping records," Jonathan said. "Then again, she may have nothing to do with this at all. The only person who really knows is Father Rouge."

Ivy sighed. "She seemed happy to see you, at least."

"Did she?" he asked. "I wasn't really paying attention."

Ivy rolled her eyes. Sometimes guys downplayed the fact they were attractive to the opposite sex ironically, because they knew exactly what they were doing. But in Jonathan's case, she really did think he was oblivious. It was sort of endearing, in a way. "You said someone else on that list lives out here somewhere?"

"Douglas Lefler," Jonathan said as Ivy started the car. "He used to run a huge law firm here in town. But last I heard— from my mother—he had moved out to the coast."

"Shouldn't be too hard to track down an address if you're up for another drive."

"Sure," he replied. "Who doesn't like a Sunday afternoon trip to the beach?"

Chapter Fifteen

IT TOOK another two hours and multiple phone calls on
Jonathan's end, but they finally managed to locate Douglas
Lefler's home. As they pulled up, Ivy was stunned by the
grandeur of the property. The house itself sat up on a cliff
overlooking the Pacific Ocean, surrounded by manicured
grounds on one side and massive rocks that led down to the
beach on the other. A long staircase wound from the top of
the cliff all the way down to the wide beach itself, and looked
at least six stories tall as they approached.

They'd had to stop at a small guard house at the entrance
to the neighborhood and show their credentials before they
were allowed in. And Ivy had no doubt in her mind that the
guard called ahead to tell Lefler they were coming.

"I'm going to go out on a limb and say Lefler was a
successful lawyer," Ivy said.

"Ambulance chaser," Jonathan said under his breath. "I
never met the man personally, but I know his reputation. He
would do anything and everything to get a client's money. It
obviously served him very well. His son was a grade-A asshole
back when I was a kid."

"I'm starting to see why you left this life behind," Ivy said.

"If you'd followed your family fortune you'd have been forced to become a dickhead."

He went to say something she was sure would be a rebuttal before he realized she was joking and he chuckled instead. "Yeah, I guess I would have."

As they pulled up to the circular driveway, Ivy caught sight of a man in white pants and a tan sweater standing on the stairs to the house, leaning on a wooden cane. He looked to be in his late sixties or early seventies and wore a pair of sunglasses to block out the afternoon sun.

"Target acquired," Jonathan said as Ivy killed the engine.

"That's him?" she asked. "He looks like John Hammond. Minus the beard."

"Yep." He stepped out of the car as Ivy followed and addressed the man. "Mr. Lefler."

The man made his way down the stairs one at a time. Though he was slow, he didn't break eye contact with Jonathan or Ivy. "I figured I'd save you the time, detectives. I don't have anything to say that can't be communicated through my lawyer."

"You don't remember me, do you?" Jonathan asked as Ivy circled the car, joining him.

"Should I?" Lefler asked.

"Jonathan White. I'm Constance Garson's son."

Lefler removed his sunglasses, revealing one of his eyes was cloudy, like someone had covered it in old milk. But the other was a bright and sharp cobalt. "My God. Johnny White. Well, you certainly grew up, didn't you?" He reached out his hand and Jonathan took it, shaking it briefly.

"This is my partner, Detective Bishop."

Lefler nodded at Ivy but thankfully didn't reach out to shake her hand. She wasn't sure if that was a slight or not.

"Joined the force, huh?" Lefler said. "Not what I expected from you. Not at all."

"We have a few questions we'd like to ask," Jonathan said, ignoring the man's comments.

Lefler only smiled. "As I said, you'll have to speak to my lawyer. If there is one thing you learn in thirty years of defense work, it's to never talk to the police. No offense, of course."

"Of course not," Jonathan said. But Ivy could tell he was doing everything he could to keep his cool. She hadn't realized what kinds of wounds speaking with these people would open up for him, but it was clearly affecting him.

"How is your mother?" Lefler asked.

"Same as always," Jonathan replied. "I'll let her know you said hello."

"Tell you what, why don't you come in for a quick drink? You've driven all the way out here. No sense in you leaving so quickly." He turned and began heading back up the staircase.

"That's very generous, but—" Ivy stopped Jonathan from protesting. This man was offering them a look inside his house. He might not be willing to answer any questions, but she didn't want to lose this opportunity.

"Thank you, we'd love to," Ivy said.

"Tell me about yourself, Detective," Lefler said, taking the stairs one at a time. He favored his left side, leaning heavily on the cane. Ivy was curious as to his injury but wasn't about to ask.

"Not much to tell. I've been with the police for a couple of years now, was just recently promoted to Detective."

"And how do you like police work?"

"I like it just fine," she said. "Not everyone likes the police; I understand that. But I think we do more good than harm."

Lefler turned and gave her a rueful smile before nodding. "Good for you." He pushed open one of the two double doors to his home. Ivy followed him in while Jonathan brought up the rear.

Inside the home was expansive, and almost entirely white. It featured a two-floor opening that looked out onto the ocean. The ceilings had to be twenty feet high, and the windows were flanked by the tallest curtains Ivy had ever seen.

The entire house screamed money, and Ivy took a moment to examine all the details while Lefler made his way over to the wet bar that was inset to one of the bookshelves in the room. "What will you have?"

"Whatever is easy," Ivy said.

"Just water for me," Jonathan said.

Lefler chuckled as he turned to start the drinks. "Tell me, Johnny. How did your mother react to you becoming a cop?"

"She tolerates it," he replied.

Lefler chuckled again. "Not well, I'd imagine. Boy, I would have loved to have seen her face. Your mother and I, well…we have something of a history."

"She's told me on multiple occasions," Jonathan replied. Ivy wasn't sure what Lefler was alluding to, and she didn't care. She'd spotted something on the bookshelf that had taken her attention.

"She's a good woman, your mother," Lefler said, handing Jonathan a water. He started making his way to Ivy but she met him halfway instead, taking the drink from him. He'd made it strong and she could only take one sip before setting it down.

"Thanks," Jonathan said. It was clear to Ivy he was uncomfortable with this conversation. Not only that, but she couldn't figure out why Lefler had wanted to bring them in here. Did it have something to do with his prior relationship with Jonathan's mother? Regardless, Ivy had what she needed.

She looked dramatically at her pocket, pulled out her phone and tapped the screen. "Bishop. Ok, got it." She put the phone back in her pocket. "We got a lead."

Jonathan arched an eyebrow, then set it glass down,

shaking Lefler's hand again. "Sorry, we'll have to cut this short. Thanks for the drink."

Ivy made her way back to the door as quickly as she could without running as Lefler and Jonathan said their goodbyes. Though she noted the older man followed them out to the top of his steps before watching them drive away.

"What was that about?" Jonathan asked. "I thought the whole reason we went in there was to try and wear him down so he'd answer some questions."

"No need," Ivy said. "We got what we needed."

"Which was?"

Ivy pulled out her phone and showed him the picture she'd snapped while looking over Lefler's library. "Look what he had on his shelf."

Jonathan's eyes widened. "A Torah?"

"Yep."

"But that doesn't mean—"

"I checked the inscription. It was a gift from his parents," Ivy said. "His very *Jewish* parents. You know what this means."

"He's not Catholic," Jonathan said. "Just like Whitney Green."

"Bingo."

∾

BY THE TIME THEY RETURNED TO OAKHURST IT WAS DARK. After finding out two of the most prominent names in Rouge's ledger weren't members of the same faith, Ivy had a hunch that most of the people on the list probably weren't. Which opened up even more questions. A list of parishioners she could explain away, that Father Rouge was either keeping track of donations or visits or some other metric. But given the first two people they'd looked into didn't even belong to the church, Ivy couldn't help but wonder just *what* the ledger was for.

If the sample from the desk tested positive for cocaine, then a very simple answer presented itself: the ledger was a list of customers. But Ivy couldn't imagine Whitney Pearson or Douglas Lefler driving all the way down to Oakhurst to get a drug fix, not when there had to be a dozen better options in Portland alone. So what was the reason? Not to mention the implications of a priest distributing illegal drugs. All of a sudden, Lana Orellio's theories didn't seem so far-fetched.

"Well, I was hoping that would be a little more productive," Jonathan said as Ivy pulled up to his place to drop him off. "Sorry to make you drive all that way."

"It wasn't a total waste," she said. "At least we have something of a pattern now. Maybe we'll get lucky and find out none of the names on that list are members of the church."

He yawned, causing Ivy to yawn in response. "I have a feeling that's only going to make it more complicated. Start again early in the morning?"

She nodded. "We still have forty-eight more names to go."

He got out and gave her a quick wave. "Have a good night."

She waved back, then drove off as soon as he disappeared around the corner. The prospect of going to forty-eight different people didn't appeal to her. Not to mention it would take forever, and it was very possible their killer might strike again. They needed a way to nail this guy down and fast.

As she drove back to her apartment she had a thought. She grabbed her phone and hit the second number saved in her contacts. Unfortunately, it went to voicemail.

"Oliver O'Toole. I don't answer from numbers I don't know. Text me what you need." She'd never heard Oliver's voicemail before and couldn't help but laugh at its brevity. She wished she could record an away message like that, but she had to be available for witnesses or victims. She couldn't just turn her phone off.

It was pretty late, maybe Oliver had turned in early. Though in the past he had always answered her calls. Still, she would check with him first thing tomorrow before she met up with Jonathan. Maybe he'd made some progress on the mutilation angle. He might even have a shortcut that would make this investigation easier. At the very least he could help her search for any other similarities between the names.

Resolved that she couldn't do anything else about the case tonight, she finally let her mind wander the rest of the way home. But as soon as the case was off her mind, Jonathan's news about Alice replaced it, front and center.

The only way she would not end up thinking about this twenty-four seven was to find Alice Blair and confront her. She needed to hear it from Alice's own mouth, but also, she wanted to know how much Alice knew about her case. In a weird way, Ivy felt like the woman had invaded her privacy, and she was determined to get it back. At a minimum she could demand Alice stop looking into the case and to let Ivy handle it.

At the same time, she was disappointed in herself. Hadn't she been the one to swear to herself that once she made detective she would spend all of her free time working on finding out what happened to her family? She had begun the process, but life and cases continued to get in the way. And by the time Ivy got home in the evenings, she was so dead tired that she just wanted to sleep, because she had to do it all again the next day.

Still, that was no excuse. Especially if they were still out there somewhere. Ivy owed it to them to find out what happened and to track them down. She'd hit a few roadblocks already with the case file, given how small it was. But now that she and Nat were on better terms, maybe they could work together to find out what happened. If what Alice suspected was true, and Nat really was hiding something, the best way for Ivy to find out would be to face it head on.

By the time she pulled into her small garage that sat across from her apartment building, Ivy had formulated a plan.

She'd find and confront Alice Blair, get as much information from her as possible, then speak with Nat.

At the same time she would work the case with Jonathan. It was a lot, but she could handle more than one task at a time, right?

That's what the job was all about.

Chapter Sixteen

Ivy PULLED up to Oliver's house at a quarter past seven. She was due to meet Jonathan at eight, which gave her about thirty minutes to convince Oliver to check into the names on the ledger. Though he'd never really put up much of a fight in the past. He'd complain, but she was pretty sure she'd be able to elicit his cooperation.

The bigger issue was she was becoming reliant on someone not part of the police force in an official investigation. But the truth was that Oliver could get into places she couldn't, and he could make certain judgement calls that she might find...objectionable, were she to be aware of them. Jonathan didn't approve of Oliver's involvement, which was why she wasn't planning on telling him. Still, it gnawed at her that she was even going down this road in the first place. She resolved that not only would this be the last time, but she would insist that Oliver stick to the letter of the law in his search. It was time to stop looking the other way.

She'd tried calling again this morning, but he wasn't answering. He also wasn't texting her back, which could have been alarming, if it wasn't Oliver. When they were kids, he would sometimes hide away in one of the bedrooms for a while, saying he was tired of being around the other kids so much. He was very much an introvert and introverts needed recharge time. Maybe he was in one of those cycles now. Ivy glanced at the bag of doughnuts on her passenger seat, along with a doggie treat for Hero. Hopefully they would make up for it.

But as she walked up to the house, she could already hear Hero barking inside. But it wasn't the normal, friendly bark she'd become accustomed to. This was more urgent, more intense. Immediately she dropped the bag of doughnuts and ran to the front door, banging on it.

"Oliver? It's Ivy, are you there?"

Hero began barking louder. She could hear his little feet running across the floor on the other side of the door until he was right on the other side, barking frenetically. "Oliver? Answer me!"

Nothing. Ivy bit her lip and looked around the side of the house. The entire property was overgrown and possibly covered with trip wires. But she couldn't get in on this side of the house. Her best bet was to try the far side; there was a sliding glass door on the back of the home.

The trick was getting back there. Why hadn't he just given her a key?

"Oliver, if you can hear me, I'm going around the back. Turn off whatever you have on out here so I won't get electrocuted." When he didn't respond again Ivy's heart jumped into her throat. She'd just have to risk it. On her first visit to Oliver's house, she had joked with Jonathan about what might be hidden in the yard to keep trespassers away. Now she wasn't so sure it had been a joke. Oliver could get into some shady stuff and there was a good possibility he had protected his house for that very reason.

Still, she didn't have much of a choice. She hopped over the small fence that ran alongside the walkway up to the front yard, landing in the tall grass. It came up to her hips, probably having never been cut since he moved in.

She moved carefully, but with purpose, looking for anything that could be nestled in the grass, or the reflection of any wires as she quickly made her way across the yard. Her foot snagged on a vine and she almost went down, but managed to right herself in time. As she came up to the corner of the house, she backed up against the brick, and checked the blind to make sure she wasn't walking into something worse before proceeding.

Thankfully there was no one there. And there was another fence on the side of the yard. She hopped over this one easily enough, landing in more manicured grass. This side of the house was actually well-kept. Oliver must have had to clear the back yard for Hero.

But the fuzzy thought was fleeting as Ivy made her way around the back to the sliding glass doors on the small concrete patio. She noted nothing looked out of place back here, and the glass doors were locked from the inside. As soon as she began yanking on them, Hero appeared, barking at her from the other side. He jumped up, his little paws on the glass, trying to get to her.

"Oliver! I'm going to break your door. Last warning to let me in," she yelled. She looked into the dark house, but none of the lights were on and she could barely see a thing due to the reflection.

With no response, she didn't have a choice. She pulled out her service weapon and used the butt of the weapon as a hammer, slamming it against the sliding pane away from where Hero was standing. The glass cracked, then shattered all over the inside of the house.

Ivy ran inside just as Hero was about to run on the glass and picked him up, holding him under one arm like a football. "Where's your papa?" she asked, her weapon still in her other hand as she surveyed the scene. What was even more alarming was there had been no response to the door shattering. At the very least that should have set off a security system. And knowing Oliver, it should have done much worse.

"Oliver!" she called out again but there was no answer. *Shit.* She backed up against one of the walls with Hero under one arm and her weapon in the other. "If there is anyone in this house, show yourselves right now. This is the police!"

Silence.

Ivy checked the corner into the living room, but it was empty. She reached over and flipped on a light with the barrel of the gun, but nothing in the room seemed out of place. The curtains had been drawn, blocking out any light from outside, but that was normal for Oliver. As far as she knew, every room in the house had its curtains drawn.

She made her way through the kitchen slowly as Hero panted under her arm. At least he'd stopped barking. She set him down so he could get some water from his bowl, which she noted was almost empty. He lapped up what was left quickly. "Stay," she said in a hushed tone. Hero put his butt to the floor, but watched her with worried eyes. It looked like Oliver's training had paid off.

As Ivy continued through the house, she checked the corner of each room before entering, finding more of the same. Had he just left and not told her? He wouldn't leave Hero here all alone; she was sure of that. But if it was the case, she had just destroyed an expensive sliding glass door for nothing. Though, she had to assume if he had left, he would have switched on one of his many alarm systems.

Before she could make her way down the hallway, Hero bolted past her. "*Hero*," she whispered, but he ran all the way down to Oliver's office and began scratching at the door. There were two other rooms down here and Ivy had to check them to make sure she wasn't walking into an ambush. But the little dog was telling her everything she needed to know.

Ivy ran to the office door and picked up the dog again so

he wouldn't go running inside. With her weapon in her other hand she turned the handle, pushing the door open. She checked the corner, sweeping her weapon back and forth, but there was no need. There was only one person in the room and he was lying on the floor. Ivy set Hero down, who ran over to Oliver, whimpering and licking at his face.

Oliver was face-down on the floor, splayed out. Ivy rushed over beside him and without even thinking, placed two fingers against his neck to feel for a pulse. Thankfully, the steady rhythm of his heartbeat told her he wasn't dead.

"Oliver, can you hear me?" she asked. But there was no response. She had no choice but to try and turn him over and get him conscious. She put her gun in its holster, then tried to get up under him to roll him. Her adrenaline was burning so hot she didn't even flinch at the contact. But as she began to roll him, she caught a glimpse of his face, which was black and swollen all over. He was bleeding from multiple cuts. It looked like he had been in a boxing ring. He groaned as she tried to move him.

"Okay, I won't move you," she said, setting him back down.

"Vee?" he asked, weakly. Hero continued to lick at his face. Ivy tried to move him back so he wouldn't lick Oliver's blood.

"Yeah, it's me," she said, pulling out her phone. She dialed 911. "This is Detective Bishop, badge eleven-three-six. I'm at 4486 Roslyndale in need of an emergency response unit. I have a male victim, approximately twenty-seven years old, unconscious and semi-responsive. Appears to have sustained multiple blunt force trauma injuries to the head and torso. Significant bruising and lacerations observed. Requesting immediate EMS response. Possible robbery in progress. No visible weapons on the scene, but evidence of a struggle. Securing the area, standing by."

The operator on the other side confirmed paramedics were on the way.

"Who did this?" Ivy asked as soon as she was off the phone. "What happened?"

Oliver only groaned softly. He probably wasn't even conscious. Ivy needed to clear the house. Whoever had done this to him could still be here. "You stay here," she said. "I'll be right back."

He groaned again as Ivy carefully stood and returned to the hallway. Her heart was about to burst out of her chest, but she took a few breaths and managed to center herself. She didn't have time to wait for backup. If there was someone else in this house, it was her responsibility to detain them. She checked the first room, finding it was empty as the rest of the house. The next room was nothing but storage boxes, but a thorough search revealed no one inside.

When she came to the final room she took one more deep breath, opened the door and took cover. The room was where Oliver kept all his servers, usually with hundreds of fans running to keep it all cool. Except now the room was silent. Ivy fumbled for the switch, and when the light came on, she gasped.

The entire room had been destroyed. Parts of computers were strewn all over the place. It looked like someone had taken a wrecking ball to the room. Not a single unit seemed to be working. The windows on this side of the home had also been broken. She assumed it had been how the home invader had left the property. If she'd come around the other side of the house, she would have seen this immediately.

One thing was for sure: there was no one left in the house. She'd checked every room, every nook and found nothing. She returned to Oliver and Hero.

In this distance, Ivy heard sirens approaching. She got up and headed to the front door, making sure the path was clear. She also unlocked the gates leading up to the house and flagged down the approaching ambulance.

"Where is he?" the paramedics asked as the jumped out of the van.

"Back bedroom," Ivy said. "There's also a small dog inside. The path should be clear." The paramedics nodded as a patrol car came charging down the street, pulling in behind Ivy's car. Ivy returned inside and grabbed Hero to get him out of the way while the paramedics worked on securing Oliver. She returned him to the kitchen, blocking off the area so he wouldn't run down the hall again. She also refilled his water bowl, which he took to greedily.

"Bishop?"

"In here," she called back. She looked around the corner to see Alan Wilcox, her old partner from when she'd been a beat cop. "Alan."

"Hey," he replied. "What's the situation?"

"Looks like a B&E with assault," she replied, stepping over the makeshift barrier for Hero. "I had to break in through the back door. The victim is Oliver O'Toole, age twenty-seven."

"You know the victim?" Wilcox asked, pulling out his notepad.

She nodded. "Old friends. I cleared the house, looks like they might have escaped through the back bedroom. It's a mess back there. Not sure how they got in, though."

"Ma'am," one the paramedics said as they wheeled the gurney down the hallway with Oliver still on it. "We're taking him to County General."

"How is he?" Ivy asked.

"Too early to tell," he said. "Would you like to follow us over there?"

Ivy glanced at Wilcox. "Go," he said. "I'll take care of this here. Pendleton is on the way to assist."

Ivy glanced at Hero, water dripping from his jowls. "Do you know anything about dogs?"

"I know I'm allergic to them," he said, taking a step back.

She couldn't just leave him here at a crime scene, especially not in this condition. Ivy grabbed the leash hanging on the small hook by the back door and picked up Hero in her other arm. "That's okay. Just let me know what you find out, will you?"

"You got it," Wilcox said. "I hope your friend is ok."

As Ivy headed for the door; her arms full, she noticed the bag of doughnuts discarded on the porch. This was not how she'd expected this morning to go. "Me too."

Chapter Seventeen

As Ivy stood outside with Hero, watching him do his business on a small patch of grass near the hospital, she saw Jonathan's car pull into a nearby parking spot. After notifying Nat of the situation—and conveniently tucking the conversation she needed to have with the woman away—she'd called him on the way to the hospital to let him know she wouldn't be in this morning and to start without her. She hadn't expected him to actually show up.

"Hey," he said, trotting up, shooting a quick glance at Hero. "What's the news? Is he ok?"

"Still waiting to hear," Ivy said. "They're still evaluating him. Jonathan, he was beat to hell. Someone really took it out on him."

"Robbery?" Jonathan asked.

"I couldn't tell, it was so crazy over there," she replied. "Wilcox is working on it."

"That's good," Jonathan replied. "He's reliable. How did you find out he'd even been attacked?"

Ivy swallowed. She hadn't been looking forward to this. "I went over there to see if he could help with the case. I thought maybe he could cut down on some of the names on Rouge's ledger."

Jonathan nodded, though it was obvious he wanted to say something about Ivy's decision. Instead, he motioned to Hero. "Is *he* ok?"

"Seems to be," she said. "He isn't injured as far as I can tell. But maybe I should take him to the vet anyway to make sure? I don't know. I've never had a dog before."

"You have to pick that up, you know," Jonathan said, pointing at what Hero had left behind. The little dog kicked up some of the grass as he finished his business.

Ivy sighed. "Here," she said, handing Hero's leash to Jonathan. She pulled a glove from her pocket and deftly picked up the remains, depositing them in a nearby trash can. "I'm going to head back inside. Are you ok working the case on your own today? I don't want to leave until I get an update."

"I'll stay with you," he said. "We can keep going through the list. Might take your mind off things."

She nodded. Hero led the way back into the hospital through the automatic doors. "I just can't figure out who would want to attack Oliver," she said as they walked. "What do you think he was into?"

"Could be anything," Jonathan said. "He runs in dangerous circles with dangerous people."

"But he always keeps himself anonymous," she said. "That's kind of the point. So people couldn't find him."

"Looks like he ran into someone as good, if not better than he was."

Ivy didn't want to think of the implications of that. Oliver was a pro at computers, something that had always eluded Ivy. If he'd gotten himself in with someone who was even *better*, then he could have a target on his back for the rest of his life. But they could worry about that later. Right now she just wanted to make sure he would see tomorrow.

As they headed back into the waiting room, a doctor was emerging from the double doors leading to the back. "Detective Bishop?" he asked, pulling down his mask.

"Here," she said. Hero pulled on the leash trying to get to the doctor.

"I'm Dr. Brachman. You came in with Mr. O'Toole?" Ivy nodded. "I wanted to inform you we're taking him in for surgery. He has a punctured lung, a ruptured appendix and could be bleeding internally. How long ago was the attack?"

"I don't know," Ivy said. "We're still investigating. Is he going to make it?"

"If we can stop the bleeding, I believe so. I need to get back in there, but I wanted to give you an update. We're prepping him now."

Ivy nodded. "Thank you."

Brachman turned and headed back into the unit while Ivy collapsed into a nearby chair. *Internal bleeding, a ruptured appendix and lung?* None of that sounded good. Not to mention the other injuries he sustained.

Jonathan took a seat beside her, neither of them saying anything for the moment. She was glad he was here. Somehow, Oliver's condition *felt* like her fault, even though she knew that was ridiculous. If she hadn't gone over there this morning, he might have died right there in his house. At the very least she gave him a fighting chance. Still, she felt like she might throw up.

"Wilcox will speak to the neighbors," Jonathan finally said. "Someone might have seen something. And I seem to remember Oliver had cameras everywhere."

"Yeah," Ivy said. But given the state of that computer room, she wasn't sure if any footage from them would be recoverable. "Someone wanted to send a message."

"Why do you say that?" he asked.

"Nothing else in the house was disturbed. Just the server room. Hero was fine. Whatever Oliver did to piss someone off, they wanted him and him alone to feel it. They attacked him, then destroyed the thing that allows him to run his business."

"I'm not about to pretend I know how it all works," Jonathan said. "But I'm pretty sure he can stay in business without that server room. Was his main computer still there?"

Ivy tried to remember. She was so preoccupied with helping Oliver and trying to keep him awake she hadn't noticed. "I don't know." She glanced down at Hero. "I don't guess you could tell us what happened." Hero just stared at her in return, panting lightly.

"You're not the first person that wished dogs could talk, trust me." Jonathan reached down and scratched the little dog behind his ears. "What are you going to do with him?"

"I'm not sure," she replied. "Even if he does pull through, I doubt Oliver is going home anytime soon."

THREE AND A HALF HOURS LATER, IVY WOKE TO FIND SHE'D fallen asleep in the chair, her head precariously close to Jonathan's shoulder. She snapped awake, rubbing her eyes. She'd wrapped Hero's leash around her leg so he wouldn't escape, but when she looked down, she found he'd curled up in a small ball under the seats.

"Hey," Jonathan said. "Get any rest?"

Ivy rubbed her eyes. "You shouldn't have let me fall asleep."

"You seemed to need it," he replied. "I've managed to narrow down some more of the names on the list. They're more local, thankfully. But there are still about ten that I can't track down."

"That's good," Ivy said. "Should we start calling or—"

The doors to the back opened again, revealing the same doctor as before. Ivy immediately stood up, her heart in her throat.

Dr. Brachman's mask was already down and his scrub cap was off. "Good news, we were able to stabilize Mr. O'Toole. We repaired the damage to his lung, stopped the bleeding and removed his appendix. He's resting comfortably now. But as you know, he's been through a severe trauma."

"Is he awake?" Ivy asked.

"Not yet. We're keeping him under for the time being. Fortunately, despite the damage to his face, I think most of it is superficial and will heal on its own. But I want to rule out a concussion, which will take some time."

"What happens now?" Jonathan asked.

"Now, he gets some rest. If all goes well, we'll try waking him in the morning. But we're going to keep close observation on him for the next twenty-four to forty-eight hours to make sure he's completely stable."

Ivy took a breath of relief. That was all good news. "When can I see him?"

"Let's see how the next twenty-four hours go. If you leave me your number, I'll call you with an update tomorrow."

Ivy pulled a card from her wallet and handed it over. "You can call that number anytime."

Brachman nodded. "Thank you. You're welcome to stay, of course. But there's little you can do here. He won't be awake any time soon. Is there any other family we need to notify?"

Ivy shook her head. "Just me."

Brachman nodded. "I always like to make sure. You're listed as his emergency contact, so I'll be relaying everything through you."

"Oh," Ivy said. She hadn't realized Oliver had done that, but she guessed it made sense. Who else was he going to list?

After speaking a little more with the doctor, Ivy decided staying any longer at the hospital would be a waste of time. Oliver wouldn't know she was there and there wasn't anything she could do. Instead, she was anxious to get back over to his house to see if Wilcox had managed to uncover anything about the incident.

"Hey," she said to Jonathan as they left the hospital, Hero continuing to lead the way. "I know we're supposed to be working this thing. But I'm going to run back over there to check on their progress. I just want to know if they've found anything."

"Sure," Jonathan said. "I'll tag along. I'm sure Wilcox won't mind a few more eyes on the scene."

She smiled. "Thanks. You don't have to do that."

They headed back over to the house in both cars, Hero riding shotgun in Ivy's vehicle. The whole way she kept trying to figure out what she was going to do with him. She had been the one to convince Oliver he needed a dog in the first place, so wasn't he her responsibility?

But spending all day alone at her apartment wasn't ideal either. One of the reasons she didn't already have pets was because she was never home. It wouldn't be fair to them. Hero needed companionship during the day, not to mention she was pretty sure pets weren't even allowed in her building.

When they pulled up to the house, two police cruisers were still on site. The area had been marked off with yellow police tape, and Ivy caught sight of a white van parked in front of Wilcox's cruiser. She got out of the house and saw Wilcox trotting down the steps of a nearby neighbor across the street, shoving his notepad in his back pocket. He signaled to her and Jonathan to meet him over at the front of Oliver's property.

"How's your friend?" he asked as the trio met back up.

"He's stable for now; they're going to keep him sedated. It was pretty bad."

Wilcox nodded. "Forensics found some blood in the house. We assume it belonged to the victim, but they're taking samples just in case."

"Anything else? Any witnesses?"

"Lady across the street thought she heard a commotion

early this morning, but she said it could have been the TV her husband always leaves on all night. We also have the neighbor two houses down who says they saw a black car drive away around five-thirty."

"What kind of black car?"

He pulled out his notepad again. "Couldn't say, witness stated *it was darker than the inside of a mine shaft.*" He flipped the notepad back and shoved it in his pocket again, pointing along the road. "No streetlights on this road. Any light would have had to have come from a nearby house and they were what… fifty yards away?"

"Any other evidence inside the house?" Jonathan asked.

"Bishop said she was the one who broke in the back door," he said. "But it looks like she was right. Our perp probably left out the side window. Why they didn't just leave out the front I don't know."

"Oliver is known to…be a little eccentric when it comes to his house," Ivy said.

"Are you kidding? I've been in there. I can tell," Wilcox replied. "Still. I didn't see any reason why they couldn't have used the front door."

"Hero," Ivy said. Both Jonathan and Wilcox turned to her. "They didn't want to let Hero out. Maybe they were afraid he'd run out the front door if they tried leaving that way."

"Why would someone who beat the ever-loving snot— excuse the term—out of Mr. O'Toole, care about the dog?" Wilcox asked.

Ivy shrugged. "Hero wasn't harmed. Maybe there's a reason for that. You might be looking for an animal lover."

Wilcox jotted it down. "Noted. I guess that makes sense."

"Speaking of which," Ivy said. "I need to go get some things. Mind if I…?" She pointed at the house.

"No, go ahead," he replied. "Burns's people are just about done anyway."

"Here," Ivy said, handing Hero's leash to Jonathan. "Hold

onto him for a sec." She left the two men at the front of the house and made her way inside. There she ran into the same tech who had been on the scene at the church.

"Detective Bishop," he said. "Twice in as many days. That's got to be a record of some kind."

"Find anything useful?" she asked.

"Couple of prints, blood and some fibers. We'll have to test it to make sure it belongs to the victim. Whoever they were, it doesn't seem like they were too worried about leaving evidence behind. Found a steel bat in the back room. We think that's what caused all the damage back there. It's already on its way back to the lab."

"Might have been the assault weapon as well," Ivy said. She described Oliver's injuries to him.

"I'll coordinate with the hospital and get a medical report. See if we can't start matching some of this up."

"Thanks," Ivy said. "I really appreciate it. This one is... personal."

"No problem." He gave the tip of an imaginary hat and headed in the opposite direction. Ivy went into Oliver's kitchen and started gathering up supplies. She grabbed a bag of Hero's food, a nearby dog bed, some toys, his water bowl and another bag of treats from the pantry.

"Moving out?" Jonathan jested as she emerged from the house with all of Hero's stuff.

"If he's going to live somewhere else, he needs his effects," Ivy said.

"You're taking him to live with you?" Jonathan asked.

"Nope, with Carol. She's home all day; he'll have company."

"Does *she* know about this?" he called after her as she trotted his things to her car.

"No, but she's about to."

Chapter Eighteen

"WHAT'S ALL THIS?" Aunt Carol asked, opening the door. Ivy was sure she looked like a madwoman, all of Hero's things in her hands, and the little dog, by himself on a leash at her feet.

"I need your help," Ivy said.

"Well, come on in," Carol said, holding the door for both of them. "What's happened?"

Ivy took a second to bring everything into the house and set it all down. She then tried to explain to Aunt Carol what had happened to Oliver, though she found now that her adrenaline was beginning to wane it was becoming more difficult.

"Here," Carol said. "Just come with me into the kitchen. Sit down." She took Hero's leash from Ivy, unbuckled it, and let the dog start roaming free in the house. Ivy trudged her way into the kitchen and practically fell down into one of the chairs, completely exhausted.

Why was she so tired? She hadn't done a thing all day except get up a little early and then spend most of it sitting at the hospital. She'd even fallen asleep there. So why did she feel like her eyes were about to snap shut on their own?

"Here," Carol said, pushing a glass of water in Ivy's direction. She then took Hero's water bowl and filled it up, placing it on a small towel at the edge of the cabinets in the kitchen. The little dog was still sniffing out the living room, but eventually made his way into the kitchen, exploring every corner of the room.

"Now tell me what happened," she said.

Ivy started at the beginning, though she left out the part as to *why* she had gone over to see Oliver. She tried to remember every detail, but now that she was out of the moment, she found it more difficult to concentrate. But she managed to get through it.

"He's going to make it," Carol said. "Don't you worry about that."

"You don't know that," Ivy said. "There's a chance he won't."

"You have to believe he will."

Ivy didn't have time for Carol's *positive thinking* class. "Regardless of what happens, I need someone to take care of Hero if...until Oliver gets better," she said. "I would do it, but—"

"Say no more," Carol said. "Believe it or not, I kind of figured it out when you showed up with all that gear in tow."

"Do you mind?" Ivy asked. "Otherwise, we'd have to put him in the pound or—"

"I already said yes," Carol replied. "It's no trouble, really. Has he eaten today?"

Ivy knew she hadn't fed him, other than a quick snack here and there. "No, I don't think so."

"Have you?"

Ivy glanced to the side.

Carol got up, heading for the stove. Ivy moved to get up too, but Carol stopped her in her tracks. "You sit right there and relax a second. I can take care of this."

"His food is in one of those bags," Ivy said.

"I'm not letting him eat bagged dog food," Carol said. "He'll eat something real." She pulled out her cell phone, typing away. "Ah, that's easy enough." She grabbed some supplies from the refrigerator.

"What are you doing?"

"Fixing him a real meal," she said.

"You can't do that," Ivy said. "At least not right away. He's used to one kind of food. If you change it too suddenly, he'll get sick." She got up and retrieved the bag of food from the hallway. Hero started jumping up and down as soon as he saw it.

"I didn't know you were so well-versed in animal care," Carol said, standing to the side as she watched Ivy pour Hero a serving into his bowl. She set it down beside the water and the little dog went to work.

"I guess I just picked it up watching Oliver," Ivy said.

"I can at least fix you something to eat," Carol said. "And I'll make sure not to change up his food too much. Now please, sit down. You look like you're about to fall over."

Ivy did as she was told. A few moments later Carol handed her a cup of earl gray. "How is your other case going?" Carol asked halfway through preparing dinner. "The one you were called away on the other night."

"Oh," Ivy said, taking another sip of the tea. "Complicated. You saw what happened on the news?" Carol nodded. "Well, it's more than that. I can't say why, but let's just say they don't make it very easy for us."

"If it was easy, dear, everyone would want to do it."

Ivy supposed that was true. "To be honest, I haven't been able to concentrate all day. Jonathan and I went up to Portland yesterday to interview some potential witnesses, but didn't come back with much. We were supposed to keep working on it today, but then this happened and…"

"—threw everything off track," Carol said, already plating

some of the food from the skillet. Hero had long ago finished his meal and was looking up at Carol with ravenous eyes. "Do you have any idea what happened to Oliver? Who might have done this?"

"I don't ask too many questions about his business," Ivy admitted. "But now I wish I had. As far as I could tell there was no forced entry."

"That means he knew whoever came in, right?" Carol asked. She set a plate of goulash in front of Ivy. It smelled so delicious she was at risk of drooling.

"Usually. But not necessarily," Ivy said. "Someone else may have had access to the house. A key, or a passcode. But knowing Oliver, that's unlikely."

"If he were to give anyone a key, I'd think it would be you," Carol said.

"Still, I don't know a lot about his life now. We've only started to get to know each other again after fifteen years of not speaking. There are sure to be things he hasn't told me— either because of my job or because he's afraid I might judge him."

Carol took a seat next to Ivy, a small plate of cooling hamburger in front of her. She picked up a small piece, rolled it around in her hand a minute, then put it in front of Hero's nose. He chomped it so quickly Ivy was afraid he'd taken one of Carol's fingers off. "I don't know much about the boy," Carol said. "But from what you've told me, he's only ever wanted to impress you. I think you might be onto something."

Ivy shook her head. "Right now, I don't even care what happened. I just want to make sure he's going to be okay. I can figure out what happened afterwards. Plus, it's not even my case. Wilcox is working it."

"Your old partner?" Carol asked.

Ivy nodded. "I know he'll do a good job. If we'd been promoted at the same time we'd still be working together."

"So what does Jonathan think about all of this?" Carol glanced at Ivy under hooded eyes.

"He's been really supportive," Ivy said. "But that's it. Nothing else."

"Okay," Carol said, holding up her hand. "Just curious." She fed Hero another small piece of hamburger.

As Ivy sat there eating, her mind kept falling back to what Jonathan had said yesterday. Had that only been yesterday? It seemed like a week ago now. She couldn't decide if she wanted to bring it up to Aunt Carol or not, but after everything that had happened today, maybe it was better if she saved it for another time. With so much going on, Ivy's attention was being split a hundred different ways. She needed to get back on the Rouge case.

"Did you know him? Father Rouge?" Ivy asked.

"Not personally. I knew *of* him, but I never met the man," Carol replied. "Always heard good things."

"That's what everyone seems to say," Ivy said. "The man had no enemies." She'd made it about halfway through her meal and was already stuffed. Or maybe she just didn't feel like eating very much.

"Well," Carol finally said, getting back up from the table with Hero close behind. "Don't worry about us. We'll be perfectly fine here. And I'm happy to take care of Hero for as long as necessary."

"Thank you. That's a big help," Ivy said. "I really should get going. It's been a long day and—"

"My darling, you don't have to explain yourself to me," Carol said. "Go. Do what you need to do. I'll call if I need anything. But we should be just fine here."

Ivy nodded, picking up her plate. "Leave that right there. I'll take care of it."

"Thanks, Aunt Carol," Ivy said. "This really means a lot."

"Think nothing of it," she said. "We'll be thinking good

thoughts for Oliver. You'll let me know if anything happens?"
Ivy nodded. "Then drive safe back home. And get some rest."

As Ivy headed back to her car, she reflected on just how lucky she was. Not everyone got an Aunt Carol in their lives. Some people didn't have anything.

Chapter Nineteen

"GIVE ME A SITREP," Nat said, circling her overcrowded desk
and sitting in the worn leather chair behind it. She'd called Ivy
in first thing this morning after Ivy had informed her of what
had happened with Oliver. While Ivy had been keeping her
abreast of their progress on the Rouge case, she hadn't actually seen Nat in a few days, not since before Jonathan told her
about Alice's suspicions. And ever since then, Ivy hadn't been
able to stop thinking about it. Even now, as she sat across from
the woman who rescued her as a teen, who had supported her
joining the force and even hired her to the Violent Crimes
Unit, Ivy couldn't help but see someone with two faces.

"We're still interviewing the people on Rouge's list," Ivy
said. "The first couple were no-gos, but I have a feeling we'll
make more progress with the locals."

Nat opened her laptop and tapped a few keys. "You and
White went up to Portland? Why?"

"Detective White recognized two of the names on the list
as former...acquaintances," Ivy said. "He thought we might
have more luck with someone he had a personal connection
to."

"And?" Nat asked.

"Both denied knowing Father Rouge. Though Jon— Detective White believes they're both hiding something. We also discovered neither are Catholic."

"Very well," Nat said, tapping a few more keys on the computer. "I'm getting calls from the diocese about when we'll relinquish the church and the body. They want to have a funeral as soon as possible and are even discussing burying him in the church's graveyard."

Ivy thought back to the old graveyard behind the church with its askew and barely legible epitaphs. Digging a new plot back there would be a feat. "I think we have everything we need from Burns. I don't see any reason we can't release the body."

"Bishop Bain will be happy to hear that. He's been a relentless boil on my ass."

"We met him," Ivy said.

Nat shot her a smirk. "What about the church?"

"We're still trying to figure out who could have had access. I know forensics has done their work, but I would feel better if we held off from letting anyone in there for a few more days. At least until we narrow the suspect list."

Nat sighed. "Well, get on it. Armstrong is fielding daily calls from the press and you know how much he enjoys dealing with them."

A mention of the press made Ivy's stomach drop. She recalled the recent notice that banned any media person from the building. "I saw the email."

"Email?" Nat said, then corrected herself. "Oh, yes. Given how certain members of the media seem to think this office is their personal playground, we thought it was prudent."

"You're talking about Alice Blair," Ivy said.

"If you want to put a name to it," Nat replied without a hint that she'd had a personal conversation with the woman. Nat had one of the best poker faces Ivy had ever seen. "But it applies to anyone. If anything, she did us a favor."

"Did something happen?" Ivy asked.

Nat stopped. "What do you mean?"

"I was just wondering if this was in response to a particular incident." She kept her voice cool and level, not letting on to the fact she knew more than she did. This was dangerous territory, and she needed to be careful. She hadn't even expected to bring it up, but as soon as Nat opened the door, she couldn't help but walk through.

"Nothing in particular," Nat said. "But in all honesty, it's something that should have been instituted long ago. Starting when she broke into your workstation."

"I wouldn't say she *broke in.*" Ivy adjusted herself on the seat. "And that was my fault for not closing it down properly."

"Regardless, it was a breach and we should have taken care of it then and there." Nat paused. "Why the interest in Alice Blair all of a sudden?"

"She's been at the church a lot," Ivy lied. "And I keep thinking about that night on the cliff."

Nat nodded, understanding dawning on her face. "You're not questioning what you did?"

"Well," Ivy said, leaning forward. "If it weren't for me, she never would have been in that position. *I* put her there by being careless."

"And you helped save her," Nat replied.

Ivy locked her gaze with Nat's. Did she know? Ivy could come right out and confront her with the accusation. But it would surely be shot down in an instant and possibly damage what little of their relationship they'd rebuilt. Ivy didn't want to admit to herself how precious that peace was to her. How much she cherished it, even if it was a lie. But confronting Nat head on wouldn't do her any good. The woman's demeanor was hard as stone. Trying to get anything from her was an exercise in futility.

Ivy just needed to find a way to crack it. Because if there

was any truth to Alice's suspicions, Ivy couldn't keep herself blind to the truth forever.

"Put it out of your mind," Nat finally said. "Otherwise, you'll end up looping it in your head forever. You can't change what happened any more than anyone else. Best thing you can do is forget it and move forward. And don't forget, everything worked out in the end." She held Ivy's gaze a moment too long before turning back to her computer.

There it was. Ivy had overplayed her hand. Her attempt at subtlety might as well have been a wrecking ball. And Nat had seen right through it. Alice was right, she *was* covering something up. Something she believed she was justified in obscuring. Maybe an outsider wouldn't have recognized the exchange for what it was, but Ivy knew.

"How is your friend?" Nat asked as if nothing had transpired between them.

"Um…I heard from the doctor this morning," Ivy said. "He did really well overnight and is already awake. I was going to go see him this afternoon."

Nat nodded, keeping her attention focused on her computer as she typed. "I read Wilcox's initial report. I'd say it looks like a simple B&E except for the fact nothing was taken. At least, as far as they could tell."

"Didn't look like a burglary to me either," Ivy said, her heart sinking. There was no way she was ever going to get Nat to tell her what was really going on. The woman had been lying to her for so long she believed she was completely justified in doing it. Ivy's only choice at this point would be to start investigating Nat herself. A course that would be wrought with danger. Like swimming with crocodiles.

"Don't worry, he'll get to the bottom of it," Nat said nonchalantly. "I'm just glad your friend is okay."

"You remember him, don't you?" Ivy asked, causing Nat to glance up. "From Mrs. Baker's house? He was there when you dropped me off."

"Oh," Nat said. "That was so long ago I don't really recall." She glanced over the edge of her laptop again. "Was there anything else?"

"No." It was as if all the air had disappeared from Ivy's lungs. Were anyone else to watch the conversation between the two of them they'd probably say it was completely normal. But Ivy knew Nat too well for that. And that was part of the problem. Nat knew Ivy too. It was as if there were two invisible forces, pushing against each other, neither of them moving in either direction, so they looked like they were standing still. But to the two people behind those forces, they were using everything they had to push as hard as possible.

"Ok, keep me updated on the Rouge case. We're on the clock here."

"You don't need to remind me," Ivy said, anger beginning to bubble up inside her. "We're doing the best we can."

Nat looked up a final time, her face as emotionless as a granite wall. "Then go do it."

Ivy stood and left the room, barely managing not to slam the door behind her. *God damn* her. Her superior attitude. Her smugness. She was getting away with murder and she knew it. And Ivy wasn't going to take it any longer. She thundered down the stairs, headed for the parking lot before running into Jonathan, who was having a discussion with Pendleton. She barely saw the two of them, instead she made a beeline for the doors. She needed air.

"Ivy, wait up," Jonathan said from behind her, but it was accompanied by a buzzing in her ears that was turning everything fuzzy. She pushed through the double doors out into the morning air, crisp and clean. Somewhere behind all the clouds above, the sun was shining, but Ivy couldn't see it. All she could see was a sea of gray above. Still, she took five deep breaths, closing her eyes. It was all she could do not to scream.

"Are you okay?" Jonathan asked from behind her.

"Alice was right," Ivy said without opening her eyes. "She's deliberately hiding something."

She could feel his presence beside her. Even though she couldn't see him, she could *sense* him. "Are you sure? Alice even said she didn't have any real evidence."

"I've never been more sure of anything in my life," she replied. "I should have seen it earlier. But I was too preoccupied with keeping the peace. With *hoping*, for once, we might actually be able to have a real relationship again." The words came out through her teeth and she took another deep breath, willing herself to calm down. If she didn't, she might end up punching the closest thing to her and she didn't want that to be Jonathan.

"Then that's a God damn fucking shame," he replied.

Her anger disappeared. It was like a warm wind had come through and blown it off her, taking it far into the distance. She opened her eyes and turned to him.

A smile lit up his face. "I always pay my debts."

Ivy grinned, despite herself. In fact, she almost felt like laughing.

"C'mon," Jonathan said. "I have news."

Chapter Twenty

"GOING ON YOUR HUNCH, I decided to try and connect the names on the list," Jonathan said. "We know Whitney Pierson and Douglas Lefler weren't Catholic, so why did Father Rouge's have their names in a drawer?"

"Right, and?" Ivy asked. Since he'd more than likely won the bet, it was only fair to let him drive for once, and she wasn't about to argue. Even though she felt a lot better than she had fifteen minutes ago, she didn't trust herself behind the wheel right now. Driving too fast had become an easy way to burn off her anger, but at the same time, it put her and other people at risk. The best thing she could do right now was ride shotgun.

That, and keep thinking about what Jonathan said outside the station. What she wouldn't give to have that on repeat.

"Donations to the church?" he said. "No. I checked with Eloise Banner. She didn't know either of them. So then I thought maybe it would be a good idea to check with some of the volunteers. We interviewed the employees, but not the weekly volunteers. The deacons, the choir, the people who *see* the attendees on a weekly basis."

"That...makes sense. But when did you have time—"

"Yesterday, and last night," Jonathan said. "I managed to schedule some quick interviews while we were waiting at the hospital and went to see them after we left Oliver's house yesterday."

"Why didn't you tell me?"

"Because you had enough to deal with," he said. "You'd been through a stressful situation, we weren't sure what Oliver's condition was, and I wasn't going to pile more on you in the moment. You needed to take yesterday to *not* think about the case."

"You…didn't have to do that," she said, her voice growing smaller. "I could have handled it."

"I know you could have," he replied. "But you're the kind of person who will run yourself into the ground to your own detriment. And it wasn't like I wasn't going to ever tell you. In fact, I knew you'd feel like we were behind if we didn't make any progress yesterday."

That was true. As much as she hated to admit it, she tried to keep thinking about the case yesterday, even during the crisis just so she wouldn't feel like she was letting it fall by the wayside. But Jonathan had picked up the slack and already done the work. She wanted to be angry, but in truth, she was grateful.

"What did you find?"

"That our two friends up in Portland weren't as ignorant as they led us to believe," he replied. "I showed their pictures to two different members of the choir I spoke with last night. They remembered seeing both Pierson and Lefler at Wednesday night services in the past two months."

"Wait a second," Ivy said. "They were attending services?"

"According to these witnesses, yes. Even going as far as to receive the Eucharist."

"That's where everyone goes up for the wine and cracker thing, right?" Ivy asked.

Jonathan grinned. "Yeah. More or less."

"Do you think they just spontaneously changed religions?" Ivy asked.

"I don't know," he replied. "I guess it's possible. Maybe every person on that list is someone who converted to Catholicism secretly for some reason."

Ivy tried to play it over in her head. It's possible, she supposed, someone could convert without telling anyone. Some families were very strict about which religions their children or spouses belonged to. Maybe Pierson and Lefler wanted to keep their beliefs secret from other people in their families or social circles.

"Where are we going?"

"To visit the Deacon," Jonathan said. "I want to see if his recollection matches up with the choir members."

"Finally," Ivy said. "I assume he's back from his... sabbatical?"

"I know," Jonathan said. "Convenient timing. But maybe we can kill two birds with one stone. Eliminate him as a suspect and see if he can confirm what we've heard so far at the same time."

"I guess we can hope," Ivy said.

TWENTY MINUTES LATER THEY PULLED UP TO A SMALL, modest house on the west side of town. It was a rancher, nestled in the middle of a quaint neighborhood. It looked like the kind of place where kids played in the cul-de-sacs and people walking their dogs would wave at each other as they passed.

The house itself was well-kept, with brick-bordered flower beds underneath the two windows flanking the house. No flowers were in the beds yet, or perhaps they had already been planted and were waiting for spring. Regardless, the house seemed well-taken care of.

"Nice place," Jonathan said, noting the four-door Mercury in the driveway.

"It's a little small," Ivy said. "I don't think it's any bigger than my apartment." They made their way up the walkway, but before they could climb the two steps to the porch, the front door opened, revealing a man in his early forties. He had on frameless spectacles and his blonde hair had begun to bald. But his eyes were bright and he had prominent cheekbones, giving him the look of a cherub.

"Deacon Lutz?" Jonathan asked.

"Detective White," the man said, holding out a hand. Jonathan shook it. "Thank you for coming."

"This is my partner, Detective Bishop," Jonathan said.

Ivy nodded. The deacon extended his hand for her and for a split second, she almost fell back into her old habit. But something felt different, and unexpectedly, she took the man's hand, giving it a hearty shake. She'd expected it to feel like grabbing a live electrical wire, but the sensation was dulled and she couldn't figure out why. Though she did notice Jonathan give her a curious look. "Pleasure," she said.

"Would you like to come in?" Lutz asked, holding the door for them.

"Thank you," Ivy said, leading the way into the home. Inside it was as she expected. There was minimal furniture, all of it probably a hand-me-down, though it was all clean and in good shape. A worn carpet covered the main living area, which she noted had no television anywhere. Just two couches and a few other pieces of furniture. A bookcase at the end of the room was stacked with all different kinds of books. As Ivy investigated the titles, Deacon Lutz closed the door behind them.

"Please have a seat. Would you like something to drink? I have tea, water, or I'm happy to brew some coffee."

"No thank you," Jonathan said. "We'll try not to take up too much of your time."

"Very well," the man said. Ivy joined Jonathan on one of the couches while Lutz took a seat on the other.

"Quite a variety of books you have," she said.

"Thank you. I try to be well-read."

"I wouldn't have expected a Catholic Deacon to be a science fiction fan."

The man laughed. It was a jovial sound, filling the room. "I guess that's my one vice. I grew up on Star Trek. I guess in many ways I never let it go."

"You just returned from Deer Ridge Correctional facility, correct?" Jonathan asked.

"Yes, I was on a short sabbatical there with the prisoners," he replied. "Our incarcerated population is one of our most overlooked. People often forget there are real humans in there, many with mental health issues. We try to help where we can."

"Did you happen to speak to a prisoner named Kieran Woodward?" Ivy asked.

Lutz furrowed his brow. "I don't believe so. Who is he?"

"No one," Ivy said. "Just curious."

"Is taking sabbaticals to the prison something that's a regular part of your schedule?" Jonathan asked.

Lutz sat back in the couch. "I wouldn't say it was a regularly scheduled. But it was something Father Rouge and I spoke about many times. He would send me when he could, when things at the church were slow."

"When was the last time you saw Father Rouge?" Ivy asked.

"Last Monday. I was helping him prepare for Wednesday Mass," he said. "I left Oakhurst the following morning and didn't return until last night."

"Even after you'd heard the news?" Ivy asked.

"Matthew wouldn't have wanted me to leave," Lutz said. "And I was in contact with Bishop Bain. He assured me that I should finish my time at Deer Ridge. The church would be here for me when I returned."

Ivy leaned forward. "Does that mean you'll be taking Father Rouge's position?"

"Oh, no, that's not a role for me," he said. "I'm what's known as a permanent deacon. I can't become a priest. No, Bishop Bain will assign someone from the diocese to come and take over."

Well, there went motive. "We've already spoken to Mrs. Banner and Mr. Suntree about the incident. But do you happen to know anyone who might have wanted to harm Father Rouge?" Jonathan asked. "Anyone who was angry with him?"

"Not personally, no," Lutz said.

Ivy narrowed her gaze. "What does that mean?"

He turned to her; his hands open. "Just that the church hasn't had the best...reputation as of late. A lot of people blame all Catholics for the actions of a few...misguided individuals. That blame can transform into anger."

"But Father Rouge had never faced accusations like that," Ivy said.

"Of course not. If he had, the Bishop would have removed him from the post. Father Rouge was as aware as anyone of the church's optics. He did everything in his power to be as transparent at all times, making sure no one could ever accuse him of anything."

"How did he do that?" Jonathan asked.

"By making sure whenever he was with children, there was at least one or more other adults close," Lutz said. "Even though Father Rouge never would have taken those kinds of actions, he wanted to make sure the community felt safe in the church."

"What about members that weren't children?" Ivy asked. "Would he still meet one-on-one?"

Lutz looked between them. "Well, yes. It was necessary for

confession, obviously. But his reputation was untarnished. I hope you're not looking to place unfounded blame—"

"Nothing like that," Jonathan said. "We're just trying to figure out how he related to the members of the church. Maybe members who…wanted their relationship with the church kept secret?"

Lutz raised an eyebrow. "To keep one's relationship with God a secret is to live a lie."

"Which plenty of people do, every day," Ivy said, pulling out her phone. She showed Lutz the pictures of Pierson and Lefler. "Have you seen these two in the church before?"

He took the phone and studied the pictures. "Yes. They're regulars on Wednesday nights. I've spoken to them a few times, but I don't know their names."

"Every Wednesday night?" Jonathan asked.

"No, I'd say once a month or so."

"For how long?"

He handed the phone back to Ivy. "Maybe the last year or two," he replied.

"But never on Sundays," Jonathan said.

Lutz shook his head. "Nor for our Saturday evening services."

Ivy pulled up the picture of names from the ledger, handing it back to Lutz. "Do you recognize any of these names?"

He frowned. "This is Matthew's handwriting."

Ivy nodded. "We know."

He turned back to the list, looking at it carefully. "Yes, Karen Stokes. I've spoken with her a few times. Recently started coming to service."

"How long ago?" Ivy asked, taking the phone once again.

"Two months, I believe," he replied. "Also one of our Wednesday night family. The other names I don't recognize."

This was only becoming more confusing by the day. Maybe what everyone on the list had in common wasn't that they were secretly joining Catholicism, but instead that they were all Wednesday night visitors only. The question was, what happened on Wednesday nights that didn't happen on Saturdays or Sundays?

"Were you a part of Wednesday night services?" Ivy asked.

"Usually," he said. "Except in cases when I was out of town, like this past Wednesday."

Ivy glanced at Jonathan. They were running out of questions. Something was happening here, and it was becoming harder and harder to nail down. "I'm sorry, I'm not very familiar with Catholicism. Can you walk us through a typical Wednesday evening service?"

"Well, since our church is smaller than most, we elect to have evening Mass on Wednesdays instead of every day. That was a change made in the mid-nineties when attendance began dropping. It just didn't make sense to have an empty Mass daily. And people seemed to like the evening Mass. Everyone is welcomed in, then we have the Introductory Rites, before the Liturgy of the Word. Then we move on to the Liturgy of the Eucharist before the Concluding Rites. It's all very simple. I can provide you with a full schedule if you like."

"That would be very helpful," Ivy said. Lutz had just thrown a lot of words at her, half of which she didn't understand. She'd never participated in a Catholic Mass before and had no idea how it worked. Lutz stood and headed back into the kitchen before returning with a small pamphlet a moment later.

"This is a typical schedule for Mass," he said. "Sometimes there will be small changes, but they're superficial. We Catholics don't like to deviate much from the source material." He offered a warm smile.

Ivy flipped the paper back and forth. It seemed pretty

straightforward. "So your Wednesday Mass is pretty much the same as the Sunday Mass," she said.

"More or less," he replied. "There's a little more pomp and circumstance on Sundays, you understand. But they're practically identical."

She had to admit, she was deflated. She had been hoping there was something fundamentally different about the two that would support her theory of why some people only came on Wednesday nights. But she had to face the fact it was possible that it was nothing more than preferred schedule. Maybe some members couldn't come on Sundays, especially if they were hiding their beliefs from their families. But Wednesday nights were much less conspicuous.

"Deacon," Ivy said. "This might seem like an odd question, but was Father Rouge into anything… strange?"

The man frowned. "Strange how?"

"Anything that might be…looked down upon if the community found out."

"I would certainly hope not," he replied. "Not only would that be catastrophic for the church, but it would seriously undo the reputation he'd worked so hard to establish."

"Then you don't know anything about any drug activity in the church."

The man looked as if someone had splashed him with cold water. "Drugs? Of course not."

"I didn't think so." She glanced at Jonathan, hoping he had something else. But he seemed to be at as much of a loss as she was.

Jonathan turned to Lutz. "Thank you for your time, Deacon," he said. "We know these aren't the most pleasant of circumstances."

"It is no trouble at all," he said. "I'm sure your job necessitates unpleasant visits all the time. I only hope this one was more comforting than most."

Ivy had to hand it to him, the man did have a disarming

demeanor. And despite the alibi, she wasn't ready to dismiss him from the suspect pool just yet. Even though, if what he said was true, Father Rouge's death didn't seem to help him in any way.

Just as she was feeling like they'd run into yet another dead end, her phone buzzed with a text.

"Who's that?" Jonathan asked. "And why are you smiling?"

"Just got the word from Burns. They confirmed the substance in Father Rouge's desk was cocaine after all."

Chapter Twenty-One

Ivy took a bite of her burger without really tasting it. She was thinking about how Father Rouge could have been involved with illegal substances without anyone knowing. Even his right-hand man, Deacon Lutz, seemed to have no knowledge of what he'd had been hiding in his desk.

"The question is, do we believe Lutz?" Jonathan said. "Or is he in on it? He said himself he was there for every service."

"And as Deacon, he would have been the closest person to Father Rouge most of the time," Ivy added. "But he seemed pretty shocked when we brought up the drug angle. I'm not sure he knew about it."

"Then Rouge was playing a different kind of game," Jonathan said. "Maybe it was as Orellio suggested, maybe he kept it there for addicts who were trying to come down." Ivy shot him a look as she grabbed a couple fries. "I know. That's about as plausible as an elephant that can fly. And we already know Lutz's alibi is rock solid."

"I think we need to go back to Pierson," Ivy said. "We already know she lied to us. And out of the two names we've found on that list so far, she's the only one who hasn't invoked a lawyer. Not to mention, I think we can use her attraction to you."

"What?" Jonathan asked, looking up. His mouth was full of chicken sandwich.

"You didn't notice. But she was eyeing you," Ivy said. "I think between that and the fact that Lutz recognized her, we can pressure her to talk."

"It's worth another shot," Jonathan said after he swallowed his bite. "I just wish it wasn't such a long drive."

"I also want to start checking some of the other names," Ivy said. "He had to be getting his supply from somewhere. I'll talk to Conroy over in Vice."

"You know what the lieutenant is going to say," he replied. "We still don't have a killer. Or a motive."

"I don't give a shit what she thinks at the moment," Ivy spat. "We'll never figure out who killed him if we don't know what he was into. But I am sure that his death has something to do with that list. I don't know how, but they're connected."

"I don't disagree, but it could take us months to figure out what really happened that night. That's more time that a killer is loose in our community. A killer the police department can't catch. I don't think Armstrong would be above calling in the FBI, do you?"

"He'd never want the embarrassment," Ivy said. "And it's not like we're dragging our feet. But sometimes these things take time. We can only go as fast as we can go."

"Why don't we split the work?" he suggested. "I can drive back up to Portland and interview Pierson again, while you try to figure out where he was getting his supply."

As much as she hated to admit it, splitting the work would make it go faster. But Jonathan usually wasn't so preoccupied with speed. Was there some reason he didn't want her going back to interview Pierson again? Maybe she'd been too hasty in her assumption that he didn't know she was flirting with him.

Ivy shook her head. Where had *that* come from? And what did she care if Jonathan wanted to hook up with someone he knew in his youth? That wasn't her business. She had her own problems, this case top among them.

"Sounds like a plan," she said. "Can you drop me back off at the station?" She balled up what was left of her food and tossed it in the nearby receptacle.

"I guess I'm done," he said, gathering up his sandwich.

"You can eat on the road," she said. "Let's get a move on."

ONCE IVY WAS BACK AT THE STATION, SHE TRACKED DOWN Conroy and put a bug in his ear about the cocaine they'd found in Rouge's desk, or at least the residue. They hadn't found his "stash" but she was much more willing to believe Lana Orellio now. Maybe the whole murder had been nothing more than a cover for the perp to abscond with Rouge's drug stash. Ivy became more and more convinced that if they could track down the drugs, they would find their killer.

Unfortunately, Conroy hadn't heard any rumblings about a large amount of cocaine from the normal sources, but he promised her he'd let her know the minute that changed. With Jonathan out of town, Ivy suddenly found herself without any more leads to follow.

Sure, she could always look into the list again, but even she had to admit she kept getting distracted thinking about Oliver. Instead of heading back to her desk, she made her way over to Wilcox's station, though he wasn't around. But Perry, his new partner, informed her they hadn't gotten very far. It seemed not very many of Oliver's neighbors liked him, so they were having a hard time finding witnesses. That and the early hour was making the investigation more difficult.

They had managed to get some partial prints off the baseball bat, though. But so far there hadn't been any hits in the system.

She thanked him and headed back to her desk, fully intending to return to the case, only for Oliver's situation to keep popping up in her mind. She also couldn't rule out the similarities between her case and his. Two attacks, one fatal, one not. But both against a single, white male during the night. She needed to speak with Oliver to find out what he knew about the attack. She told herself that it was because it might help her in her own case, but the true reason was much more selfish.

She was worried about him, about what he was into. And she needed him to come clean with her. It was the only way she could help him.

Avoiding Nat's office, she headed back out to her car and rushed to the hospital.

She checked with the nurse at the front desk to make sure Oliver had been moved from the ICU first, and upon obtaining his room number, headed down to the elevators. She was just thankful they'd managed to wake him this morning without a problem. No doubt he was worried about Hero, and she told herself the reason she was doing this was just to make sure he was okay, allay any worries he might have and then she would get back to work.

Ivy stepped off the elevator at the fourth floor and headed down the corridor, passing a nurse helping a patient walk along the hallway. Neither looked up as Ivy passed. The rest of the floor was relatively quiet, and when Ivy reached the room, she noticed a small piece of paper had Oliver's name written on it beside the door.

The door itself was cracked and the room looked dark inside. She knocked a few times.

"Yeah?" his weak voice replied.

Ivy pushed open the door slowly, stepping inside. Oliver was on the bed in the darkened room, a blanket covering the bottom half of him. The blinds had been drawn and the television above the bed was on, though it was muted.

As soon as he saw her, he winced, his swollen face exaggerating his features. "Ivy," he said. "What are you doing here?"

"Glad to see you, too," she replied. She understood some people didn't want others to see them in a vulnerable state. She could understand it better than most. But she was also pissed at him. And if this was uncomfortable, that was too bad.

"I...didn't mean it like that," he said, turning back to look at her. "I just...how did you know I was here?"

"Who do you think found you?" she asked, coming into the room fully. A recliner chair sat on the other side of his bed but she elected to stand.

"I guess I should have figured," he replied. "They said the cops found me but they didn't specify...where's Hero? Is he okay?"

She nodded. "He's with Carol. She said she's happy to take care of him for as long as you need."

"Thank you," he said. "I was so afraid...I thought they might..."

"Oliver," Ivy said approaching the bed. "What happened? Who attacked you?"

"It doesn't matter," he replied. "I just need to heal and get back home."

"The hell it doesn't," she snapped. "You're going to press charges and we're going to bring whoever—"

"Ivy, stop," Oliver said. "These aren't the kind of people you charge with assault. If I do anything else...it will only make things worse."

"Then you knew who it was," she replied. "That explains the lack of forced entry."

He lifted one hand, but it didn't stay up for very long. "Yeah. Look, thank you for helping me. I didn't want you involved in this. Just…let me heal and then I can put all of this behind me."

"It's not that simple," Ivy said. "There's a formal investigation."

"What?" he asked.

"What choice did I have?" she refuted. "You were about to die right there in my arms. I had to call for backup. How was I supposed to know you just wanted me to sweep it all under the rug?"

"Wait," he said. "I was in your arms? Really?"

She sighed. "I'm not surprised you don't remember. You were barely conscious."

"You…actually touched me?"

"I was trying to save your life, you idiot," Ivy replied. Something in the atmosphere between them changed. She couldn't put her finger on it, but there was a definite shift. Ivy sighed, putting her hands on her hips. "What did the doctors say?"

"I've got another few days in here," he said. "By then most of the swelling should start to go down. Dr. Brachman thinks I can go home by the weekend. Then he said another four to six weeks of healing at home."

"I'd say that's a pretty good improvement, considering you were on your actual deathbed yesterday."

"I've always been a fast healer. You know that," he said. He was right; she'd forgotten. When he'd sliced his hand open on a kitchen knife back at Mrs. Baker's house, it had healed in only a few days. Compared with the two weeks it had taken for Ivy's arm to heal when she fell out of one of the trees in the backyard and torn it open on a nearby rock.

"If you won't tell me who attacked you, can you at least tell me why?" she finally asked. He looked away again. "They trashed your server room. It's a total loss in there."

He winced, but didn't respond. He hadn't known about that. No one had the opportunity to tell him until now.

"Were they looking for something? Or did they just beat the hell out of you for no reason?"

"Ivy…"

"You have to give me *something*," she said. "Because the less you say, the more suspicious it looks. And I'm not working the case. Wilcox is. If he finds something illegal in there, or figures out—"

"Okay, okay," he said, relenting. "I was supposed to be receiving a payment."

"At five-thirty in the morning?" Ivy asked.

"Yes. Don't ask why. That's why I thought they were there. Okay?"

"Why did they attack you?"

He let out a long breath, which seemed to pain him. "Because I threatened them."

"Oliver," she said. "What—"

"I know, I know," he said. "Not the smartest move. But you have to be firm with these people, Vee. Otherwise they don't respect you."

"Or they come and beat the shit out of you," she replied. "Why were you threatening them?"

"Because they hadn't paid," he said. "I always, *always* require payment upfront. But they'd come via a reputable source and had a good reputation so I thought…it was my own fault. I broke my rule…and this is what I get for it."

"You're telling me they came and beat you within inches of your life and destroyed your server room because *they* didn't pay for a job that you did?" she asked.

He sighed. "That's about the long and short of it."

She wasn't buying it. There was something else going on here, but she wasn't sure what. Oliver was protecting someone, whether that was himself or someone else she couldn't say. But he had put himself *and* Hero at risk. And that was inexcusable. "What kind of work did you do for them?"

He shook his head, even though she could see it pained

him to do it. "I don't want to get you involved. The less you know—"

"Cut the bullshit, Oliver," she replied. "You could have died."

"I know," he replied. "But I didn't. You were there."

"Only by chance," she said. "If I had been much later, I would have found a corpse. I deserve the truth."

He bit his lip. "I've told you the truth."

"You're a real piece of work, you know that?" Whatever he was protecting, he wasn't about to give it up. "Don't expect me to save you again."

"Ivy…"

But before another lie could slip through his lips, she turned and left the room, her anger from earlier having only multiplied. Why did everyone think it was okay to lie to her? First Nat, and now Oliver? Who was next, Aunt Carol? What was it about her that made everyone think they could just keep her in the dark and she'd sit around and take it?

Oliver could go fuck himself. If he wanted to play in quicksand, then she wouldn't be there when he got sucked down. At least Hero was safe. And the next time he asked her for a favor, she wouldn't even bother responding.

Chapter Twenty-Two

JONATHAN STEPPED out of the car, and looked up at the imposing house. He'd called ahead and scheduled an appointment with Whitney Pierson this time instead of just showing up. Fortunately, she had asked him to meet her at her home, which was situated northwest, on the far side of the mountain. Driving up the winding roads, he got a gorgeous view of the valley below. Normally he wasn't impressed by things like this, having grown up in it, but as he'd driven up to the house he couldn't help but appreciate the scenery. The house itself must have one hell of a view.

"Jonathan!" Whitney waved to him from one of the two large double doors.

"Good afternoon," he called back, recalling what Ivy had said about the woman flirting with him on their last encounter. He hadn't seen it, though that meant very little. He was often oblivious to things like that until they were right in his face. But now that he was looking for it, he could already see the smile on her face was a little over-enthusiastic. No one should be that happy about a cop showing up at their house.

"Come on in. It's freezing out here," she said. She was in a tawny sweater and white pants, looking every bit the heiress she was. The Pierson Empire had once been built on lumber, then logistics, and now they were partners in one of the largest shipping operations across the country. All of which had set her up for life long before she was born, giving the woman free reign over which direction she wanted her future to take. Before the other day, Jonathan hadn't seen her since grade school, since before she decided to go off to study in Europe for the remainder of her education.

That wasn't to say he hadn't been in a similar position. But he had known even then he wasn't going to follow the path that had been laid before him.

"Thanks," he said, coming into the large, white foyer. Her arm brushed his as he entered, and Jonathan didn't think that was an accident. But he didn't linger on it. Instead, he surveyed his surroundings. The house was reminiscent of Lefler's home, except was decorated much more tastefully, with warm colors and softer accents everywhere. A large rug that looked like it had been hand-stitched ran the length of the foyer.

"It's good to see you again. I'll admit, I wasn't expecting you to call back after the other day." She led them into the living area, which was off to the right of the foyer and was expansive, filled with multiple couches, a fireplace large enough to walk into, and a massive television mounted on the wall.

"I just had some follow ups from our conversation," Jonathan said, remembering he needed to play nice. He spotted the spyglass from the auction had already been placed inside a glass case that was on one of the built-in shelves. "I see it made it in one piece."

Whitney turned, glancing at the artifact. "Oh, yes, they just delivered it this morning. I thought it was a great piece. What better way to buy something than to do it knowing the money goes to charity?"

Jonathan took in the rest of the room. Unsurprisingly, it

had an even better view than the one he'd spotted coming up here. "You've done well for yourself."

"You mean my *family* has done well for themselves," she said, heading into the adjoining kitchen. "Something to drink? Sparkling water? Espresso?"

"Just tap water is fine, thanks," he replied, taking a seat on one of the couches.

"Here you go," she said, handing him a bottle of water. She took a seat beside him, just barely far enough away it wouldn't be considered inappropriate. Still, given how much seating was in the room, it was interesting. Ivy had been on to something.

Jonathan glanced over to the family portrait that hung on the wall. Whitney and her husband, along with three children, all probably under the age of six, dressed in beige and white. Behind them Cannon Beach stretched out on a sunny day. "Just you in the house today?"

"Most days," she replied. "Mark is in Vegas for a work conference, and the kids are with the nanny or in school. This place will be a madhouse in a few hours when they get home, though."

He looked around, not seeing any evidence the house *had* children. "You keep it clean."

"That's the housekeepers," she said. "But I'm more interested in what you're doing these days. Police detective. I still can't believe it."

"Didn't think I could do it?" he asked.

"Honestly, I'm surprised anyone could get out from under Constance's thumb. But I guess if someone had the guts it would have been you. You always had a strong character." She repositioned herself on the couch just infinitesimally closer to him. It was enough to confirm Ivy *had* been right after all.

"Thanks," he replied. "That means a lot."

"How's your sister?" Whitney asked, leaning forward just a little. Marie hadn't been diagnosed until about six years ago, so Whitney had no reason to know about her illness. And Jonathan saw no need to tell her.

"Just fine, thank you." She smiled warmly at him. Now was as good a time as any. "We've been doing some more digging into Father Rouge," Jonathan said. He noticed this time she didn't seem as on edge as she had before. She might be more prepared, which could make this harder.

"Did you find out what happened to him yet?" she asked. "I looked up the story after you left. It's terrible."

"We're still working on it." He cracked open his water and took a sip. "The thing is, we suspect he might have been part of a larger drug operation."

She did her best to look shocked, but he could tell part of it was a cover. Where she had been able to feign ignorance before, now she was deliberately putting on a show. And since that was the case, there was no reason to hold anything back. "And we know that you had direct contact with him."

At this her eyes went as wide as saucers. "What?"

"We have a witness who puts you in Oakhurst Catholic Church on Wednesday nights. Not every Wednesday, but at least once a month. For perhaps the past year."

She had gone completely still; her earlier warmness having completely evaporated. "Well, that's just not true."

"Trust me, the character of our witness is above reproach," Jonathan said. "The question is, why did you lie to us the other day? And why are you still lying now?"

Whitney stared at him a moment before biting her lip and pulling back into the couch, as far away from him as she could get. "You don't understand. How could you?"

"Try me," he said.

"Look at you. Police detective. Working murder cases. Going out and actually doing something with your life. While I'm stuck here, spending my parents' money on things that don't matter for charities I'll never see."

Jonathan set his water down and focused all his attention

on her. She clearly had something she needed to get out, and he wasn't going to stand in the way of it. "You're feeling purposeless."

"More than that, I feel *stuck*," she replied. "You got out. I never had that kind of courage. And now, everything is written for me. I love my kids, I really do. But being a mom and a wife to a husband who works all the time means this is my job. Alone. For the next twelve years plus. And by the time they're out of the house it'll be too late."

"Too late for what?"

"To make a difference," she replied. "So excuse me if I need something to take the edge off every now and again."

"What did you need to take the edge off?" he asked.

Her face turned even more serious. "Are you going to arrest me? Do I need to get my lawyer?"

Jonathan scooted a little closer to her on the couch. "Look, I'm not interested in arresting anyone except who killed Father Rouge. And I seriously doubt you were a part of that. But I do need to know what he was into, so I can at least follow a direction. Because all I have right now is a body, and a drawer full of residue."

Whitney sighed. "You promise you won't hang me up for this? These kids need a parent around, and God knows Mike is never here."

"I promise," Jonathan said. "You can trust me."

She stared at him a moment longer, apparently coming to a decision. "Fine. He was my dealer."

"Dealer for what?"

"Mostly coke. But it was never a lot. Just enough to get me through some of the tougher days. And sometimes when I'd have friends over. Mike doesn't know."

Jonathan pulled out his notepad. "How often would you buy?"

"Once a month," she admitted. "I'd drive down to Oakhurst. Attend services. Come back home."

"Why Oakhurst?" Jonathan asked. "There have to be a dozen better options in Portland alone."

"Why else? I didn't want the wrong people finding out. You know what kind of a gossip community exists for people like us. I figured if I went down there no one would get on my tail about it. Little did I know you were working in the same town." She opened her own water, taking a large swig. She almost seemed disgusted with herself.

"How did you meet Father Rouge?" he asked.

"A mutual friend. Someone who already knew what he could get." He arched an eyebrow at her. "Believe me, I thought it was crazy too. Getting drugs from a priest? But my friend swore by him, and he turned out to deliver."

"Who is this friend?" Jonathan asked.

She shook her head. "You get my statement, that's it. I'm not implicating anyone else."

"Do I know them?" he asked.

"Jonathan…"

"Okay," he said. "Let's go back to the meetups. Where did they happen?"

"During services," she said. "It's a Catholic thing. Everyone goes up to receive communion. He would pass the packet to me when giving me the bread."

"And no one else saw? The Deacon?"

She shook her head. "He was always facing the audience."

"Why didn't Father Rouge just meet with you in private?"

"I don't know," she admitted. "I was just told this was how it was done. My friend gave him my name, I assume he made sure I wasn't a cop or whatever, and then he started delivering on a regular basis. Anytime I would show up. I never even spoke to the man."

Jonathan thought back to what Deacon Lutz said about Rouge's desire to keep his behavior always looking above board. Maybe he didn't want to be seen going into private with an attractive young woman. Then again, maybe he just thought this way was safer. After all, who would believe a Priest was handing out cocaine during communion? It sounded ludicrous enough.

"And that was it?" Jonathan asked. "No other exchange of information?"

She shook her head.

He had to admit, it was pretty efficient. "Do you know how many other people were receiving?"

"No idea," she replied. "All I know is I couldn't show up on Saturdays or Sundays and expect the same thing. It was Wednesdays only."

That lined up with what they knew so far. Jonathan had good reason to believe that every person on the list was receiving their "communion" from Father Rouge on Wednesdays. He hadn't wanted to believe it was possible at first. "Any idea how long he'd been doing this?"

"Nope. But he seemed to be...what's the term? Old hat? If it bothered the man, he didn't show it. He never even made eye contact with me."

Jonathan flipped his notebook closed and replaced it in his pocket. "I don't guess you happen to have a sample of what you bought from him?" She glared at him like he was stupid. "Just thought I'd ask. Still, this has been very helpful." He stood.

The disappointment on her face was palpable. "I guess I shouldn't be surprised," she said.

"About what?"

"That you really did just come here to talk about the case. I thought maybe you felt the same spark I did the other day, that maybe..." She began to reach for him, but pulled herself back. "That was just me being dumb."

"I'm sorry if you thought this was something else," he said. "But my first duty is to my job."

"I know," she replied. "And I respect you for it. Plus, I saw the energy between you and your partner. That's not something I could compete with."

"I'm sorry?" he said again, this time genuinely confused. "Energy?"

"Yeah, you know. It's like electricity, when two people are attracted to each other but they're trying to do everything they can not to acknowledge it. It's like trying to keep two magnets apart. There are forces at work."

"You're saying me and Ivy—" Sure, they had a few moments of closeness, particularly that night at Carol's house, but he thought that had been nothing more than partners getting to know each other. Then again, if he was really honest with himself, he *had* felt something.

"Wow, for a detective you sure miss a lot," Whitney said, smiling.

Jonathan stood, holding up the notepad in an attempt to obscure his embarrassment. "Thank you for this. It was a big help."

"You're welcome. I hope you find the person you're looking for." She smiled as she stood. "Safe trip back and..." She inclined her head at the bottle on the table. "Don't forget your water."

Chapter Twenty-Three

Ivy was having a difficult time keeping her eyes open. After leaving the hospital she had come back to the station to try and make some progress on the case. Her best bet was to try and track down some of the other people on the list, but it was proving difficult. Some of them had moved away, others she couldn't find at all, and some even looked like they might be dead. She hoped Jonathan was having better luck than she was, because as far as she could see, this case was looking more and more like it might turn cold unless they found something major.

She was about to call it a night when her phone pinged with a text.

Plz don't delete this. Can we talk?

Ivy's eyes went wide as soon as she saw who the text was from. She grabbed her phone and texted back.

Depends. What do u want?

In person.

Ivy took a deep breath. Her heart had picked up its pace and any semblance of tiredness had disappeared like a thief in the night. There was only one reason she could think that Alice Blair would want to see her, and it had to do with the woman who sat in the office at the other end of their department.

When? Ivy asked.

The sooner the better.

If that wasn't ominous, Ivy didn't know what was.

IVY SAT IN THE NEARLY EMPTY CAFÉ, A CUP OF COFFEE COOLING between her hands. Alice had said to meet her at nine, and the clock on the wall showed ten past. The woman had been MIA ever since that night at the church and all of a sudden she shows up demanding a meeting? If Ivy hadn't already confronted Nat, she might not have agreed. After all, she was suspicious of Alice's motives.

But she had also been curious to meet with the woman ever since Jonathan had relayed her suspicions. Then again, all of this could be nothing but a fact-finding mission for Alice, who had been permanently barred from the station. Maybe she was just looking to get back at Nat and Armstrong. Either way, Ivy was going to get some answers.

If the woman would actually show up.

The café was almost completely empty, save for one patron at the far end of the bar on the other side and the waitress working the late shift. The sign on the front said they stayed open until eleven, but Ivy was pretty sure if she and the other patron weren't already here, they'd be closed by now.

Just as Ivy was about to leave a five for the waitress and call it a wash, a car pulled into the parking lot. Alice Blair stepped out and hurried around to the front of the building, letting herself in. She spotted Ivy and made her way over.

Her hair, which was normally pulled back into a perfect ponytail was flat and matted, and she wasn't wearing one of her normal "reporter" outfits. Instead she came to Ivy in a pair of dark jeans and a simple sweatshirt under a heavy jacket.

"Sorry for making you wait," she said, pulling off the jacket and tossing it into the booth before sitting down. "I got delayed."

"Big story?" Ivy asked.

"Family," she replied. "It's not important." She pushed a cluster of stray hairs out of her face as the waitress came over. "Just coffee," she said.

"Warm yours up?" the waitress asked Ivy.

"Sure," Ivy said.

The waitress grabbed a nearby pot and filled another cup, setting it in front of Alice before refilling what little Ivy had drunk from her own cup. "Ya'll want to order anything?"

"Nothing for me," Alice said.

"I'm good," Ivy replied, her complete attention on Alice.

"Just wave me down if you end up wantin' something," the waitress said and headed off for her other customer.

"Thanks for meeting with me," Alice said as soon as the woman was out of earshot. "I wasn't sure you'd agree to it. I assume Jonathan spoke with you?"

Ivy nodded. "He told me your theory."

"And?" Alice asked, leaning forward.

"The question that pops in my mind is, what axe do you have to grind with Nat?"

Alice sat back abruptly. "What?"

"Why else would you suspect her of a coverup? Why not anyone else in the office?"

Alice stared at Ivy a moment before leaning forward again. "Because she was…and still is the case officer. For *your* case. No one else could be responsible."

"So then you really believe it," Ivy said.

"Don't you? Otherwise, I don't know why would want to meet." Ivy took a deep breath and turned her attention to the window, the slats of light created by the shade falling on the table like prison bars.

"I know something is going on," Ivy finally said. "But I don't know that it's a coverup. And I need to know your stake in this. Because if you're just fishing for a story—"

"Look," Alice said. "I know there is something here. And I think I can prove it. Am I after a story? Absolutely. But that doesn't mean I don't think we can help each other. When I found out about your…situation, something just didn't seem right to me. How is it that a family just…disappears into the night? No evidence left behind? No trace of what happened? Tell me I'm not crazy. You've had the same thoughts, right?"

Of course she had. It was all Ivy thought about for the first few years after everything happened. But as time went on and as she tried to move on, Ivy thought about it less and less. And eventually it just became a part of her past, something she didn't question as much because to her, it didn't seem that strange anymore. She'd allowed herself to become used to the idea. And that had dulled her search for the truth. Maybe she'd become too complacent. "Ever since I was twelve, all I've wanted is to know what happened that night. But the file is—"

"—empty, I know," Alice said. "Another strange anomaly, don't you think? Shouldn't there have been something in there? Follow-ups with missing persons? Calls to other states and districts looking for them? A paper trail as to what happened to your family's finances?"

"Finances?" Ivy asked. "Everything was sold to help pay off the debts. There were no finances."

"Really?" Alice asked. "Because I can't find any record of it. I have the house sale, but no idea where those proceeds went."

"No, that can't be right," Ivy said. "I remember meeting with the realtor as a kid. And…"

"…and the then Detective Natasha Buckley, right?"

"…Yeah…" Ivy replied. "But that doesn't mean there was a coverup. Files get lost. I don't remember a lot from that period in my life."

"Now you're just making excuses," Alice said, taking a sip of coffee. "Look at the evidence. Even without bodies, there should be a lot more in that file."

Ivy winced when Alice said *bodies*. She wasn't stupid. To suspect that her family could still be alive after all this time was wishful thinking at best. But still, it hurt to acknowledge they were probably dead.

"Sorry," Alice said. "Sometimes I don't have the best tact. But tell me you see it, too. Whoever has control of that file must have done some major editing."

"That's a felony," Ivy said. If Nat were responsible, she was putting her career, and her freedom on the line. And for what?

"Here's what I know," Alice said. "Your parents and your brother disappeared August 23rd, 2007. You were found wandering the streets by Detective Natasha Buckley the following morning, August 24th, at 2:30am in some kind of trance. You were taken to the hospital, where you were in a coma for a solid week before coming around. You were then placed with the Baker family foster home until you were adopted eleven months later by Carol Chamberlain. The investigation into your family was national news for a few weeks, but with no leads, the police were eventually forced to move it to the cold cases, where it has remained ever since. Sound about right?"

"Yeah," Ivy said, staring at her mug. Of course, there was one detail that Alice didn't know. That apparently no one knew. Ivy had been found covered in blood. But not her own. At least, that's what that psychopath Kieran Woodward had said. And maybe she wouldn't have believed it if she hadn't had such vivid dreams about it.

"Did you ever investigate the file yourself?" she asked.

"There was nothing to investigate," Ivy said. "No witnesses. No one saw a thing. There was no evidence left behind at my house, nothing that could have been used, anyway. Somehow, I left my house in the middle of the night and ended up over six miles away. Like something just picked me up and deposited me in the middle of the street."

"Well, what if I told you that I have proof Detective Buckley intentionally omitted information from that file?" Alice said.

Ivy looked up. "What do you mean?"

"After I spoke with Jonathan, I knew there was no way you'd ever believe me unless I brought you proof. So that's what I've been working on the past four days, not that my mother will ever let me hear the end of it, but that's not important right now."

"Alice," Ivy said, pushing her mug to the side. "What did you find?"

"First I need your word you're going to keep me in the loop on this," she said. "I already tried going to your boss. She wasn't very receptive."

"Accusing someone of a coverup tends to have that effect."

Alice shrugged. "Can you blame me? I don't like to beat around the bush. My best stories have always come when I've confronted people directly."

"Nat's not like that," Ivy replied. "She's not someone you can bully into giving you information."

"So I found out. But I need your word, Bishop. I've done the legwork here. Don't cut me out when you find out what's going on."

Ivy didn't see she had much choice. If she wanted answers, she was going to have to make a deal with Alice, whether she liked it or not. "You have my word."

Alice grinned, pulling out an old newspaper. It was dated August 26th, 2007. She opened it to the second page, where there was an article stating: *Police continue to look into Disappearance of Missing Family*.

Ivy had seen the article before, but there wasn't any substance there. Just a standard report from the police that they still didn't have any leads. "I've seen this before."

Alice pointed to the byline. It had been written by Russ Shackleton. "Russ is my boss. He runs the newsroom. What I didn't realize is he was the reporter assigned to your case back in the day. Back before I moved to Oakhurst."

"Okay," Ivy said. "But the paper never reported anything substantive."

"Doesn't mean they didn't have something." She winked at Ivy. "It took a fair number of drinks and a night later than I'd be willing to admit, but I got him talking. It turns out he suspected that something wasn't right back then as well. Enough that he was tailing your boss."

"He *what?*"

"Well, first he hounded the crap out of her about the story. Every day, peppering her with questions, but she never had anything new for him." Ivy could relate. Reporters like Alice, and apparently Russ, could be relentless. "But he noticed she would take long absences from the station soon after the case. Enough that it was suspicious."

"What kind of absences?"

"The kind that make it look like you're not really working," Alice replied. "So he started tailing her. And believe it or not, she was going to the same place every time." She pulled out a smaller piece of paper with an address listed on it.

"What's this?"

"It's where Nat was spending so much time back in 2007," Alice said. "When she was supposed to be working on your case. It's out on the far east side of town, in the woods."

"What was she doing there?" Ivy asked.

"Russ told me he spotted her meeting up with a man a couple years older than her. He witnessed them meeting on more than one occasion and eventually concluded Nat was skipping work for a hookup."

"But Nat's—"

"—gay, I know. But *he* didn't know that back then. After that, he stopped investigating, because he just assumed she wasn't giving the case any attention. And he couldn't prove the affair, so he just let it go. But you and I know that isn't the case. So the question is, why was she meeting with this man so much the week after you were found?"

"Who is the man?" Ivy asked.

"No clue. Russ couldn't remember what he looked like. Just that he was a few years older than Nat. He found that odd enough to remember, for whatever reason."

Ivy had to admit, it seemed strange. But just because she was meeting with someone in a rural house doesn't mean it was connected to Ivy's case. It could have been part of another case she was working at the time. Or it might have been something personal after all, though Ivy couldn't fathom what that might be. Nat's father was dead, had been for decades. Could it have been another family member?

"That's not all," Alice said, tapping the piece of paper with the address on it. "This house? This house is less than one mile as the crow flies from where you were found."

Ivy's eyes went wide. "What?"

Alice nodded. "I thought that might get your attention."

Ivy pulled out her phone and immediately put the address into her maps. The location came up, showing a run-down old cabin of a house in the woods just like Alice said. But looking at it from a bird's eye view, Ivy could see it wasn't far from the industrial area where she'd been picked up. A short walk through the woods would put her right there.

Alice sat back, obviously satisfied with herself. "I wish I'd had this when I confronted her a few weeks ago. I'd like to see her wriggle her way out of that one."

Ivy continued to stare at the house, trying to remember it

in any way, but nothing was coming to her. She had no memory of that place. Maybe if she saw the inside. "What's there, at the house? Did you go inside?"

"That's as far as I've gotten," Alice said. "Kind of figured it wasn't my place. Plus, a police officer will have a much easier time obtaining access to a privately owned home that I will."

"You found the owner?"

"Still working on that. It's owned by an out-of-town corporation. But I'll be sure to let you know what I find out."

"Alice…" Ivy said, looking at everything the woman had dropped in her lap. "I don't know what to say, other than… why?"

Alice's face softened. "I know I come off as a bitch sometimes…well, most times. And I don't always make the right decision in the heat of the moment, but I'd like to think I'm a good person at heart. And what you went through…it didn't sit right with me when I found out. Not to mention you've been fighting this fight by yourself all this time. I thought maybe you could use an ally."

Ivy couldn't hold in her surprise. She hadn't expected Alice of all people to be the one to help her find out what happened to her family.

"And, you have to admit," Alice said, leaning forward conspiratorially again. "It'd be one hell of a story."

"Yeah," Ivy said, staring at the address. "It really would."

Chapter Twenty-Four

"THE QUESTION IS, do you think she could be right?" Aunt Carol asked, as she set a bowl of fresh food down in front of Hero. The small dog dug right in.

Ivy hadn't gotten much sleep. Her mind was too preoccupied with Alice's news. She'd decided to try and sleep on the information to see if anything looked different in the morning. But in the cold light of day, the facts had seemed just as clear as they had been last night. Nat knew something about Ivy's circumstances…something she hadn't told her over the course of fifteen years. It wasn't concrete, but it was too much to dismiss as coincidence.

"I think I do," Ivy said. "Assuming Russ Shackelton's memory wasn't faulty, he might have just blown this whole thing wide open."

"The question is, how do you prove it?" Carol asked. "If Nat isn't talking, then the only way to confirm what Alice told you was true is to find this mystery man."

Ivy nodded. "A man with no description, whom only Nat can identify. And if she's kept this from me for this long, I doubt she's going to just tell me who he is if I just come out and ask." This was the first real lead about her own case that she had ever encountered. The only problem was it was nearly impossible to go any further. Not without involving Nat. Still, she planned on looking into the house. Ivy wanted to get a look inside there, figure out how it connected back to her family's disappearance. What would a cabin in the middle of the woods have to do with anything?

"I just don't know," Carol said, taking a seat across from Ivy as Hero enjoyed his breakfast. "Nat has always been there to protect you. Why would she hide all of this?"

"You didn't see what she was like yesterday," Ivy said. "I might as well have come out and accused her in flashing neon letters and she didn't even flinch. I'm not surprised Alice wasn't able to get anything out of her. The woman can't be broken."

"But she has *always* been on your side," Carol said. "She could have cut off communication after she dropped you off with the Bakers, but she didn't. She could have declined your application to the police, but she supported it instead. She even put you on her own squad."

Ivy balled her hands into fists, staring through the table, a realization coming to her. "She wanted to keep me close. She wanted to keep an eye on me."

"Now you're just being paranoid," her aunt said.

"I don't think so," she said. "Otherwise, why doesn't she just tell me the truth?"

"Have you considered that maybe she *is* telling you the truth? That none of what this reporter saw fifteen years ago actually happened? You said yourself things between the two of you had really improved in the past few weeks. Are you really willing to give all that up on the word of someone you don't know?"

"If it gets me to the truth, absolutely."

Hero finished his meal, but continued licking the bowl, pushing it around the floor until Carol finally picked it up and deposited it in the sink. "I think you need to take some time to think about this."

"I *have* thought about it," Ivy insisted. "I've thought about it every day for the past fifteen years. What if I can find out what really happened to them? What if...what if I can find them?"

Carol let out a long breath, then took a seat back in front of Ivy. She reached out with both hands, before grimacing and pulling them back again. It killed Ivy to see Aunt Carol desperate to connect with her. She deserved a daughter she could comfort and support. Ivy had never been that daughter.

"I just don't want to see you let down again," she said. "You've been through so much. I was hoping you might be able to put all of this in the past. But if there is new evidence out there, you *have* to pursue it. You owe it to yourself."

"Thank you," Ivy said. She knew she didn't need Aunt Carol's permission to look into her own past, but somehow it just felt right. The woman had been for her in a time when she had needed stability. And Ivy had repaid her in some of the worst ways, by breaking her curfews, hanging out with the wrong crowds, or just generally being a horrible person. After she'd left that life behind and joined the force, it had given her a new perspective on her adoptive mother. One where she could finally see what Carol was trying to do for her all those years. Everything she sacrificed for Ivy, never asking anything in return.

It was a debt Ivy wasn't sure she could ever repay. But she would damn well try. And that started by keeping Carol in the loop about what was going on with her case.

"I know one thing is for sure. Nat would never have an affair," Ivy said, changing the subject. "She was too devoted to Samantha. Whatever Alice's boss saw, it wasn't that."

"Agreed," Carol said. "But why would she be meeting with this man so often around your case?"

"I don't know," Ivy said. "And I don't know how to find

him. Or if he's even still alive. And if he is, who's to say he isn't living in Mexico or Europe somewhere?" Ivy hit her fist on the table. How was she supposed to track down someone with no name or description? It could literally be any human male on the planet.

"You'll figure this out," Carol said, offering her a warm smile. "I know you will. You're too stubborn not to."

Ivy grinned despite herself. "Thanks." There was a way forward here, she just needed to find it.

But as she was thinking, her phone vibrated in her pocket. She pulled it out, seeing Jonathan's name on her screen. Shoot. She should have called him this morning already. She'd need to inform him about her discussion with Alice yesterday. He'd been right all along.

"Hey," she said, picking up. "I'm heading to the office in a few minutes. Need me to pick up anything?"

"Nope, but you're not coming to the office. Head to lockup instead."

"Don't tell me you have a suspect in custody." She'd been so worried about her own case she'd been neglecting the one she'd been assigned to. Could Jonathan have done that much legwork already?

"Not quite," he said. "But I think you'll be pleasantly surprised."

Chapter Twenty-Five

IVY STRODE down the hall of the Oak Creek Jail, having deposited her weapon and signing in with the sergeant at the front. Jonathan was at the other end of the hall and as soon as he saw her, headed in her direction. She wasn't sure what it was, but there was something different about him. Something...lighter. Like he'd just swallowed an endorphin pill.

"I'd hope you might have stopped for doughnuts," he said, a large smile on his face.

"If you wanted doughnuts, you should have asked for them," Ivy said. "Now what's going on?"

"Conroy called me first thing this morning. He informed me the sample we pulled from Father Rouge's desk matched a sample of cocaine they seized last week. Chemical composition was almost identical, close enough that it probably came from a sister batch."

"His supplier?" Ivy asked, her eyes going wide.

"I think so. And you'll never guess who it is." She could tell he was enjoying drawing this out. But she wasn't.

"Just spit it out already before I kick you in the shins for being so damn smug."

Jonathan had to work to hold in a laugh. "Your old

buddies, the Black Pistons. Apparently, Vice managed to infil-
trate and break up a drug deal on the outskirts of town. The
Pistons thought they were selling to Japanese nationals here
from Tokyo."

"You're kidding," Ivy said. She hadn't heard a word about
that. "When did that happen?"

"Six nights ago," Jonathan said. "They kept it completely
under wraps, though. Lieutenant Ayford was afraid if word
got out in the department it might leak somehow. Not even
Armstrong knew what was going on."

"Holy *shit*," Ivy said. "That was the same night Rouge was
killed. Has there been any other connection with our case?"

"Looking into that now," he said. "But your buddy Red is
in custody with his lawyer right now, working on a plea deal. I
thought you might want to be here to see this. Conroy is about
to go in there and see if he can't force a confession out of him
on Rouge."

As if on cue, Conroy came around the corner with a
paper cup half full of coffee. "Ah, Bishop," he said. "Glad you
could make it. You know this scumbag Blackwater?"

Ivy nodded. For a short time she'd associated with the
Black Pistons, back in her rebellious days. Never enough to
fully join the gang, but she'd been close. And she'd seen the
kind of harm they'd caused. Knowing that Marshall "Red"
Blackwater was in jail and probably would be for a long time
was nothing short of a relief. "Yeah, we've crossed paths. You
think he looks good for Rouge's murder?"

"I wanted to ask you that," Conroy replied. "He ever show
any inclination to disemboweling anyone?"

"No," Ivy said. "He's more of a hands-off kind of person,
or that's what I've heard. I've never actually witnessed him
killing anyone before. But there are stories."

"Oh yes, I've heard the stories," Conroy replied before
sipping his coffee then tossing into a nearby can. "The man
has made quite the reputation for himself over the years. But

we've got him and his cronies dead to rights on possession, trafficking and illegal distribution of a class C narcotic. His lawyer's trying to slick talk his charges down, but I'll be happy to take it to court if they want. I just wanted to check with you first, make sure you didn't have anything to add."

Ivy shook her head. She never would have put this on the Pistons; it wasn't their style. But she wasn't about to stop Conroy from going in there and trying to get something out of Red. If the substance was a match, maybe they really did have something to do with Rouge's death.

"Alright then," Conroy said. "Enjoy the show."

"C'mon," Jonathan said. "I can't wait to see this."

"Did you have any luck with Pierson yesterday?" Ivy asked as they walked. Conroy would probably be interviewing Red in one of the adjacent "conference" rooms. The feeds for those rooms were all at the front of the jail.

"I did, actually," he said. "She confirmed she'd been buying from Rouge. Which makes me think Lefler and all the rest were too."

"Damn," Ivy said. "Father Rouge was a bona fide drug dealer. Did she say why she came all the way down here to do it?"

"Anonymity. She didn't think anyone from Oakhurst would recognize her. She's pretty well-known in Portland. It makes sense."

"How did she ever find out about him?" Ivy asked as they passed back through security and gathered up their weapons from the lockup.

"A mutual friend, apparently. She wouldn't give me a name, but I'm betting it was someone else on that list. How did you get along yesterday? Make any progress on your end?"

She was about to tell him no, that as far as the case was concerned, she hadn't made much of a dent at all. But she didn't want to get into her discussion with Alice, not right now.

It was too much and they had other things to worry about. She'd tell him when they were in a less public place.

"Not much, unfortunately. I only managed to track down three more of the names. The others are going to be more difficult to find. The DMV records can only get you so far."

"Well, with any luck, we won't need them," Jonathan said, pushing through another door on the far side of the building. They entered into another secure area, though this one didn't have any prisoners. "Morning Derek," Jonathan said.

"Detectives," the officer replied as he buzzed them through. "Here for the show?"

"Gotta make sure Vice doesn't screw up our case," Jonathan replied. Ivy couldn't help but notice just how *happy* he seemed. This was far from a slam dunk. The odds that Red was involved with Rouge's death were about fifty-fifty in her opinion. So what was causing Jonathan to act this way?

Ivy followed Jonathan into the viewing room which had a monitor showing the feed from the other part of the jail. On the screen Red sat at a metal table beside his lawyer, towering over the man. Part of Red's reputation came from his imposing six-nine height, which was complemented by two hundred and eighty pounds of muscle. Conroy sat across from them, far enough that if Red tried reaching across he wouldn't be able to grab the man, despite his large wingspan.

"—a few more things we need to clear up before I talk to the D.A.," Conroy said. They were looking at the back of the Detective, which gave Ivy a perfect view of Red's face. The man's dark moustache and beard looked practically black on the image, though it was in reality a crimson color. Ivy was sure he dyed it, adding to his overall menacing appearance. Of all the Black Pistons, he was one of the most intimidating. At their last meeting, Ivy's sophomoric attempt to question them about the recent deaths at a nearby beach, Red had all but threatened to kill her. And it had been a threat Ivy had taken seriously, not that she liked backing down from a bully. But Red was Vice's problem. And they had delivered.

"Can we please move this along," Red's lawyer said. "My client has been more than cooperative."

"Your client has been belligerent and an asshole," Conroy said. "This takes as long as it takes."

That elicited a chuckle from the other officers watching in the room. Ivy couldn't help but think she should be the one in there, interrogating Red. But it wasn't her case, so she crossed her arms and watched, hoping for a miracle.

"Tell me what you know about the Catholic Church, Mr. Blackwater," Conroy said. Red narrowed his eyes while his lawyer looked like he might have swallowed something sour.

"What the hell is this?" the lawyer asked.

"Maybe I should be more specific," Conroy said. "Tell me about Father Matthew Rouge."

"Who is that?" the lawyer asked.

"Ask your client," Conroy replied. "Trace amounts of your client's property was found at the scene where the man was killed. I'd like to know how it got there."

"Wait a second," the lawyer said. "Is this about that priest who was killed last week?"

Conroy nodded. "Coincidentally, he was killed the same night as the raid which landed you here." He nodded to Red. "I'd like to know what you know about the man. We might need to add a murder charge to the list."

"This is ridiculous," the lawyer said. "My client has nothing to do with any murder. This is a possession charge, plain and simple."

In a second Conroy was on his feet, causing even Red to pull back at the speed and ferocity of his movement. "This is *not* a simple possession charge," Conroy growled. "Your client is facing multiple prison sentences for distribution of a schedule two narcotic, trafficking charges, conspiracy, money laundering, racketeering—do I need to go on? Now I'm happy to add murder here and call it a day. I doubt a judge *or* jury will feel much pity for someone in your position, Mr. Blackwater. That's *if* you even get to trial, which I doubt."

Red turned to his lawyer. "You said you would help me. This don't look like helping." The way in which he said it sent a shiver down Ivy's back. She remembered when he'd talk to other members of the Pistons like that. Odds were, the next day they'd show up with a broken arm, or missing a finger or two. Always blamed it on an accident, but Red wasn't the kind of man who allowed mistakes. Ivy couldn't even imagine what he'd be like in prison.

The lawyer looked between Red and Conroy and swallowed, hard. "I—if my client did happen to know anything about this *priest*, we expect some leniency."

"I'll speak to the D.A. about it," Conroy said. "But your client is in no position to deal here. If you stonewall us on this, things only get worse. If you cooperate, they stay the same. Understand?"

"That's a raw deal," Red said.

"It's what happens to criminals," Conroy replied, sitting back down. The room fell into a silent standoff. Finally, the lawyer leaned over and whispered into Red's ear. The man's face, which had already been sour to begin with, seemed to grow even darker. Ivy had to admit, Conroy was good at his job. He wasn't letting Red intimidate him.

"What do you want to know?" Red finally said.

"What was your association with Father Rouge?" Conroy asked.

"We sold to him," Red replied. "He wasn't a big client. But he was a regular."

"How much?" Conroy jotted something on the notepad in front of him.

"About a hundred grams a month."

Ivy couldn't help but be surprised. That wasn't an insignificant amount. And far more than Lana Orellio had discovered in his desk. Was he really distributing all of that to the public? If so, that was a Class B felony on its own.

"How long had you been selling to him?" Conroy asked, bringing her back to the present.

"About three years," Red replied.

"When was the last time you or any of your men saw Father Rouge?"

Red sighed. "During the monthly exchange. Couple weeks ago. I can't remember which day."

"And no one approached him since?"

"Never had any reason to," Red replied. "He always paid. Wasn't like he owed us anything."

Conroy and his people would have to scour through anything they seized from the Pistons' place of business, but Ivy already had a sinking feeling. Red wasn't the kind of person to go after someone for no reason. If Father Rouge was behind on his payments, or he was in debt to them in some other way, then maybe they would have given him a shakedown.

"Did any of your men have anything to do with Father Rouge's death?" Conroy asked.

"No," the man replied with a straight face. Obviously if the raid was happening at or near the same time, they wouldn't have had a chance. Not unless Conroy's people missed one of Red's men.

Ivy tapped the shoulder of the man running the feed, breathing through the shocking sensation. "Can he hear you?"

"Yeah, he's got an earpiece in," the officer said.

"Tell Detective Conroy to ask him if he's running anyone outside the gang. Anyone who might retaliate for them."

The officer relayed the question to Conroy who stopped, inclining his head back towards the camera for a second as he listened. He then turned back to Red. "Anyone still out there? Running things in your absence? Anyone who might want to get revenge out of spite?"

"No," Red said, staring Conroy down. Ivy wasn't sure she believed him or not. There could be someone who had an affiliation with the gang, even if they weren't a full-on member who might be looking to make a name for themselves now that Red and most of his cronies were in lockup. But why they would go after Father Rouge was still a mystery. There had to be half a dozen better options out there.

"I think that's enough, don't you, detective?" The lawyer said. "You've asked your questions and my client has been more than cooperative."

Conroy looked at his notepad, then nodded. "Yeah. We're done. I'll speak to the D.A." He stood and exited the room.

Jonathan turned to Ivy. "What do you think?"

"It's not looking very likely," she said. "Unless he's got someone out there trying to clean up all their clients. But unless I'm wrong, we haven't had any other major drug-related deaths in the past week. And even if he did, why not just shoot them or cut their throats? Why stage the organs?"

"Yeah," Jonathan said. "It was a long shot. But at least now we can confirm Rouge's activities. *And* we know who was supplying him."

"Better than nothing," Ivy agreed.

A few moments later Conroy came in, carrying the notepad. "Sorry I couldn't get more from him. We'll run his records though, see if we can't find Rouge's name in there anywhere."

"Thanks anyway," Ivy said. "You handled him well."

"These guys are all alike," Conroy replied. "I'm just glad we were able to finally nab him. Thanks for the assist, by the way."

"Assist?" Ivy asked.

"Didn't Lieutenant Buckley tell you? We used some of your intel from your experiences with them to set up the sting. It really came in handy."

Ivy gave the man a tight smile. "She must have forgotten to mention it."

"Well, regardless. It was a big help. Probably wouldn't have gone as smoothly without it."

Ivy and Jonathan mingled with the remaining officers for a few more minutes before departing. But Ivy wasn't really listening. Her mind was on other things. Nat had gone behind her back *again*. And she'd had enough.

"What are you thinking?" Jonathan asked as they headed back out to their cars.

"I need to make a stop," Ivy said.

Chapter Twenty-Six

Ivy STORMED into the office on a mission. She had been blind to what was really happening for too long. No, *willfully ignorant*. She had traded truth for comfort, hoping that a better relationship with Nat would somehow magically fix everything.

But it had only made things worse. It had made her a doormat, one that Nat felt like she could walk all over. And Ivy was done with all of it. She couldn't suffer living in the dark anymore and it was time to finally confront the woman.

She took the stairs two at a time, not seeing anything else in her mind's eye except Nat's office with its files all over the place and stale smell of coffee. The woman she had once called a friend, a *protector*, sitting there, stabbing her in the back this entire time. It was time to put an end to all of it.

When Ivy reached the landing and spotted Nat's office across the room, she made a beeline for it, ignoring everyone else in the unit. Nat's door was slightly open, but when Ivy reached it, she didn't even bother knocking. She pushed it aside, storming into the room. Her boss, who was on a phone call and typing on her laptop at the same time, looked up, surprise on her face. Ivy slammed the door hard enough that it should have shattered the glass emblazoned with her boss's name, but for some reason didn't.

"I'll call you back," Nat said and placed the receiver on the base.

"How dare you," Ivy said, practically shaking.

Nat closed her laptop, focusing all of her attention on Ivy. "What's going on?"

"I thought you were my friend," Ivy said. "I thought we had moved past all of this."

"I'm your *boss*," Nat said. "But I also like to think of us as friends. We've known each other a long time."

Ivy pushed the chair in the room out of the way. "You're right. Long enough that I should have known better than to trust you. Something about the past few weeks hasn't felt right. And it's because you've been lying to me the entire time."

Nat sat back in her chair, glaring at Ivy. She always fell back into her stoic "stone-faced" routine. But she wouldn't get away with it this time.

"Pretend you don't know what I'm talking about all you want. But you and I both know you haven't been telling me the truth from day one."

"Look, if this is about the Vice case I was going to let you know, but we were under strict—"

"*I'm not talking about the Vice case*," Ivy yelled. Her heart felt like it was on fire, her lungs like they couldn't get enough air, and yet wanted nothing more than to scream. Sweat had formed at her brow, but she did nothing to wipe it away. "I'm talking about what happened to me fifteen years ago. The night my family disappeared."

"Ivy," Nat said, remaining unperturbed. "How many times are we going to ride this merry-go-round? I have told you everything I know. There's no other way to say it."

"Then tell me about the man," Ivy said. "Tell me about the man you met at the cabin on Winding Way Road. Who was he? And why did you meet with him so much that week?"

Nat's eyes flashed. It had been the first response Ivy had elicited from the woman. And in that moment, Ivy knew she'd hit something. Alice's boss had been on to something real, he just hadn't known it at the time.

"Yeah, I know about him," she said. "And I know about the house. What I don't know is why you didn't tell me about it. How every time I asked you if there were any updates on my case you never mentioned it."

"Look, Ivy, you don't know what you're talking about," Nat said. "I don't know where you've been getting your information but—"

"Don't you dare lie to me again," Ivy snarled, and she thought she almost saw Nat flinch. Was that *fear*? Nat had never been afraid of anything. But there was something about this that scared her. If that was the case, added bonus.

"There never was a man," Nat said. "I don't know what you're talking about."

Ivy slammed her fist on Nat's desk, causing the files on it to shake, and a couple to slip off and hit the floor. "God *damn* you."

"Detective Bishop, this is not proper behavior for an officer of the law," Nat said, her voice changing its timbre ever so slightly. She'd shifted back into boss mode. "And this is not how you speak to a superior officer."

"Superior officer my ass," Ivy said. "You've been stabbing me in the back since day one."

"You're on suspension," Nat said almost too quickly. "Effective immediately."

"Yeah? That how you want to play it?" Ivy asked. "Why not go ahead and fire me? And explain it to Armstrong while you're at it."

"I'm sorry, but your erratic behavior gives me no choice," Nat said like she hadn't even heard Ivy. Though her voice almost shook as she said it. "Hand over your badge and your sidearm." There it was again. That undercurrent of *fear*. Was Nat really so scared of the truth?

Ivy pulled out her weapon and placed it on the desk, followed by her badge. "I can't believe you'd do this to me," she said. "After everything you put me through. You never cared about me. I just can't believe I was so blind to it until now."

"Ivy—that's not…" Where she seemed to soften for one brief second, it was gone almost immediately. "I'm sorry it's come to this. I'll be putting your behavior under review. Expect a call from Internal Affairs."

So that's how it was going to be. The second Ivy tried to get to the bottom of what was really going on, the hammer came down. *This* was why Nat had wanted her so close and on her team. So that if Ivy ever stepped out of line, she could wrangle her back in. "You might want to have them examine your behavior as well. Don't think I'm taking this lying down. Unless you're ready to arrest me, you can't stop me from looking into this. And you can bet I'm going to find out what happened in that cabin."

Nat's eyes flashed again and it took everything Ivy had not to smile. Nat talked a tough game, even played a hard hand, but deep down, she really was afraid. Now all Ivy needed to do was find out what was driving that fear. And it wasn't as if she was just pontificating here. She really and truly was going to look into the address Alice had given her. Especially now that she apparently had nothing else do to.

"Expect a call in the next few days," Nat said. "Until then, I'd make sure not to leave town."

"Trust me, everything I need is right here," Ivy said, not breaking eye contact with the woman.

"Dismissed," Nat finally said.

Ivy turned to leave, opening the door.

"And, Detective," Nat added, causing Ivy to turn back. "Don't believe everything you hear. That's what children do."

Ivy just narrowed her eyes at the woman before storming back out. She headed over to her desk and grabbed a few items, just in case she would never be able to step foot back into the department again. Everyone else in the squad watched as she gathered up her stuff in a small box and headed out. It didn't surprise her no one came up to ask what was going on or to console her. She was sure half of them had heard it through the thin door of Nat's office. And the other half frankly didn't care. Ivy hadn't been in the department long enough to make a lot of friends.

She headed back down the stairs and outside to her car where Jonathan was standing, his breath visible in the cool air.

"How'd it go?" he asked as he opened Ivy's door so she could put her box inside.

"About like I'd expected," Ivy said, her anger seeping away. "Though I didn't think she'd get IA involved."

Jonathan whistled. "You sure this is a smart idea?"

She turned to him. "Trust me, it's the only way."

"So, what now?" he asked.

"Now we sit back and wait," she replied. "Or I should say, *I* sit back. You have a case to work."

Chapter Twenty-Seven

As NAT SAT at her desk, she couldn't keep her hands from shaking. Had that really just happened? She could hear Ivy outside her office, gathering her things. It took everything Nat had to calm herself while she waited. Her heart was going a million miles per hour and her breathing was ragged. She knew this day coming was a possibility, but part of her had never expected it to actually happen.

Then again, things had been more volatile than normal lately, starting with that Kieran Woodward case. That had been the first crack of the shell. Then when Mrs. Baker and the kids went missing, it only compounded things. Nat had thought she'd gotten a handle on Ivy, that she'd managed to lull her into a false sense of security over the past few weeks. She'd realized, perhaps too late, that she'd distanced herself too far from Ivy. And that distance had only contributed to the problem. Maybe if she'd been closer with her over the past fifteen years, maybe if she'd built a stronger relationship with her, none of this would have happened.

She'd tried, but it had been too late. When they found Ivy's name carved into Mrs. Baker's body, Nat knew she had one of two choices. Either side with Ivy, or against her. And she chose the safer option at the time, despite not knowing the truth. It had been a hail mary that had, for the most part, worked.

Up until now.

And now, it could all fall apart. How much was Nat willing to sacrifice? This business had already cost her marriage. Was she willing to let it take her job too? But what was the alternative?

She stared at Ivy's badge and gun on her desk. Did Ivy own any other firearms? She couldn't be sure. But making sure she wasn't packing was the first order of business. Her threat about IA had been an empty one, and Ivy probably knew it. The fact was, Nat could only keep Ivy off-duty for maybe a week before it started to look suspicious. She couldn't actually *charge* her with anything, could she? And even if she could, it would probably only make the situation worse.

Nat was screwed. Royally screwed. Ivy knew about the house. And she knew about Mike. Somehow, she knew about Mike.

Opening the top drawer of her desk, Nat pulled out an old pack of cigarettes. It had been illegal to smoke in this building since sometime in the early two-thousands, but she didn't care. She propped open her window, lit a cigarette and sucked in a long breath.

As she exhaled, she immediately felt more relaxed. There was a way around this. There always had been. She just needed to find it. Because if Ivy learned the truth, it would destroy everything. Her, Nat, everything she'd built over the past fifteen years, all of it.

Nat took a few more drags on the cigarette before putting it out on the desk itself, leaving a small, black mark in the old wood. She couldn't just sit here and wait for Ivy to find the truth. She had to do something. And she couldn't do it alone.

Nat pulled out her phone and dialed a number she hadn't dialed in almost fifteen years.

~

Nat stared at the floor of the small bar. She'd taken a booth on the far side of the building where she could watch the door. A glass sat in front of her with a finger of bourbon warming within. She'd already had one to try and calm her nerves, but didn't want to get too sloshed before the meeting. Just as she was contemplating knocking it back and ordering a third, the door to the restaurant opened.

Nat spotted the man at the same time he saw her. He'd gained a little weight around the middle and now had *no* hair on his head instead of just a little, but otherwise he hadn't changed much. He still wore the signature scowl she'd become accustomed to and his eyes were sharp and clear.

She didn't bother signaling to him as he made his way over to her, taking a seat across from her in the booth.

"This wasn't the deal," he said in a gravelly voice.

"The deal has changed," Nat said.

"We had an arrangement. One where you never contacted me again."

Nat just stared at her drink. She had gone back on their agreement. It was supposed to be over. But Nat was the one who had to look at Ivy every day. The one who had to watch her and see the pain on her face as she struggled for just one ounce of truth.

"She knows."

The man across from her just stared back.

"Did you hear me?"

"I heard you," he said. "What does she know?"

"She knows about the cabin. And she knows about you."

This news didn't seem to particularly bother him. As far as Nat could tell, his posture hadn't changed. He didn't even seem surprised. "You don't seem to understand what I'm saying here, so let me spell it out. Ivy Bishop is on the cusp of discovering everything."

"Okay," he said in that maddeningly nonchalant tone of his. "What do you want to do about it?"

"I don't know," Nat admitted. "I thought you might have some ideas. Which is why I called you."

"Does she know about you yet?"

Nat let out a long breath and knocked back the bourbon. "I dunno. Maybe."

"Then I'd do yourself a favor, and get out of town," he said.

"I can't do that," Nat said. "I'm not going on the run for the rest of my life."

"Okay. Then you have to come clean with her."

Nat shook her head. "Not an option."

The man shifted forward slightly. "I warned you about this fifteen years ago. I told you it would come back to bite you in the ass. I did my part. Leave me out of it."

Nat ran her hands down her face. "There has to be another way."

"Sure there is." He stared at her.

It took half a second for Nat to realize what he meant. It was a possibility that had haunted Nat for fifteen years. Ever since that night she found Ivy, walking in the middle of the street. "No. She doesn't deserve that."

"Those are your options," the man said. "That's it. You tried to cover it up, but it's falling apart. And now, you've put yourself— and me— in the crosshairs."

"What would you do if you were me?" Nat asked.

"I told you. What I'm doing as soon as I leave here," he said. "I'm packing a bag and I'm leaving. Forever. Because if you're right, then I'm not going to be here when she learns the truth."

"You can't just *leave*," Nat said. "We have to fix this."

The man stood. "I did my part. Fifteen years ago. And now it's time for me to go. I suggest you do the same. Before it's too late."

Before Nat could argue, he headed back towards the door, passing the waiter who was on his way to bring over a menu. The entire conversation had taken less than three minutes.

"Would you like to hear about our specials?" the waiter asked, coming up to the table.

"No, just get me the check," Nat said.

Chapter Twenty-Eight

THROUGH THE BINOCULARS, Ivy watched as Nat sat in the restaurant, speaking with the mysterious man. He'd just come in and sat down, but from the way he was sitting, Ivy didn't think he would be staying for very long.

There had been no question in Ivy's mind that if she confronted Nat, the woman would never tell her the truth. That much was obvious. Which meant Ivy needed to force the situation in another direction.

After leaving the jail, she headed back over to the hospital to have a little *discussion* with Oliver. Despite his condition, she had been pretty sure he'd be able to help her out. After all, he owed her now. She'd not only saved his life, but she'd been complicit in covering up his less than legal activities. If anything, he owed her as many favors as she could ask for.

She'd gone straight over to the hospital from the jail and floated the idea of tracking Nat using her cell phone. At first, Oliver had balked at the idea. But it really hadn't even taken that much convincing for him to come around. The only problem was all of his equipment had been destroyed. At least, all of the equipment the attackers could find.

With special instructions, she'd headed back over to his

house to find he had a hidden safe that had been built into the floor below his office. Thankfully all it had required was a sixteen-digit code instead of a retinal scan or thumbprint. Inside was a laptop, along with a lot more cash than Ivy had expected, and a couple of things she hadn't recognized. When she returned to the hospital with the laptop, she hadn't mentioned the items, even though both of them now knew they were there.

For the moment, Ivy didn't care about Oliver's activities. She could deal with that later. All she wanted to do was make sure she could track Nat's movements. Her plan depended on it.

Phase two had been the "show" in the middle of the precinct. She'd pushed Nat harder and farther than she ever had before, in hopes of eliciting some kind of reaction from the woman. She had a fifteen-year shield to break and knew it wouldn't be easy. Ivy figured she'd leave that office with nothing less than a reprimand, though the suspension and threat from IA were surprises.

Finally, phase three was to wait. Ivy had seen that fear in Nat's eyes, but even she couldn't have predicted Nat would move as quickly as she had. It had barely been two hours since their confrontation, and here Nat was, meeting with someone Ivy had never seen before. Very possibly the person Alice's boss had seen all those years ago.

It had taken a lot of convincing, but after she'd told Jonathan what Alice had revealed, he finally relented. He hadn't been on board with the whole "throw your career away on a hunch" plan, but at least Ivy knew he wasn't going to rat her out. She also convinced him he needed to continue to work the case, and to keep up appearances. She didn't want Nat to figure out what she was really planning.

But as Ivy watched the two of them through the window of the restaurant, she wished Oliver could have found a way to activate Nat's microphone and not just ping her GPS signal.

He'd called Ivy from the hospital, letting her know Nat was on the move. Ivy had stayed a comfortable distance away, but no more than ten minutes away from the precinct. But this place was a good thirty minutes outside the city. Somewhere, much like Whitney Pierson had hoped, where no one would see or recognize Nat. Little did she know Ivy had eyes on her the entire time.

The man got back up from the booth and made his way outside, heading back for his car.

"Shit," Ivy said. She watched as Nat stayed in the booth. It looked like she would be there for a bit longer. Ivy pulled out her phone and texted Oliver.

I have a lead. Keep tracking her and let me know where she goes. I have to check something out.

K. Be careful, he replied.

Ivy put the binoculars away and started her engine, though she left her lights off for the moment. She was on an adjacent side street. But depending on which way the man pulled out of the parking lot, she might have to drive past the restaurant. And she didn't want Nat recognizing her car.

Fortunately, when the man pulled out in his nineties Crown Victoria, he turned right, headed in Ivy's direction. He passed where she was "parked" without a glance in her direction. She pulled out slowly like she was leaving a nearby business and flipped her lights on, following the Crown Vic.

She was too far away to get a good view of the license plate, but was pretty sure it started with an "E" followed by a "6". It didn't matter much, she would get a good look later, when she figured out where the guy lived. Then she could run a DMV check and a property search and find out just who this man was. Maybe she could even show his driver's license picture to Alice's boss, find out if he was the same man he'd seen all those years ago.

However, while Ivy was following him, she noticed he wasn't making any turns. Instead, he was just heading straight down the road, like he was leaving town. They were already pretty far outside of Oakhurst; how long was she committed to following this guy? What if he'd come in from somewhere else? Nat had met him within two hours of their discussion, so he couldn't be *that* far away.

It didn't matter. Ivy would follow the man as far as necessary to find the truth. She had a tank that was three-quarters full. That should be enough.

At least, she hoped it would be.

But the longer she followed the strange car the more uneasy she felt in the pit of her stomach. Ivy couldn't put her finger on it, but something about this felt wrong and she wasn't sure what it was. Even worse, she no longer had her sidearm, and thus had no way to defend herself if something *did* happen.

But before she could figure out how she wanted to proceed, the car ahead of her pulled off the main road into a gravel parking lot. Ivy only had a split second to decide, and even though it went against all her instincts as a cop, she pulled in behind the man, though she positioned the car where she was a good thirty feet from the other car, which was pointed towards the woods.

There was no question about it, she had tipped her hand, and the mysterious man knew someone was following him. But she couldn't let this opportunity pass her by. She might never get another shot at this guy for as long as she lived, and if she had just driven on by, there was a good chance she would have lost him forever.

The other car shut off its engine and lights, and the driver door opened to reveal the man. He got out, walking around the car to face Ivy's vehicle, standing right in the headlights. He probably wasn't much taller than Ivy, and had something of a stocky build. He wore a heavy jacket but even Ivy could tell there was a firearm tucked under there.

"Why don't you come on out, Ivy." His voice wasn't

threatening, nor was it angry. In some strange way it was almost comforting, like that of a grandfather.

Ivy opened her door, but stayed behind it, using it as a shield. "Who are you?" she asked.

"No one you need to worry about," he said. His tone was very nonchalant, almost bored, even.

"Then why were you meeting with Nat?"

He scoffed. "She wasn't kidding when she said you were determined."

"Look," Ivy said. "I just want answers. What happened to me fifteen years ago? What did Nat do?"

"I can't answer that," he said. "I only came in after. To help clean up."

"Clean up what?" Ivy asked.

"I think you know," the man replied. "And if you don't, you know who does."

A thousand possibilities ran through Ivy's head at once. "Do you know what happened to my family?" Ivy asked.

The man put his hands on his hips and stared at the ground for a minute. Then he took a few steps forward.

"Stop. That's far enough," Ivy said.

"Kid," the man replied. "I don't want you dead. If I did, we wouldn't be standing here having this conversation."

"Then why are we?" Ivy asked.

"I may not have all the answers you're looking for, but I think you're a good person. That's not an opinion everyone shares. If I were you, I'd watch my back very carefully."

"Why? What's going to happen?" Ivy asked.

"All I know is the closer you get to the truth, the more dangerous it gets. For you. Take care of yourself, kid. I hope you find what you're looking for." He turned to head back to his car.

"Wait," Ivy said, coming out from around the door. She knew it was stupid the second she did it, but the man didn't turn back. He just got back in his car. "Wait, *please*." She reached his side door and tugged on the handle, but it was locked.

From inside the car the man gave her a sad kind of smile, then backed up, and pulled out of the parking lot, headed back in the original direction he'd been going. Ivy took a second to memorize the plate, then hopped back into her car and peeled out after him.

But as soon as she got on the road, there were no taillights anywhere ahead of her. She scanned the roadside to see if he'd pulled off somewhere, but there was nothing but woods on either side of the road. Ivy floored it, thinking he'd just left her in the dust, but as the Datsun reached ninety, she was forced to back off or risk the tires coming off the road on a sharp curve.

The man was gone. She was alone out here.

Chapter Twenty-Nine

THE ENTIRE DRIVE back to town, Ivy was sick to her stomach. The man's words kept repeating in her head.

Watch your back.

I came in to clean up.

Ivy believed he *had* been the man Alice's boss had seen working with Nat. He'd been in that cabin fifteen years ago. And he'd been there because Nat had brought him in.

But for what? And was he speaking literally, or figuratively? She needed to get inside that cabin and figure out what happened in there. It was her only way forward. She had the license plate from the man's car, but she was pretty sure if she asked Jonathan to run it, it would come up with nothing. The man had easily figured out she was following him. And he'd disappeared just as easily. Ivy had a feeling if he didn't want to be found, he wouldn't be.

Her plan had worked, but it had only led to more questions than answers. And did he really mean what he said when he told her to watch her back? No matter how she sliced it, Ivy kept coming back to the same conclusion: He'd meant Nat was coming for her.

In her wildest dreams, Ivy wouldn't have suspected Nat of

trying to kill her. The woman had been like a big sister to her, a mentor and a friend. But other than the past few weeks, her behavior towards Ivy during her entire tenure in the VC had been ambivalent at best. Downright antagonistic at worst. That was fine. People grew apart, stopped getting along. But would Nat actually *harm* Ivy? She must be missing something. He'd meant something else. Nat was a police officer. She wouldn't kill someone in cold blood. Right?

Then again, Ivy still had no answers to what really happened to her all those years ago. For all she knew, Nat had a hand in what happened to her family. And if that was the case, she had everything to lose by Ivy finding out the truth.

She didn't want to get ahead of herself. Nat being behind her parents and brother disappearing was almost too much to believe. Still, the entire drive, she kept checking her rear-view mirror, worried that she'd see Nat's car appear and attempt to run her off the road. Her mind was spinning out of control and she was growing more paranoid by the second.

Finally, she called Oliver.

"Hey," he said, his voice still weak. "Did you find what you're looking for?"

"No," she said. "Where is she right now?"

"Headed back to her house, it looks like," he said. Ivy took a breath, realizing just how anxious she'd been. "Listen, I don't know how much longer I can watch her. The nurse has already come in here and tried to take my laptop three times."

"Make sure she gets back to her house and then call it a night," Ivy said. "We'll pick it back up tomorrow."

"What are you going to do?" he asked.

"Don't worry about me," she replied. "And don't think I've forgotten about that little hidey-hole of yours. We need to have a discussion after all this is over." *If it's ever over.*

"Can't wait," Oliver replied.

She wanted to jump on him for being a smartass, but right now Oliver's business activities were the least of her worries.

First things were first. She needed a way to defend herself. Ivy hung up with Oliver and made a sharp right turn onto the nearest side street, pointed in the direction of Aunt Carol's house. She was being erratic and she knew it, but how was she supposed to feel? She'd just learned the person she had once trusted most in the world may be coming to stab her in the back... literally.

Everyone always lets you down in the end.

It was something she'd learned early on, though she hadn't actually put words to it until much later. There was only one person she could count on to get her out of this: herself.

Twenty minutes later she pulled up to Aunt Carol's house. All of the lights were off except for the porch light and one light on in the living room, which Ivy knew she kept on all night so the house wasn't so dark. But Ivy couldn't wait until morning. Time was of the essence. There was no guarantee Nat would stay at home once she got there. Maybe after this she needed to swing by the hospital to grab Oliver's computer. That way she could track the woman herself.

Ivy hopped out of the car and ran up to the door, fumbling with the keys. It took her a second to unlock the door, but as soon as she did, she heard barks coming from down the hallway. She flipped on the light just as Hero came around the corner, barking his little head off. As soon as he saw her, his eyes lit up and the barks changed from threatening to excited. Ivy leaned down to pet him on the head quickly before opening Aunt Carol's hall closet. Inside was the shotgun, still covered by the blanket. Ivy grabbed it.

"Ivy?" Aunt Carol called from the hallway.

"Yeah, it's me," Ivy called back, cracking open the shotgun to make sure both barrels were loaded. Two sat in the chamber. She looked around the closet for addition ammunition, but couldn't find any.

"What are you doing?" Carol said, coming around the corner. "You scared me half to death."

Where was the damn ammunition? There was nothing in here but unused pillows and old coats. "Where do you keep the extra shells?"

"Ivy Katherine Bishop," Aunt Carol said, causing Ivy to stop in her tracks. The woman rarely raised her voice and it was in that voice that Ivy heard not just anger…but pain.

Ivy turned to look at the woman who had taken her in as a teen. Who had nurtured her, who'd done her best to raise her. And who had received little in return. Ivy had resolved to do better for Aunt Carol, to at least try to give her a piece of what she deserved: love from a daughter. And now, she'd effectively broken into her house in the middle of the night, probably scaring the poor woman half to death.

As Ivy looked at Aunt Carol, realizing what she'd just done, she couldn't help but well up with tears. She set the weapon down against the wall. "I'm so sorry," she whispered before holding up her hands. Tears broke the surface and streamed down her cheeks. "I…I didn't…I'll just…" She turned back towards the door.

"Stop," Carol replied. Ivy complied. "Turn around." Again, she did as she was told. "Tell me what is going on. You wouldn't be here in such a state if something hadn't happened."

Ivy shook her head. She couldn't tell Aunt Carol. She wouldn't believe it. No one would. Plus, this was *her* problem. She had to figure out a way to solve it. She put her hand back on the door handle.

"Come in right now or I'm calling Jonathan."

Ivy looked up, wiping her eyes. Aunt Carol's face was completely serious. "Don't think I won't do it." Her cell phone was in her hand, probably ready to call 911 if Ivy hadn't answered her.

Finally, Ivy relented. It was as if exhaustion had just taken over her body and she could barely stand up. She headed into the kitchen, led by Hero.

"Sit," Carol said as she went over to the sink and filled a kettle with water. She put it on the stove to warm.

"You know they have machines that can do that without needing to use a stove," Ivy finally said.

"Doesn't mean it works any better," Carol said. "I prefer my tea the old-fashioned way. And I think you do too."

Ivy wiped her eyes again, but couldn't help but smile. Hero laid down at her feet in a ball. Carol nodded at him. "He's been so protective since he's been here. Oliver picked himself a good dog. Even if he's a little on the small side."

Ivy looked down at the animal. "I'm just glad he wasn't hurt when Oliver's house was...raided."

Ivy could practically feel Carol's eyes on her. But the woman wasn't saying anything. Ivy expected her to pepper her with questions: why was she here at this time of night, what did she want with the shotgun, etc. But there were no questions. No judgement.

Finally, the tea kettle began to whistle and Carol pulled it off the stove, pouring the water into two mugs. She dipped a chamomile tea in each and handed one to Ivy. The warm mug felt good in her hands. Hero sniffed the air at the floral smell, only to lay his head back down.

Carol took a seat across from Ivy at the table...their normal places. She sipped on her tea carefully, relishing the taste. Ivy did the same, finding the sensation was more comforting than anything.

Finally, she couldn't stand it any longer. It all poured out of her like a waterfall. Everything that had happened since the jail...her plan to expose Nat, the mysterious man and his warnings, and everything she'd found at Oliver's. Not to mention the fact a killer was still on the loose and Jonathan was probably overworked trying to track him down by himself.

The entire time Carol sat and listened, never interrupting, only taking a sip of tea occasionally. When Ivy was finally done, Carol set the mug to the side. She regarded Ivy with soft, kind eyes. "I see now why you needed the shotgun."

Ivy couldn't hold her surprise in. "You believe me?"

"Of course I believe you," Carol said. "Why wouldn't I?"

"Because it's Nat," Ivy said. "It's...*I* barely believe me. I feel like I'm going crazy."

"Darling," Carol said. "You have had to deal with so much. Adding all of this on top of your plate is more than most people could handle. You're fighting a war on three different fronts. No wonder you feel backed into a corner."

"It's not just that," Ivy said. "But what if this man is right? What if Nat has been involved with everything from the beginning? That means she lied to me for fifteen years."

"Lied to *us*," Carol said. "You're not the only one in this situation. If that's true and Nat really is behind this in some way, then I don't blame you for wanting to protect yourself."

"What do you think I should do?" Ivy asked. "I mean, what if she's coming for me?"

"First you need to inform Jonathan," Carol said. "He'll help you."

Ivy shook her head. "I can't. He's working the case...I can't ask him to risk his career too. I'm already on suspension. If he gets involved...it won't go well for him."

"Let him make that determination," Carol said. "But you can't go up against Nat alone."

"The problem is I don't have any proof," Ivy replied. "Nothing but the vague word of a mystery man who I doubt I'll be able to track down, and a fifteen-year-old recollection of something that may or may not have happened. I already tried confronting her. All that did was give her a heads-up."

"But it also confirmed your suspicions," Carol replied.

Ivy couldn't help but be a little surprised at her reaction. "You're not taking this like I thought you would. You've always defended Nat, even as recently as yesterday. You said she had always been on my side."

"That was before you managed to force her hand," Carol said. "Innocent people don't go to clandestine meetings outside of town. I had *hoped* Nat had another explanation for all of this. But given what you've found so far...I don't see how that's possible."

"Me either," Ivy said. "And it isn't like I haven't given her a chance to come clean. She just doubled down."

"Then you don't have a choice," Carol said. "You're going to have to use everything at your disposal to expose her. You need to find the proof."

Ivy nodded. "I would have taken pictures of her and the man in the restaurant if I'd been close enough. But all I had was my cell phone and with it being dark out, the picture was too grainy to tell what was going on. Maybe what I need is a professional."

"A private investigator?" Carol asked.

Ivy nodded. "I'd get Oliver to do it, but with his injuries I don't want him out following anyone. But that doesn't mean we can't use what he's already developed."

"That sounds like a start," Carol said.

Ivy let out a breath. "I just hope I can find something incriminating before she decides to make her move. The man wasn't exactly precise about when she may make her move." Ivy shot a glance back towards the hallway where the shotgun sat.

"I think you should stay here tonight," Carol said. "Maybe for the next few nights. Just to be safe."

"That's not being safe," Ivy argued. "That's putting you and Hero at risk. If she's willing to come after me, I'm not sure she'd be too concerned about collateral damage."

"Again," Carol said. "That's my risk to take. Not yours."

"I can't—"

"Stop," Carol said. "I won't hear any more of it. You'll sleep here tonight. Hero will be able to warn us if anyone tries to get in. He was awake before you even got to the front door."

Ivy wanted to argue that she hadn't been trying to be quiet and that Nat was a trained officer. If she wanted to approach a house without anyone knowing about it, she'd be able to. But odds were, she would take a few days to at least prepare. If she really was coming after Ivy, she'd need to make it look ironclad. It couldn't just look like a robbery gone bad. Nat was a detail-oriented person. She'd make sure all the angles were covered, that no one could poke holes in her story.

At the very least, that gave Ivy some breathing room.

"Okay," she finally said. "You win."

"Great," Carol replied. "I'll get your room ready."

Chapter Thirty

IVY DIDN'T SLEEP MUCH. And when she *had* managed to sleep, she kept seeing Nat in her dreams. But she was always in the shadows, never quite there fully, like she was lurking in Ivy's subconscious, just waiting for the right moment to strike.

Waking early, Ivy set herself up in Carol's living room, keeping a watch outside the window for any strange cars that might pass the house. But she didn't see anyone other than Carol's neighbors, people heading to work, out taking their dogs out for a morning walk. People who weren't possibly being hunted down by someone they trusted.

Around seven, she started getting texts from Jonathan asking if she'd made it back ok last night. Carol was rummaging around in the kitchen, feeding Hero and making breakfast as Ivy contemplated her words from the night before. Telling Jonathan the truth meant pulling him into something she couldn't take back. But hadn't he already gotten himself involved, when he told her about Alice's theories? Carol was right, he'd done it to help Ivy. Because he cared for her. Maybe what Ivy had felt the other night in this very house hadn't been in her imagination after all. Though, if that was the case, she wasn't going to use

Jonathan's feelings against him to pressure him into helping her further.

It was better to leave him out of this.

She texted him back that she was fine, that nothing of note had happened last night and she was still waiting for Nat to make a move.

"Hungry?" Carol said, startling Ivy who shoved her phone back in her pocket. "I made waffles."

"Yum," Ivy said, though she didn't have an appetite. She needed to get back over to the hospital and speak with Oliver again. He knew plenty of people in town who could do the job she needed done. It would just be a matter of arranging the funds. But Ivy could take care of that later.

She ate quickly, though she ended up leaving a lot on the plate.

"What do you plan on doing?" Carol asked.

"Talk to Oliver," Ivy said. "He'll know someone who can help. And figure out a way I can keep an eye on her at all times. That way I'll know when she's coming."

Carol nodded. "Just be careful. I don't like the idea of you out there without a way to defend yourself."

Ivy realized her earlier plan wouldn't work. "I think you should keep the gun," she said. "In case someone comes here looking for me. Your safety is more important."

Carol shot her a knowing look. She got up and opened the cabinet above the refrigerator, pulling out a .357 Magnum in a holster. She handed it to Ivy.

"*Aunt Carol*," Ivy said. "How many guns do you have in this house?"

"A few," she replied. "Never can be too careful. Now you take that in case you need it."

Ivy looked at the weapon. It was a monster. But it could stop just about anything out there. "Thank you."

"I still don't like having them," Carol said. "But sometimes we have to do what's necessary."

Ivy nodded. She took the weapon and strapped the holster to her belt. "I need to go. The sooner we get started…"

"I understand," Carol replied.

Ivy finished a few more bites of waffle, petted Hero again and headed out to her car. She couldn't help but check her surroundings, just in case someone happened to be out there waiting for her, but there was no one. Still, she felt slightly better with the weapon attached to her hip.

As she was on the way to the hospital, her phone buzzed in her pocket. She pulled it out to see it was Jonathan.

"Good morning," he said, answering. "I wanted to update you on the case."

"You don't have to do that," Ivy said. "I'm on suspension. I'm not supposed to have anything to do with any active cases."

"Be that as it may," Jonathan replied. "You're still my partner which means you still get updates." Ivy smiled, shaking her head. He was *still* in a really good mood. She was glad she hadn't ruined it with her news from last night. "I managed to track down a few more people on Rouge's list. We now have three full confessions of people that bought drugs from him."

"Great," she said. "How does that get you any closer to finding out who killed him?"

"Well, we already know it probably wasn't his distributor. I double checked with Vice. They managed to confirm all members of the Black Pistons are accounted for during the timeframe when he was murdered. Not only that, their associates were so focused on making sure the deal with the 'Japanese' went well, they didn't have time to go out and clandestinely murder someone. So it's unlikely the Pistons have anyone out there doing any kind of cleanup. Their other customers, for instance, haven't been attacked and it's already been a week."

"Are you thinking maybe it was someone on the list?" Ivy asked.

"It's my leading theory. Someone was upset with him for some reason. That's either going to be a competitor or a customer. And since I doubt anyone was interested in moving in on the 'Catholic Parishioner' cash cow, my guess is it had to be a customer."

"So all you have to do is find an alibi for everyone on the list," she said. "Easy."

"Unfortunately not," Jonathan said. "I still can't track down three of them. Though I've already eliminated Lefler and Pierson. Both were in Portland that night, which has been verified by security cameras and multiple individuals."

"Damn, White. You're pretty efficient when you want to be," Ivy said as she pulled up to the hospital. "I don't guess Nat assigned anyone else to the case?"

"No, she's been out of the office since yesterday. No one has seen her since. But I heard from multiple people about the blowup. Everyone is talking about it."

Good, Ivy thought. At least that gave her a little breathing room. It would look very suspicious if Ivy turned up dead after she'd just had a knock-down, drag-out fight with her boss. Nat would want things to calm down before making her move. Though it didn't make her feel very good that she'd been MIA since yesterday.

"Let me know if you hear from her," Ivy said. "But don't tell her I asked."

"Don't worry," Jonathan said. "Just keep your eye out. She'll make her move soon. Then hopefully you'll have everything you need."

It struck her as odd that while Jonathan's advice was sound, he was referring to something completely different. "Thanks," Ivy said, feeling bad she wasn't telling him the truth. If Jonathan knew what that man last night had

234 • ALEX SIGMORE

suggested, Ivy had no doubt he wouldn't let her out of his sight. "Let me know if there's anything else I can do."

"Actually," he said. "Maybe you can get Oliver to track down some of these names on the list. They're not matching any records in any system. I just need to find out where they're located so I can speak with them."

Ivy couldn't help but feel a smug sense of satisfaction. "Detective White," she teased. "Are you asking me to use unofficial and possibly illegal means to track down information for a case?" Even over the phone his energy was infectious.

"Not at all," he teased back. "Just if you happen to trip over some information…send it my way, would you?"

Ivy laughed, which was something she couldn't have even conceived of an hour ago. Somehow Jonathan always put her in a good mood. "You got it."

After she got off the phone she checked her surroundings again, her mood darkening once again. There didn't seem to be anyone out of the ordinary out there, but she couldn't be absolutely sure. Still, she stepped out of the car and headed into the hospital, taking the elevator to the fourth floor.

Oliver's door was cracked again, but this time the lights in the room were on. She knocked lightly and pushed the door open to reveal him sitting on the bed, the laptop already in his lap. His face already looked better than it had yesterday. The swelling had started to subside, though it was still discolored.

"Morning," she said, coming into the room.

"Yep," he replied. "Got some good news for you."

"Oh?"

"She's headed out of town," he replied.

Ivy screwed up her features, coming around the bed to look at his laptop. He had a map program open and on it, pinging every thirty seconds, was a little green dot that was moving farther and farther away from Oakhurst, headed south along I-5. "When did she leave?"

"Sometime in the night," he said. "I checked it first thing this morning and she was already almost in California."

Ivy took the first real breath of relief she'd breathed since last night. It looked like Nat had decided to skip town rather than face Ivy. Suddenly she felt silly for thinking the woman could ever come after her. Nat wouldn't be that brash. Whatever was going on, she must have realized she couldn't face it, so she'd decided to skip town instead. "And you're sure it's her? She didn't just toss her phone on a flatbed or something?"

Oliver turned to look at her. "You're starting to sound like me. And I don't know if that's a good thing. But to answer your question, yes, it's her. I caught her image on two different traffic cameras." He pulled up the images, which had been time-stamped. And there, in the driver's seat of her car, was Nat.

"Do you think she suspects you're tracking her?" Ivy asked.

"I don't see how she could," he replied. "I've been tracking you too and you haven't noticed, have you?"

"What?" Ivy said, taking a step back. "You're tracking me?"

"I thought it was the safe thing to do," he said, defending himself. "I figured if I knew where you and she both were, I'd know if you ever got close to each other and I could warn you."

Ivy screwed up her face. "I guess that makes sense. You should have told me."

"Jeez," he replied. "You're acting like I'm not on your side here."

"Sorry," she said. "It's just been…it's been a stressful twelve hours."

Oliver pushed the laptop to the side. "What did your partner say about all of this?"

Ivy moved away from the bed and took a seat in the one

chair in the room. "I haven't told him. I don't want him risking his career for me."

"Smart," Oliver said. "Better to play your cards close. That's how I always operate."

She glared at him. "Yeah. Until you almost get killed and then no one can come help you because they don't know you're in trouble."

"I think that's a unique case, don't you?"

"I wouldn't know," she replied. "I don't know what you're into. *Is* there anyone else who might come after you?"

"Probably not," he admitted. "At least, I don't think so."

Ivy leveled her gaze with his. "Oliver. We need to talk about what happened."

"I know," he said, hanging his head. "But see? It's just like you and your partner. I don't want to tell you things because I don't want to put you in a tight spot. Your job…well, it doesn't allow for a lot of leeway in these…matters."

"Uh-huh," Ivy said. "How convenient."

"It's actually not," he replied. "It'd be a lot more convenient if I *could* tell you."

"Yeah, well, I'd like—" Her phone buzzed in her pocket. Ivy pulled it out to find the list of names had come through from Jonathan. They were the three remaining names from the ledger. She sighed. "You know you're going to owe me forever."

"I know," Oliver said.

"Good. Then you can start with this." She showed him the list of names. "I need you to find these three people. They're the last names on a list from the case I'm working. A list I was bringing to you the other day when I found you nearly dying on your own floor."

"I thought you were suspended," Oliver said.

"I *am*." Ivy glared at him. "But it doesn't mean I still can't help out."

Oliver pulled his laptop back over and started typing. "So you're still working the case?"

"Not officially. And after you get me the info on these people, I plan on heading over to that cabin to see what I can find." Now that Nat was out of the picture, this was her chance to finally get in there and get a look at the place. See if maybe it jogged any memories. She didn't really expect to find anything after fifteen years, but there was always a remote possibility.

"Just make sure you don't go alone," Oliver said. "As soon as they clear me I'll—"

"—keep your ass in bed for four to six weeks like your doctor ordered," Ivy replied.

He grimaced. "I want my dog back."

"You'll have to talk to Carol about that," Ivy said. "He's pretty comfortable over there. Plus your house is a mess right now. If anything, you're going to need *my* help to clean it up. Which will give us plenty of time to talk about your recent activities."

Oliver just glared at her. Ivy knew she had him in a corner with nowhere to go. She couldn't describe how much lighter she felt now that Nat was out of the picture. She wouldn't have to keep looking over her shoulder all the time. She could go home and sleep in her own bed. And she didn't have to worry about Nat going after Carol or anyone else she cared about. Was it possible the woman was out of her life forever? What if she never came back? Ivy thought that might actually be the best result. It might mean she'd have to look harder to find out what happened to her family, but Ivy was okay with that.

"Okay," Oliver said. "Julia Dufrense, Duncan McNeill and Pepper Lauren." His face formed a frown. "Hmm. Nothing is coming up."

"Yeah, I know," Ivy said. "You have to dig deeper than just the DMV records."

"Just thought I'd check," Oliver said, holding up his hands. "What are the odds they're pseudonyms?"

"High," Ivy said. "They were buying drugs from a priest."

Oliver continued typing. "Ok, McNeill...that looks like it was actually a man named Paul Forester. He's been in prison for the past year, arrested on possession last year."

"Huh," Ivy said. "He didn't give up his source. Interesting." But that removed him from the suspect list. If he didn't give up Rouge when he went to prison, why would he have the man killed? She texted the information to Jonathan so he could double-check anyway.

"These two women, though," Oliver said. "I'm having a hard time tracking them down. McNeill was relatively easy because he used the pseudonym before in various online chat rooms. But these two..."

There was a knock at the door, causing Ivy to turn. Oliver, however, kept his attention focused on his computer.

"Good morning Mr. O'Toole," the doctor said, coming in the room with Oliver's chart. He gave Ivy a friendly nod. "How are you feeling this morning?"

"Fine," Oliver said absently.

"How is he looking?" Ivy asked.

"Remarkably well," Dr. Brachman replied. "Everything is right on track, if not a little ahead of schedule. I think he'll be ready to go home this afternoon."

"Hear that, dummy?" Ivy said. "You get to go home."

"Mm-hmm," Oliver said, deep in typing.

"Sorry," Ivy said, "he doesn't have the best of manners."

"It's no problem," Bachman replied. "I'm just going to check a few vitals and I'll be on my way. Did you get any sleep, Mr. O'Toole?" The doctor moved around the bed to check the vitals from the unit that was attached to Oliver via tubes and wires. It gave his blood pressure, heartrate, blood oxygen and a dozen other statistics.

Ivy was about to start asking about Oliver's at-home care

The buried faces 239

when Dr. Brachman turned and his eyes landed on Oliver's computer. He blanched, but he recovered quickly enough. Ivy frowned, unsure of what he may have seen on the screen.

"Will he need round-the-clock care when he returns home?" Ivy asked.

Brachman looked at her like he didn't know what she was talking about. "Care? Oh, yes. Um, no, he should be able to manage most of it on his own. We'll...we'll check his mobility later today." He pursed his lips. "Will you excuse me? I...need to confer with the nurses."

"Sure," Ivy said. The man turned and left in what she would consider a hurry.

"What the hell are you looking at, graphic porn?"

"What?" Oliver asked, looking up. Ivy grabbed the laptop and turned it around. There was nothing on the screen except what looked like detailed searches for Julia Dufrense and Pepper Larson. Oliver turned it back to him. "What are you doing?"

"Did that seem odd to you?" she asked.

"What?"

"The doctor."

"I wasn't paying attention," Oliver said. "I'm too busy doing your job for you."

"Hang on a second," Ivy said, following the doctor out into the hallway. But she couldn't tell which way he'd gone. She went down to the nurse's station. "Can you tell me where Dr. Brachman is?"

"I haven't seen him," the nurse manning the station said. "He was supposed to be doing his morning rounds."

"Could you page him for me? I'm in room 404."

"Sure," she said, picking up the receiver on the phone. As Ivy headed back to the room, the page came over the speakers.

"Find anything?" Ivy asked, returning to Oliver's room. She glanced at the chart the doctor had left behind. Something didn't feel right. Why would he get upset at seeing those two names?

"Oliver," Ivy said, her stomach sinking. "Search for those names in conjunction with Dr. Phillip Brachman." She looked over at the whiteboard on the wall which listed all the nurses and doctors that were on shift to take care of Oliver today.

He turned to her. "Seriously?"

"Just do it," she said.

He worked for a minute before his eyebrows raised. "Well, it's not something, but it's not nothing either. Looks like his wife's maiden name was Larson. But her first name wasn't Pepper. It was *Piper*."

Ivy pulled out the original photos she'd taken of Father Rouge's ledger. What they'd originally read as Pepper could conceivably have been Piper, given the handwriting. At any rate, it was close enough for her. "Where is she now?"

"Dead," he replied. "She passed away three months ago, according to the obituary."

Ivy joined him at the computer, looking at the picture of a pretty, middle-aged woman above a local obituary article from their paper. "Doesn't say what she died from."

"Hang on," Oliver said and continued working. A minute later he had a dozen images of the woman, all pulled from social media. Ivy gasped when she saw them. The pretty woman from the obit photo was nowhere to be seen in these pictures. Instead it was a gaunt, pale version of the same person, with sunken eyes and sallow skin.

"Shit," Ivy said. "*Shit!*" She pulled out her phone and dialed Jonathan.

"What's going on?" Oliver asked. But Ivy ran out of the room, headed back for the nurse's station.

"Did he respond?" Ivy asked at the same time Jonathan picked up.

"No, not yet," the nurse said.

"What's up?" Jonathan asked at the same time.

"I need you to inform security you have a risk on property," Ivy said to the nurse and to Jonathan at the same time. "The hospital needs to be locked down. Dr. Phillip Brachman is to be stopped and detained as soon as he is found."

"O-okay," the nurse said, picking up the phone again.

"Ivy, what's happening?" Jonathan asked, his voice suddenly serious.

"I think I've found our killer," Ivy said. "You need to get everyone over to Oakhurst Hospital. *Right now.*"

Chapter Thirty-One

"LISTEN TO ME. You are wasting time," Ivy said. "He could be anywhere on the property. For the safety of your staff and your patients, you need to order a lockdown."

The man in the brown suit with the receding hairline shook his head for the fifth time since Ivy had located him, thanks to the nurse at the station on the fourth floor. The name on his door identified him as William Gentry, Vice President of the Hospital. However, he had been adamant that a lockdown was not necessary.

"We only initiate those procedures in an emergency," he said for the second time. "And until I am contacted by a *lawful* authority, the hospital stays open."

"I *am* a lawful authority," Ivy said. "I'm a detective with Oakhurst Police."

"And yet," Gentry replied. "You still haven't produced a badge."

"Ivy," Jonathan said, running up. "What's the situation?"

"I'm trying to get this nimrod to lock down the hospital," Ivy replied. "Brachman is somewhere in here and we need to find him before he does something rash."

"Then why haven't you initiated the protocol?" Jonathan asked, turning to Gentry.

"I was waiting for official—"

"Here," Jonathan said, showing the man his badge. "Official enough for you? Do as she says."

Gentry grimaced, then returned to his office.

The PA crackled to life with Gentry's voice. "Code Gray. All departments, this is a Code Gray."

"Finally," Ivy said. "We need to do a floor-by-floor sweep. He's here somewhere."

"Since Nat's out of the office I spoke with Armstrong. He approved two units to accompany me. They're downstairs."

"Good," Ivy said, heading for the elevators as the nurses scrambled to begin lockdown procedures. "I managed to get Brachman's information from one of the nurses before Dickhead over there stopped me. He drives a black 2015 Mercedes, which the attendant confirmed is still in the garage. And the bus that services the hospital hasn't arrived yet, so if he left, he did it on foot."

Jonathan pulled a handheld radio out from under his coat and called it in to the station, letting them know there was possibly a suspect on foot leaving the vicinity of the hospital. "What are the odds he's still here somewhere?" he asked as soon as the call was over.

They got into the elevator and rode down to the first floor. "I don't know," she said. "He looked pretty spooked." The doors opened on the ground floor, where more personnel were in the process of going through the procedures while trying not to alarm anyone. However, the people waiting in the lobby and other areas had begun to notice *something* was going on.

"Excuse me, what's a Code Gray?" a man asked Jonathan as they passed.

"Just a precaution, sir, nothing to be concerned about," he said. Once he was out of earshot Jonathan leaned closer to Ivy. "I hate lying to them."

"Better than creating a stampede because of a panic."

"True," he replied.

They met up with the other officers Jonathan had brought with him, Pawlowski and Harman, and Wilcox and Perry. Ivy was grateful they had been the ones to respond.

"Here's the situation," Ivy said. "We think the man who killed Father Rouge may still be in the building somewhere. Male, mid-fifties, five-eleven with dark brown hair and glasses. Last seen wearing a white coat over a blue button-down shirt and purple tie with brown slacks. If this man is who we believe he is, he is to be considered armed and dangerous."

"What's he armed with, a scalpel?" Harman asked, laughing.

"That's exactly what he's armed with," Ivy replied. "And a precision knowledge of human anatomy that could disembowel a man and remove all his organs before he could fight back. There is no telling what this man is capable of or what his mental state is. Proceed with caution."

Harman cleared his throat and nodded.

"Should we get clearance for this?" Pawlowski asked. "Detective Bishop was suspended."

"We have clearance," Jonathan said. "I spoke with Captain Armstrong. He said for the time being, she is reinstated while he investigates the cause of the original suspension." Ivy glanced at Jonathan, surprised. He turned to her. "Sorry, I didn't have time to grab your badge."

"That's ok," she replied. She couldn't believe he'd gone to bat for her like that. She turned to the group. "Wilcox and Perry, you start here on this floor, work your way up. Pawlowski and Harman, start up on six and work your way down. Meet in the middle. White and I will coordinate with the hospital to make sure all the exits are secure. The idea is to flush him out."

"And if he's not still here? We're wasting a lot of time and manpower," Perry said.

"Can't be helped," Ivy said. "There are too many potential hostages in here. Their safety is our first concern. If he flees...well, at least the patients and staff are safe." It wasn't an ideal situation. But they had to clear the hospital before they could proceed any further. No one had seen Brachman since he'd left Oliver's room. But that didn't mean he wasn't hiding out somewhere.

"Get moving," Jonathan said. "And everyone keep in touch." He indicated the handheld radio. They headed off to their designated areas.

"What are the odds you think he's our killer?" Jonathan asked as they headed to the main security office.

"Maybe seventy-thirty," Ivy said. "But if you'd seen the pictures of his wife...classic case of addiction. She was definitely on something. Whether or not it was cocaine, I don't know. But that and the possible name match, not to mention the way Brachman responded when he saw her name on the screen."

"But it wasn't her name," Jonathan said. "You said her name was Piper. Oliver was looking for *Pepper*."

"My guess is he recognized it anyway. You know how pseudonyms are. Once someone finds one they like, they keep using it. Maybe she really did use Pepper Larson with Father Rouge. Because I'm betting that was a nickname or maybe a term of endearment between her and Brachman."

"That's a lot of supposition," Jonathan said.

"I know. But ask yourself. If he was innocent, where is he? He'd have heard the Code Gray by now. And being a doctor, would know exactly what that would mean. He should be participating in lockdown procedures with the other hospital personnel." The first rule of any investigation was to follow the evidence. Except in this case, they didn't have any to follow. Whoever had killed Father Rouge had been meticulous to not leave anything behind. And in the absence of evidence, all they had was supposition. It was possible

Brachman was completely innocent, but they had to find the man first.

"Innocent people don't normally run," Jonathan said.

"Exactly." They reached the main security office where they were met a haggard-looking officer in his late sixties. Ivy bet when he took the job, he hadn't expected days like this.

"You two the ones who called this in?" he asked.

Jonathan nodded. "We are. Detectives White and Bishop. Oakhurst PD." He gave the man a quick overview of who they were looking for.

"I know 'im," the officer said. "Kind man. You sure you got the right person?"

"We just need to locate him," Ivy said. She couldn't explain it, but she had a tingling sensation on the back of her neck. Maybe if Brachman hadn't disappeared so quickly, or if he hadn't blanched when he saw what Oliver was looking for she wouldn't be so suspicious. But too many coincidences meant it probably wasn't a coincidence at all.

The security guard led them into the office showing the cameras for the entire hospital. There was one in the garage, which clearly showed the black Mercedes still in its spot. Another officer was scanning the feeds from each monitor.

"We've got security personnel at every entrance and exit, save the emergency ones," he said. "If those go, the alarms will sound. They're checking the IDs of anyone coming and going."

"Our people are going floor by floor," Jonathan said. "I'm sorry to say they'll be checking patient rooms. There are a lot of places to hide in a hospital."

"Still can't believe it," the guard said. "Brachman."

"Why?" Ivy asked.

"He's one of our top doctors," he replied. "One of the best in the state, actually. He could have gone to Portland or even Seattle for a bigger paycheck, but he stayed here to provide care. His patients love him."

Ivy shot Jonathan a worried look. What if she was wrong about this entire thing? It wouldn't do her any favors with Armstrong, that was for sure. Not to mention she may have accused an innocent man and scared a lot of people for no reason.

And what did she really have? A feeling? A hunch? Nothing concrete, that would hold up in a court of law, that was for sure.

Her phone buzzed in her pocket. She opened it without looking at the caller. "Bishop."

"Got something else for you," Oliver said.

"What?"

"I pulled the medical examiner's file on Piper Brachman, nee Larson. It turns out she did die from an overdose. Specifically, a cocaine overdose."

"You broke into Burns' files?" Ivy hissed. Jonathan glanced over, his eyebrow raised.

"Hey, I figured you'd want to know," he replied. "Did you find him yet? The nurse just came in here and locked my room."

"Not yet," Ivy said. "Thanks," she added under her breath.

"I'll keep looking," he said before hanging up.

"What was that?" Jonathan asked.

"Brachman's wife died of a cocaine overdose," she said.

"Motive," he replied.

"*First floor clear,*" the call came through Jonathan's radio. "*Moving to two.*"

"*Sixth floor clear,*" a second call came in less than a minute later. "*Moving to five.*"

"They're moving fast," Ivy said, watching the monitors. On them she could see the officers moving in and out of the images, checking all the rooms, accompanied by nurses and hospital personnel.

"Detectives?"

Ivy and Jonathan turned to see another security guard escorting a doctor. He was on the younger side, tall, with dark, slightly messy hair. He also wore a white coat over a button-down shirt, though his tie was a bright orange with red circles all over it. "This is Dr. Pritchett. He might have some helpful information."

The man stepped forward. "A couple of weeks ago I ran into Dr. Brachman in the basement. I was down there picking up some supplies and he came around the corner and startled me. It looked like he'd been crying."

Ivy turned to the main security guard. "This building has a basement?"

He nodded. "I thought you knew that. You said your people were searching floor by floor."

"The elevator doesn't have a button for the basement," she replied.

"It doesn't go down there. It's part of the old building. The new hospital was built on the old foundation."

"Jesus, you *have* to be kidding me." She turned to Dr. Pritchett. "Where in the basement?"

"On the west side. If you take the stairs down past the reception—"

"Did he say anything when you ran into him?"

The doctor shook his head. "No, just walked past me like he didn't even see me."

"When was this exactly?" Jonathan asked.

"Two weeks ago? Maybe three? I can't exactly remember."

Ivy gritted her teeth. "C'mon," she told Jonathan. "We need to check it."

"Do you want me to call the others?" he asked.

"No, we can handle it. They need to make sure he's not anywhere else." Though Ivy suspected Brachman might be down there, she couldn't pull the other officers from a search in-process. Any one of them could be on the cusp of finding the man and pulling them meant they'd have to start all over again.

Ivy rushed past Dr. Pritchett and the security guard, running down the hall. People were getting up from their seats, alarmed looks on their faces. She wasn't doing anything to quell their fears, she knew, but time was of the essence. Did the basement have a secret exit that Brachman had escaped through? What was his plan?

And what would they find down there?

Chapter Thirty-Two

IVY TOOK the stairs two at a time, heading down to the lowest level of the hospital. The stairwell was lit with harsh, white light that was almost oppressive. When she got to the door to the basement Ivy had to take a breath and remember not to be rash. If he was down here, they would have one chance at this and that was it.

Jonathan was right behind her, his weapon already out. Ivy pulled the .357 Carol had given her. It was heavier than her regular weapon and would go off like a cannon if she pulled the trigger, which meant she'd need to adjust for any kickback. She took a deep breath. "Ready?"

Jonathan nodded.

Ivy pulled open the door and entered into the dimly-lit hallway. Rows and rows of folding chairs and tables were stacked along the walls, making the hallway cramped. It split off in two different directions. She motioned for Jonathan to go left while she took the right side, but he shook his head.

Why? She mouthed.

Not splitting up. He mouthed back.

Fine. She took the lead, heading to the right. There were old doorways down here leading into storage rooms, though some of them were locked. She tried the doors they passed, moving on from the locked ones. Presumably Brachman hadn't locked himself inside, but in the event he did, she removed a chair from the wall and leaned it up against any locked door. If he was in one of the locked rooms and tried to leave, they'd hear the sound of the chair falling.

Above them, the old fluorescent light flickered twice before going back to normal. Ivy couldn't help but think of bad horror movies from the eighties. This was exactly the kind of situation victims found themselves in. But then again, victims weren't normally armed with a magnum.

They continued through the hall, checking every adjacent path and room they could. Eventually the hallway split off a second time, left and straight. The left hallway led into complete darkness as it looked like the lights were burnt out in that direction.

Ivy looked straight ahead, then left. Ahead was nothing more than old boxes and old equipment the hospital had discarded down here. She pulled out her phone and shone her light down the dark hallway. It was mostly clear, save for a few bits of debris along the pathway. It was hard to believe such a decrepit place existed beneath the high-tech hospital.

Sighing, she proceeded forward, her light the only thing showing the way. Her pulse was thundering in her ears. Brachman could pop out from anywhere at any second, but they had to make sure. There was no other way.

As they turned the next corner, Ivy spotted a hint of warm, glowing light up ahead of them. She pointed, to which Jonathan nodded. He had been watching her back, but now he came up beside her as she put her phone away. The light was coming from behind what looked like an old tarp that was hanging at an odd angle across some boxes that had been piled along the hallway.

They moved slowly and carefully, and as they approached

the tarp, Ivy reached out with one hand and pulled it back, her weapon extended in the other hand.

Ten feet in front of them stood Dr. Brachman, his back to them as he stood over what looked like a makeshift shrine of sorts. It was a small table surrounded by candles, which provided the light they'd seen.

"Dr. Brachman?" Ivy asked but the man didn't respond. Ivy had her weapon trained on his back, but she wasn't even sure he heard her. "*Phillip.*"

He turned and looked over his shoulder, though he didn't seem surprised. "I wanted to say goodbye one last time." He moved to the side to reveal a picture of Piper on the table, surrounded by the candles. "She died in this hospital. Right above this very spot, in room two-twelve. Which also happens to be our anniversary." The glint of a scalpel caught the light of the candle flames.

"Dr. Brachman, please release the scalpel," Ivy said. Jonathan stood beside her; his weapon trained on Brachman as well.

"You understand, don't you?" the man asked. "He had to pay."

"*Who?*" Ivy asked.

"Father Rouge," he replied. "He took her from me. It only seemed fair." He gripped the scalpel tighter.

"Are you saying you killed Father Rouge?" Jonathan asked.

"No," he replied. "I saved everyone else. You don't know what he was doing."

"We know," Ivy said. "He was distributing drugs."

Brachman's eyes flashed. "My wife...my wife was a life-long Catholic. She belonged to the church and kept it in her heart. And she trusted it. Never would I have believed that *it* would be the thing that would take her from me."

"Just put the scalpel down and we can talk about it," Ivy said.

"She *adored* Father Rouge. Said he was a pillar of the

community. That he was doing God's work. But I saw how she was deteriorating. And when I confronted her about it, she lied, telling me there was nothing wrong. Eventually she had to face the truth, and I was able to get her into rehab. She got better."

The more he talked, the more he seemed to be riling himself up. Ivy didn't like how anxious his voice was becoming. She had to find a way to diffuse this situation, but it wasn't as if she could just shoot the knife out of his hand. She'd blow his hand clean off if she tried.

"I didn't realize she'd relapsed until it was too late. I'd been watching her carefully, making sure she couldn't be buying from anyone. Little did I suspect she was getting her fix from *him*. It wasn't until she was in here, her heart failing her, that she told me where it was coming from. She still believed in him...even until the end. She said it was all part of God's plan." He gritted his teeth.

"Phillip," Ivy said.

"Don't you understand?" he said. "He was *poisoning* this community. All because that church of his was failing. Did you know he'd been *ordered* to begin distribution? That his higher-ups knew about it?" He shook his head. "The people trusted him. And he abused that trust. They all did. I should have taken care of all of them."

"Wait," Ivy said, glancing at Jonathan. "You're saying the bishop was aware of what was going on?"

"Knew about it. Encouraged it," Brachman replied. "I thought it was just Rouge, but as I was in the middle of slicing open his sternum, he finally decided to tell the truth. At least the last word out of his mouth wasn't a lie."

"Phillip, put down the scalpel," Ivy said. "We can help you. And you can help us. If you're willing to testify to what you know about Bishop Bain, the D.A. will take that into consideration."

He shook his head. "She told me she'd never go back to it.

That she was done." His eyes began to well up with tears. "Do you know what it's like to have the person you love and trust the most lie to you? To go behind your back and betray you?"

"I do, actually," Ivy said. "It's a horrible feeling. Like you've been hollowed out inside."

"Yes, that exactly," Brachman said, a small smile coming to his face. "That's exactly how I felt. How I feel every day since she's been gone. And that's what Rouge needed to feel. He needed to understand that kind of pain."

Ivy thought back to how the man had been literally emptied like a Thanksgiving turkey. She lowered her weapon, replacing it back into her holster. "Let us help you," she said, holding out her hand. "Give me the scalpel. It's all over now. Your wife can rest easy."

"No," he said. "It's almost over. There's only one thing left to do." Before she could stop him, Brachman brought the scalpel to his neck and made a quick slashing motion, cutting across his jugular.

"No!"

He dropped to his knees immediately, the scalpel falling from his hand as blood sprayed from his neck. Ivy rushed forward, placing her hands on the wound in an attempt to stop the bleeding, but there was already so much blood.

"Ivy!" Jonathan yelled.

"Just let go," Brachman managed to say, his words wet with his own blood as it began to bubble in his mouth. His eyes were locked with hers and he began choking, his lungs filling with his own blood.

"Get me a tourniquet!" Ivy yelled. Jonathan was beside her, ripping the edge of Dr. Brachman's coat as blood continued to seep through her hands, splattering them both as Brachman's heart pumped it through her fingers. His blood ran down over her hands, covering his once-blue shirt in a dark crimson as the man continued to gurgle, his gag reflex trying to take over.

Jonathan handed Ivy the piece of cloth he'd torn off and she tried wrapping it around Brachman's neck, but the cut had been too deep, too precise. With his eyes still locked on Ivy, he took his last shuddered breath before his eyes went glassy.

Ivy continued to hold the cloth in place even though it was too late. Brachman was on the ground. He'd stopped breathing and the blood continued to pool around his head as it left his body.

How had it all happened so quickly? She hadn't been able to do anything to stop it. Ivy stood, and looked down at her arms and torso, covered in Brachman's blood. And for a brief second, she saw something in her mind's eye. Like the shadow of a memory, of a place she'd never been before, of a situation she didn't remember. But one that was just like this. She had done this before.

She had held someone as they were dying, their blood covering her.

It was déjà vu of the worst kind. And as she stood back up, Ivy immediately felt dizzy. The world grew black at the edges and before she knew it, she was in Jonathan's arms.

"Hey, you're okay," he said, holding her under the shoulders. "Just take a few minutes."

She looked up at him and realized she wasn't feeling any kind of negative response at their contact. She was touching someone…and it didn't hurt.

But she pulled away, afraid…of what she didn't know. Still, she pulled back, sitting on her knees beside Dr. Brachman's body.

"You okay?" Jonathan asked.

"I don't know," she said, looking at Brachman's dead eyes, staring into nothingness. The sensation had passed as quickly as it had come on. "I really don't know."

Chapter Thirty-Three

"THERE'S insufficient evidence to connect Brachman to Rouge," Ivy said, placing the folder on Armstrong's desk. "Other than his confession to us, that is."

Armstrong, a large man with a permanent scowl, picked up the folder and flipped through everything they'd found.

"Everything we have is coincidental," Ivy said. "We even brought Lorelai Sylvester back in for a voice ID. She says the voice on the recording sounds like the one she heard that night, but it's far from a slam dunk. Burns confirmed for us that the cuts were probably made with a scalpel-like tool, and that whoever did the job needed a lot of medical experience. But—"

"—but no direct evidence," Armstrong said. "No murder weapon. No slam dunk."

"No," Ivy admitted. She looked over at Jonathan who returned a supportive smile.

"We think he stole what remained of Father Rouge's stash of drugs and disposed of them," Jonathan said. "We've had CSI over at his house looking for any remnants, but so far, nothing. The man was careful and meticulous. It's unlikely he disposed of them at his own home, given he was careful enough not to leave any evidence behind at the scene of the crime."

Armstrong continued flipping through the report. "It says here Brachman implicated Bishop Bain in the drug operation."

Ivy nodded. "Again, evidence is scant. I doubt he wrote down the order to Rouge anywhere. But we were able to look into the financials of the church. It appears up until three years ago, when Rouge started dealing—according to Red Blackwater—the church was in dire straits, bleeding money and in deep need of repair. Then all of a sudden, they became solvent again, just out of the blue."

"Interesting," Armstrong said, closing the file. "Unfortunately, I think you're right. I doubt we'll ever be able to prosecute Bain. Not unless he's stupid enough to try it again."

"He did seem *very* interested in getting back to business as usual," Jonathan said. "We should probably keep an eye on him."

"I'll let Vice know," Armstrong replied. "This falls under their purview. But with the Pistons out of commission they're going to have a hell of a time finding a new supplier. I'm sure someone will come along, but I'll leave that up to Conroy." He took the folder and slipped it into the cabinet in his desk. "Anything else?"

"We got word from Modoc County in California yesterday," Jonathan said. "They picked up a young man matching Lukas Winchell's description two days ago. He admitted to running because he thought he'd be busted for breaking and entering."

"Which is what we have his father incarcerated for," Ivy added. "But he should be back home this afternoon."

Armstrong appraised them. "I'm not concerned with a runaway kid. There's something else we need to discuss. And I think you know what it is."

Ivy shot a glance at Jonathan. "Nat."

He nodded. "According to members of your own squad, she left shortly after her...discussion...with you and hasn't been back to the office since. She's not answering her phone and she hasn't been back to her house as far as anyone can tell." He turned to Ivy. "Do you know where she is?"

"I don't," Ivy said. Oliver had continued to track Nat, but two days ago her phone had stopped moving south close to San Francisco. Since then, it had stayed local. Ivy wasn't aware Nat knew anyone in San Francisco, and maybe she didn't. Maybe she just wanted somewhere to disappear for a while. Oliver was keeping a sharp eye on her. Regardless of where she was, she wasn't about to admit to her boss's boss she had an illegal trace on Nat's phone.

"Her last communication to me was that she had put you on suspension, though she didn't give a reason," he said. "I assumed she'd explain herself in due time. But she's been gone for five days. What is going on?"

"I wish I knew, sir," Ivy replied. "She didn't tell me she was leaving."

"Why would she put you on suspension?" he asked.

"We had a... personal disagreement."

"About what?"

Ivy sighed. She looked over at Jonathan, who encouraged her to go ahead. She had tried not to think too hard about what had happened down in the basement of the hospital. But it had been at the fringes of her mind ever since.

"I accused her of covering up evidence relating to my case. The one where my family disappeared." What she didn't say is that it was also a targeted attempt to force Nat's hand, which had worked.

"Do you have evidence to support that claim?" he asked.

"I have... no..." Ivy admitted. She hadn't been able to find the man whom Nat had met with, despite having his license plate, which the system said didn't exist. And using the testimony of a fifteen-year-old memory wasn't exactly procedure.

Armstrong sat back in his chair. "You know, Bishop. This is not the first time you've been put on suspension. This... whatever it is between you and Lieutenant Buckley is obviously a problem. And it's affecting my department."

"Yes, sir," Ivy said. He wasn't wrong.

"Until she returns, consider yourself on thin ice. But when she gets back, all three of us are going to sit down and hammer this thing out. If that means moving you to a different division, then that's what we'll do. At the same time, leaving her post without notice is not a good look on the Lieutenant. So for the time being, I'm assigning her division to work under Ayford."

"What if she doesn't come back, sir?" Jonathan asked.

"Then I'll have to promote someone to her position," he replied. "But I'm not willing to go there just yet. Buckley is a good cop and she deserves some leeway. But my patience has limits." He glared at Ivy as he said it. "If you learn anything, you are to notify me immediately."

"Yes, sir," Ivy replied. "Thank you."

"I assume the two of you have plenty of other cases on your desks?" he asked. They nodded in return. "Then get to it."

Ivy and Jonathan got up at the same time, brushing elbows as they did. And just as before, Ivy didn't feel any anxiety about touching him. In fact, she kind of liked it.

"And, Detectives," Armstrong said as they reached the door. They turned to look at him. "It may not have been a slam dunk, but you both did good work on this one. As far as I'm considered, we're calling this case closed."

～

"OKAY, TAKE IT EASY," IVY SAID AS OLIVER MANEUVERED himself out of the car. Before he'd left the hospital they'd wrapped his abdomen and one of his legs, which limited his mobility. Ivy had to admit she couldn't drive him back to his house in her own car, so she'd taken his, leaving hers back at his house.

"Here, take my arm," Ivy said as Oliver leaned up against the side of his car, catching his breath.

His eyes went wide. "Are you sure?"

"How else are you going to get to your front door?" she asked.

He smiled, carefully placing his arm around hers. Ivy found she could endure the touch, though it still wasn't exactly comfortable. Not like it had been with Jonathan.

She led him to the front door, where the police tape had been removed and opened it using his keys. There was the hint of a stench in the house as they opened the door.

"Ugh," Oliver said. "I don't guess anyone cleaned out the fridge."

"I'm not your housekeeping," Ivy said, helping him into the door. She breathed a sigh of relief when he let go of her, using the wall to prop himself up as he made his way to the couch in the living room. Computer components were scattered all over the room, though that was just his general messiness, not a result of the attack.

"That's ok," he said. "I can take care of it. Just give me a second to rest."

"I'll do it," Ivy said. "Just let me go get the rest of your stuff first." She headed back outside to the car and grabbed everything else from the hospital, including the large bag of painkillers and pills Oliver would have to take for the next few weeks. As she reached the door, Carol pulled up in front of the house. Ivy waited for her as she got out of the car with Hero on a leash. The small pup was practically pulling to get back into the house.

"Oh, my," Carol said, looking at the home. "I didn't realize the condition—"

"Oliver isn't much of a groundskeeper," Ivy said, looking at the fence and overgrown dead grass.

"Okay, okay," Carol said as Hero pulled and pulled to get back to the house. He completely ignored Ivy as she led him up the walk. Finally, Carol reached down and unsnapped his leash, and Hero took off into the house.

"I guess he's glad to be home," Ivy said, carrying the rest of Oliver's things in the house. Inside they found Hero on top of Oliver, licking him incessantly. Oliver was trying not to laugh, but the little pup was relentless in his assault.

"A family reunited," Carol said, smiling. "I have all of his things in the car."

Oliver finally managed to take hold of Hero and lift the dog off him. "Thank you for taking care of him. I don't know what I would have done if—"

"Say nothing of it," Carol replied. "He was a joy. Though I may have accidentally gotten him hooked on hamburger. He loves it."

"I bet he does," Oliver said. Hero continued to lick him a few more times before jumping down, sniffing out his home, his tail wagging the whole way. Ivy helped Carol bring in the rest of Hero's things, and Ivy went about cleaning the refrigerator, which was full of expired items.

"How long has this stuff been in here?" she called down the hallway. "Some of these things expired three months ago."

"I'll clean it when I have time," Oliver yelled back. Ivy shot Carol a *Can you believe this?* look.

"Do you think he needs help around the house?" Carol asked.

Ivy frowned. "No, I'm sure he can manage. You don't need to bother yourself with it."

"It's no bother," she said. "Maybe if he cut his grass his neighbors wouldn't be so indifferent."

Ivy glared at Carol. "You are *not* coming over here to cut his grass. Plus, I wouldn't want…" She was about to say she didn't want Carol here when Oliver's customers showed up. That would be putting her in danger. Oliver still hadn't confessed who had attacked him in the first place and the investigation was ongoing. Until he decided to come clean, it would remain open.

"I just don't think you need to be doing that. He can afford a lawn service. He just chooses not to."

She shrugged. "Okay. It's just nice to have someone to take care of. And I enjoyed this little guy so much." She reached down to rub Hero's head while the dog was entranced with what might be in the fridge.

"It's a generous offer," Ivy said. "But trust me, he's fine."

Ivy and Carol continued to help get the house in livable condition again, and Ivy had made sure a contractor had come by and boarded up the broken window on the side of the house while Oliver was still in the hospital. His server room was still a mess, but it was one that could wait for later. After Carol had left, Ivy ordered Oliver a pizza before preparing to head out.

"Hey," he said as she reached the door. "Thanks. For everything."

"You'll call me if you need anything," she said. He nodded. "And we're still not done talking about…" She gestured to the back room. "But I'm not going to kick a man while he's down."

"Appreciate that," Oliver replied. "Are you doing it tonight?"

Ivy nodded. "I'm supposed to meet Alice over at the cabin in thirty minutes."

"Do you really think you'll find anything?" he asked.

She shrugged. "Probably not. But I need to at least look."

"Just…be careful," he said. And she could tell he meant it.

"Get some rest," Ivy said, looking at Hero, who had curled

up at the other end of the couch. "And for God's sake, watch a movie or something."

Oliver chuckled. "Yes, ma'am."

She gave him a final nod and headed back out to her car. There she grabbed her firearm she'd taken back from Armstrong as well as the .357 from Carol. She didn't know if Alice would be packing and if she wasn't, she wanted them both armed before they entered that cabin. Oliver had said it wasn't occupied, but one could never be too careful.

Ivy only hoped it would finally lead her to some answers.

Because all she had now were questions.

Epilogue

Natasha walked into the gas station, looking for the attendant. "You in charge?" she asked the older man behind the counter.

"It's my station," he said, somewhat rebuffed.

"That jeep out there that's for sale," she said. "How much?"

"Fifteen," he replied. "Runs pretty good. I keep her well-maintained."

"How about a trade?" Nat replied, putting her keys on the counter. The man looked around her to her Toyota Camry.

"That's almost a new car," he said. "Jeep's going on a decade now. Wouldn't be right."

"I need something that can go off-road and my car won't cut it," she said.

"But you're losing out on a lot of value," he replied. "Why not just trade it in and pocket the difference?"

"I'm in a hurry," Nat said, staring at the man. He hesitantly reached for her keys.

"Title?"

She shook her head slowly. Understanding came over his

face. He thought about it a second, then took the keys from her, and deposited two more in her hand.

"Thanks," she replied. "This helps a lot."

"This gonna come back to bite me?" he asked.

"Nope," she said and with that she turned on her heel and headed out to her car again. She grabbed the one bag she'd packed from the back and headed over to the old jeep, tossing her bag in the passenger seat. She hopped up in the cab and turned the engine over on the first try. The jeep may have been old, but the man had been right. It seemed well-maintained. She pulled out of the lot without even looking back, then headed down the mountain road, Pine trees lining both sides of the street. In the distance, the Cascades rose above the tree line, the snowcapped mountains towering over them like protectors.

The whole way she tried not to think too hard about what her next steps would be. She'd lost Mike, but that didn't mean she didn't have contacts out there. And if this was going to be a success, she would have to be very careful. Very precise. All the safeguards she'd put in place all those years ago had come undone. And now she was flying without a parachute. Ivy was on the cusp of discovering everything, and Nat had to do everything in her power to stop that from happening.

After thirty minutes of driving, she pulled on to a familiar dirt road, though it was one she hadn't seen in almost fifteen years. The road was barely a road at all, instead it was more like a well-worn path, one that had been overgrown through the years. Tree limbs scraped the Jeep on either side, confirming for her that no one used this path regularly. Which had been the whole point.

At the end of the path another black car was parked on the side. Nat pulled up in the jeep and got out. The man in the other car did the same.

"You're Natasha," he said.

She nodded. "I see you had no problem finding the place."

"Hell of a hiding spot," he replied, putting his hands on his hips as he looked around. Trees surrounded them on all sides and the sounds of the forest were the only noises out here. "So why here?"

Nat ignored him, and instead took fifteen paces to the north, then thirty paces to the east. There she came upon the three trees, all in a row. Each with a small marker that had been nailed to the trunks near the bottom. There were no words on the markers, just the markers themselves.

The man came up behind her. "Gravestones?" he asked.

Nat nodded. "These trees were half this size when they were buried."

"How do you know?" the man said.

"Because I'm the one who put them here."

To be continued...

Want to read more about Ivy?

OAKHURST IS A TOWN THAT KNOWS HOW TO KEEP ITS SECRETS, but some shadows are impossible to ignore.

AFTER THE DEVASTATING FALLOUT FROM HER LAST CASE, Detective Ivy Bishop is thrust into another chilling investigation. A family in the quiet town of Oakhurst is being terrorized by an unseen stalker—someone who watches their every move, knows their every secret, and is leaving behind cryptic messages that grow more disturbing by the day.

With her boss, Nat, still missing, Ivy is left to navigate the growing darkness alone. The case begins to unravel in unexpected ways, and Ivy can't shake the feeling that this stalker is more than just a threat to the family—it's a harbinger of something far more sinister.

As she continues to dig, each new clue draws her closer to a truth that has eluded her for years. The stalker seems to know more about Ivy's past than she does herself, and the lines between the hunter and the hunted begin to blur.

As the danger escalates, Ivy senses that the answers she's been searching for her entire life are within reach—but will come at a cost. The deeper she goes, the closer she gets to unraveling the mystery that has haunted her since that night fifteen years ago, but she must be prepared for a revelation darker than any she's faced before.

Will Ivy discover the truth, or will she be stuck in the darkness, forever? Find out in *Her Hidden Lies*, Ivy Bishop Mystery Thriller book 4.

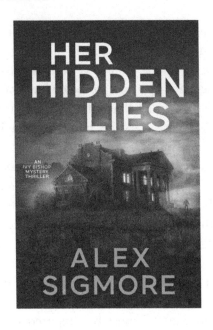

To GET YOUR COPY OF HER HIDDEN LIES, CLICK HERE or scan the code below with your phone.

FREE book offer!
Where did it all begin for Ivy?

I HOPE YOU ENJOYED *THE BURIED FACES*. IF YOU'D LIKE TO learn more about Ivy's backstory and how she became a detective, including how she originally met Jonathan, then you're in luck! *Bishop's Edge* introduces Ivy and tells the story of the case that both put her career on the line *and* catapulted her into the VC Unit.

Interested? CLICK HERE to get your free copy now!

Not Available Anywhere Else!

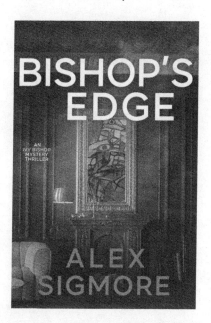

You'll also be the first to know when each new book in Ivy's series becomes available!

CLICK HERE or scan the code below to download for FREE!

A Note from Alex

Dear reader,

I first want to sincerely thank you for following along with Ivy's journey. This has been a story I've wanted to tell for a while now, and I can't tell you how pleased I am with how it's turning out.

It can be difficult to start another series, especially after the first becomes so beloved. But the response to Ivy's story has been overwhelmingly positive so far. I can't tell you how happy it makes me to continue to give you entertaining, thrilling and exciting stories that keep you up all night. We're really getting into the meat of Ivy's backstory now, so stay tuned for what happens next!

Whether you're new here, or have been following along from book one of my debut series, I want to thank you from the bottom of my heart for continuing to support me. As I've always said, *you* are the reason I write!

Because I'm still a relatively new writer with a growing following, I ask that if you enjoyed this book, please leave a review or recommend to your friends. Writing is my passion and I want to continue to bring you many more Ivy Bishop books in the future!

Thank you for being a loyal reader,
Alex

The Ivy Bishop Mystery Thriller Series

Free Prequel - Bishop's Edge (Ivy Bishop Bonus Story)

Her Dark Secret - (Ivy Bishop Series Book One)

The Girl Without a Clue - (Ivy Bishop Series Book Two)

The Buried Faces - (Ivy Bishop Series Book Three)

Coming Soon!

Her Hidden Lies - (Ivy Bishop Series Book Four)

The Emily Slate FBI Mystery Series

Free Prequel - Her Last Shot (Emily Slate Bonus Story)

His Perfect Crime - (Emily Slate Series Book One)

The Collection Girls - (Emily Slate Series Book Two)

Smoke and Ashes - (Emily Slate Series Book Three)

Her Final Words - (Emily Slate Series Book Four)

Can't Miss Her - (Emily Slate Series Book Five)

The Lost Daughter - (Emily Slate Series Book Six)

The Secret Seven - (Emily Slate Series Book Seven)

A Liar's Grave - (Emily Slate Series Book Eight)

Oh What Fun - (Emily Slate Series Holiday Special)

The Girl in the Wall - (Emily Slate Series Book Nine)

His Final Act - (Emily Slate Series Book Ten)

The Vanishing Eyes - (Emily Slate Series Book Eleven)

Edge of the Woods - (Emily Slate Series Book Twelve)

Ties That Bind - (Emily Slate Series Book Thirteen)

The Missing Bones - (Emily Slate Series Book Fourteen)

Blood in the Sand - (Emily Slate Series Book Fifteen)

Coming soon!

The Passage - (Emily Slate Series Book Sixteen)

Standalone Psychological Thrillers

Forgotten

Made in the USA
Monee, IL
11 November 2024